The door opened abruptly. Peter was standing there looking at Caroline, his face as white as the snow outside. He didn't need to speak; they could all tell by his demeanour that something had happened which none of them would want to hear. Caroline studied his face, the colour draining away from her cheeks even before he spoke. 'Darling, I'm afraid you'll have to come home. There's . . . there's been an accident. You must come.'

Educated at a co-educational Quaker boarding school, Rebecca Shaw went on to qualify as a teacher of deaf children. After her marriage, she spent the ensuing years enjoying bringing up her family. The departure of the last of her four children to university has given her the time and opportunity to write. *Whispers in the Village* is the latest novel in paperback in the highly popular Tales from Turnham Malpas series. Her latest hardback novel, *A Village Feud*, is also available from Orion. Visit her website at www.rebeccashaw.com.

By Rebecca Shaw

TALES FROM TURNHAM MALPAS

The New Rector
Talk of the Village
Village Matters
The Village Show
Village Secrets
Scandal in the Village
Village Gossip
Trouble in the Village
A Village Dilemma
Intrigue in the Village
Whispers in the Village
A Village Feud

THE BARLEYBRIDGE SERIES

A Country Affair
Country Wives
Country Lovers
Country Passions

The Village Show

TALES FROM TURNHAM MALPAS

Rebecca Shaw

An Orion paperback

First published in Great Britain in 1997
by Orion
This paperback edition published in 1998
by Orion Books Ltd,
Orion House, 5 Upper St Martin's Lane,
London WC2H 9EA

Reissued 2005

A CIP catalogue record for this book is available
from the British Library.

Printed and bound in Great Britain by
Clays Ltd, St Ives plc

The Orion Publishing Group's policy is to use papers that
are natural, renewable and recyclable products and
made from wood grown in sustainable forests. The logging
and manufacturing processes are expected to conform to
the environmental regulations of the country of origin.

www.orionbooks.co.uk

INHABITANTS OF TURNHAM MALPAS

Sadie Beauchamp	Retired widow and mother of Harriet Charter-Plackett.
Willie Biggs	Verger at St Thomas à Becket.
Sylvia Biggs	His wife and housekeeper at the rectory.
Sir Ronald Bissett	Retired trades union leader.
Lady Sheila Bissett	His wife.
Louise Bianca Bissett	Their daughter.
James (Jimbo) Charter-Plackett	Owner of the village store.
Harriet Charter-Plackett	His wife.
Fergus, Finlay, Flick and Fran	Their children.
Alan Crimble	Barman at The Royal Oak.
Pat Duckett	Village school caretaker.
Dean and Michelle	Her children.
Bryn Fields	Licensee of The Royal Oak.
Georgie Fields	His wife.
H. Craddock Fitch	Owner of Turnham House.
Jimmy Glover	Taxi driver.
Revd. Peter Harris MA (Oxon)	Rector of the parish.
Dr Caroline Harris	His wife.
Alex and Beth	Their children.
Linda	Runs the post office at the village store.
Gilbert Johns	Archaeologist and Choirmaster.
Barry Jones	Estate carpenter.
Mrs Jones	His mother.
Jeremy Mayer	Manager at Turnham House.
Venetia Mayer	His wife.
Michael Palmer	Village school headmaster.
Greenwood Stubbs	Head Gardener at Turnham House.
Sir Ralph Templeton	Retired from the Diplomatic Service.
Lady Muriel Templeton	His wife.
Vera Wright	Cleaner at nursing home in Penny Fawcett.

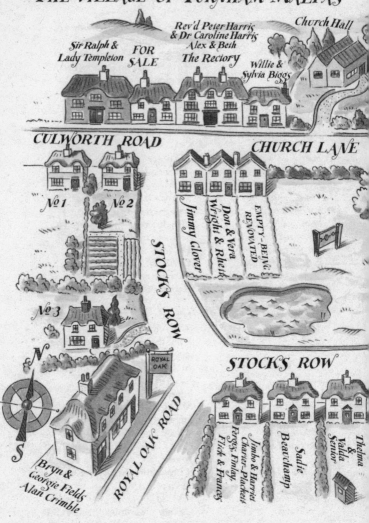

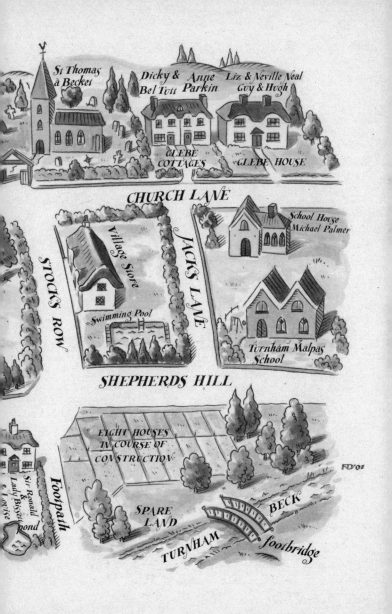

Chapter 1

Caroline slammed the rectory door behind her and tramped through the snow to the church hall. They were holding the first committee meeting for the Village Show tonight, and if she knew anything at all about village committees, it was bound to be a lively evening. Now that the kitchen there had been renovated, she didn't mind quite so much having volunteered to make the coffee. She shuddered when she remembered the old kitchen with its antique water geyser and smelly cupboards – and one never-to-be-forgotten night when she'd found a mouse nesting in the cardboard box they kept the packets of biscuits in!

While the kettle boiled she went through the members' names, counting them off on her fingers to make sure she had enough cups out. People so soon took umbrage if they felt you'd forgotten them. There was Jeremy from Turn-ham House ('the Big House') in lieu of Mr Fitch who couldn't find the time, Jimbo from the Store who'd be doing the food, Michael Palmer from the school for the children's entertainment, Barry Jones, the estate carpenter, in charge of building and erecting the stalls, Bryn from The Royal Oak, Caroline herself representing the church, Sheila

Bissett for the flower, fruit and vegetable competitions — she'd need to be kept in check or she'd be telling everyone what to do — Linda for the first-aid tent, and last but not least Louise as she called herself now, as the secretary. So that made nine.

The kettle was coming briskly up to the boil as Caroline heard the sound of early arrivals. It was Sheila Bissett with Louise, stamping the snow from their boots before they came in.

'Mother, please! I'm the secretary — I *do* know what I'm doing. I have taken notes before.'

'I just want things to go well, dear. It'll reflect on you if it isn't properly organised.'

'Well, it will be, so there. And don't forget *please* about my name.'

'I don't want to change it. I've always loved the name Bianca.'

'I haven't *changed* it, Mother, I'm simply using my first name. I've never known why you called me by my second name. Louise is so much nicer.'

'Well, it'll take me ages to get used to it after all these years.'

'You must, Mother, otherwise no one else will use it.'

Sheila tried to imprint the name on her brain. 'Louise. Louise. Louise. Heaven knows what's made you decide to do it.'

'New place. New start. I've always wanted to do it and now's the right moment. I need an entirely new persona,' Louise pleaded quietly. 'It matters to me, it's really important.'

'All right, then I'll remember. By the way, if there's any talk about the sizes of the marquees, don't forget I want a really big one for the competitions. I shall need lots of space for displaying the exhibits, you see. That Mr Fitch has plenty of money so he can dig deep for this Show.'

'The marquee for the food will be the biggest, I expect.'

'Oh well, naturally, what else can we expect? Some people, namely Jimbo, have more influence than is good for them. But let's face it, the competitions will attract the most people; they won't come all the way to the Show just to eat Jimbo's food, good though it is.'

Caroline came out of the kitchen carrying a tray of cups and a big pot of coffee. She put it down on a table. 'Hi! Would you like coffee? Milk? Sugar?' Sheila and Louise went to collect their cups.

Sheila sipped her coffee and to fill the silence said, 'Your parents have gone home today, Caroline?'

'This afternoon.'

'I met them in the Store the other day. You're so much like your mother. I didn't realise she was a doctor too.'

'Oh yes, I just wish I had half her energy. I think Peter's quite glad to see her go! She's been in his study trying to reorganise his files. He's really very patient with her.'

'They were saying how much they'd enjoyed staying with you.'

'They love seeing the children. Our two are their only grandchildren so far, you see. Their complaint is they don't see enough of them with living so far away.'

'Pity the weather wasn't a little better for them while they were here.'

'They don't really mind. Just glad to have a rest, if you can call it a rest, living in the same house as two two-year-olds!'

Sheila laughed. 'I see your point! I'm really looking forward to this Show. Such a good thing for the village, Mr Fitch coming – isn't it, Caroline?'

3

'It is. He's certainly stirring us up! First the Bonfire Night Party and now the Show. Before we know where we are, Mr Fitch will be thinking he's Lord of the Manor.' The three of them laughed, but they each acknowledged there was a ring of truth in what Caroline had said.

A cold draught announced the arrival of Jeremy. He waddled in swathed in a huge mackintosh and heavy leather boots, which made him appear more mountainous than ever. 'Hello, hello, ladies. Ah, coffee! Just what I need.'

Caroline handed him his cup and said, 'Jeremy, I don't think you've met Louise Bissett, Lady Bissett's daughter. She's agreed to be secretary for the Show. Brave girl!'

Jeremy extended his fat, sweating hand to Louise. 'Good evening, nice to meet you. Brave indeed! Having a taste of country air for a change, eh?'

'Something like that. You're Mr Fitch?'

'No, no, wish I was. My wife Venetia and I run the Big House on behalf of Mr Fitch's company. He uses it as a training centre for his staff.'

'I see. So you employ secretaries and the like?'

'Yes, we do. Is that what you are?'

'Well, I'm in banking really but I've got secretarial skills. So think of me if ever you need anyone. I'm organising the rector at the moment, lending a hand here and there, you know.'

Jeremy laughed and patted her arm. 'Lucky man to have such a charming assistant!'

Caroline agreed. 'Yes, he is. Louise is doing a sterling job with the church magazine. She's also just started distributing the new church telephone directory which she's compiled. We must let Jeremy have a copy, mustn't we, Louise, then if he needs any of us, he has the numbers to hand.'

'I'll drop a copy in for you tomorrow.' She beamed at him.

'Thank you kindly. Thank you very much. Show you round if you like when you come up.'

'Lovely! I've only seen the house from a distance; it'll be great to see inside it. Thank you.'

They chose chairs next to each other and Sheila sat on the other side of Louise. The outside door opened and in came the rest of the committee – Bryn Fields deep in conversation with Michael about the merits of being a Free House, Barry talking to Jimbo about the marquee for the food and Linda from the post office bringing up the rear on her own.

'Coffee, everyone, before we start.' They gathered round exchanging pleasantries, and then finally settled in their chairs to begin the meeting.

'As secretary, and due to the fact we don't appear to have elected a chairperson, shall I take the lead?' Louise looked round the group, meeting everyone's eyes and waiting for an affirmative. They all agreed with nods.

Louise cleared her throat, and in a decisive voice opened the meeting. 'Firstly and most importantly we have to decide on a site. Mr Fitch, who initiated this idea, has decided that he wants it on the lawns in front of the Big House and in Home Farm field. He'll open up an adjoining field for car parking, he says. Frankly, I don't think we have any choice, do you?'

Michael Palmer agreed. 'Let's face it, there isn't anywhere else at all where the ground is level enough nor where there is such good access.'

'There's always Rector's Meadow,' Bryn suggested.

'Rector's Meadow – where's that?' Louise asked.

Jeremy supplied her with the answer. 'Part of the estate.

It borders Pipe and Nook Lane behind the rectory, and runs along the back of the gardens at the rear of the Big House. It would be a good-sized area, but the access is so poor. Pipe and Nook is very narrow – let's face it, it's only an access road for the garages at the back of the rectory and the other houses. And there's no proper road from the other side, only a cart-track. At least down the main drive cars can pass each other.'

'Rector's Meadow? Isn't that where the village cricket pitch used to be, Jeremy?'

'I wouldn't know, Jimbo, sorry.'

Louise looked round the committee for enlightenment but no one could answer so she again suggested the grounds of the Big House. 'All in favour?'

'Unanimous!'

Linda giggled. 'Let's hope they clear all the cowpats away before the big day! There be dozens of cows in there at the moment.'

Jeremy frowned. 'I'm quite sure that matter will be attended to long before the day. Mr Fitch doesn't want anything to spoil the Show, he's set his heart on it being the success of the year.'

Caroline and Sheila exchanged a smile.

'Now we must settle the date. Mr Fitch suggests the tenth or seventeenth of July. Any opinions?'

Jimbo checked his diary and said he preferred the seventeenth.

Michael Palmer said he thought that by then a lot of the children would have gone on holiday. He preferred the tenth.

'It's too soon after Stocks Day,' Sheila commented.

Michael disagreed. 'Well, there's not much work associated with Stocks Day and it'll be a good chance to advertise it, won't it?' he responded. 'All those people coming for Stocks Day, we could hand out leaflets.'

'It's agreed then, the tenth?' Louise waited for a show of hands, and the decision was carried seven to two. She made a note on her pad and then expanded on Mr Fitch's ideas. 'This Show is a huge responsibility. There hasn't been one the size of this ever before, not even the ones they had before the Second World War. He wants a really big Show – an arena with events going on all afternoon, competitions displayed in a marquee, another marquee for teas and the like,' she nodded at Jimbo who inclined his head in acknowledgement, 'stalls which charities could man, ice cream, beer, you name it. He wants a Show with plenty of get up and go, not some kind of damp squib which will fizzle out halfway through the afternoon. It's got to be the show of shows, to put Turnham Malpas on the map once and for all.'

Michael Palmer said, 'Well, the school's contribution will be a display of Maypole dancing. I know it's not May Day but it looks so colourful and we have enough children for two Maypoles. Then we shall have a gym sequence by the Top Juniors, followed by country dancing. Somehow we'll need to rig up a piano and a microphone for Mrs Hardaker to accompany it.'

'I'll make a note of that.' Louise jotted down a memo.

'I'm also willing to run a children's fancy dress competition. That will bring plenty of parents.'

'Thanks, Michael, that sounds great. You're just the right person for that. Do we have any other ideas?'

Bryn proffered an idea he'd been mulling over for a long while. 'I thought one of the events we should have in the arena could be a tug of war – you know, The Royal Oak throws down the challenge to The Jug and Bottle in Penny

7

Fawcett or something – and I'd give a barrel of beer as the prize. I'd organise it. It would encourage the Penny Fawcett people to come, wouldn't it?'

Raising her voice above the babble of conversation Louise said, 'A very good idea. That's what we want, things to draw in the crowds. Could you be in charge of overseeing *all* the events in the arena, Bryn, do you think? We need someone to coordinate it all. You'll need to liaise with the organisers.'

'Well, I'm a comparative newcomer – perhaps there might be someone else who would prefer to do it? Michael?'

'To be honest I think I'll have enough to do keeping an eye on the children, and when you look round this committee, apart from Barry I'm the only person who *isn't* a comparative newcomer, so I don't see it matters. You go ahead, Bryn.'

When the question of the marquees came up, Jeremy's advice was requested.

'Well, I have the name and address of the chappie who did the marquee for the Bonfire Party we had. He was excellent, very helpful and really quite reasonably priced. I'll see to that, if you like. How many and how big?'

Jimbo asked for one the same size as the one they'd used for the Bonfire Party. 'I'm not very good at measurements, but the chap will have it in his records, won't he? That should be big enough.'

'For the competition tent, I'm afraid I shall need one much bigger than that.' They all looked at Sheila.

'Bigger than that?'

'But it was enormous.'

'Surely not!'

'It's not Chelsea Flower Show, yer know.'

Barry scoffed, 'Come off it, Sheila, what the heck! You could have got three double-decker buses in that marquee Jimbo had. Half the size'll be big enough. Next thing, Linda'll be wanting one that size for her first-aid tent.'

Linda giggled and said, 'Yes, if you like. You never know, there might be an outbreak of food-poisoning and I'll need loads of space for beds!'

Jimbo protested sharply. 'There won't be *any* food-poisoning if I'm catering, believe you me!'

Linda blushed. 'I was only joking, Mr Charter-Plackett. Me of all people should know how careful you are about food hygiene.'

'So I should think.'

Sheila turned indignantly to Barry and scathingly commented, 'And what do you know about it, Barry Jones? Nothing. If I say I want a bigger marquee, a bigger marquee I want. So write that down, Louise.' She pointed energetically at her daughter's notepad.

'Got the chairperson in your pocket, have yer, Sheila? Favouritism, that's what it is. Favouritism. We'll have a vote.' Barry raised his arm and bellowed, 'All in favour of Sheila having a marquee the same size as Mr Charter-Plackett's.'

Sheepishly everyone's hand went up, apart from Louise and Sheila.

Furious at losing, Sheila retaliated with, 'Very well then, but don't blame me if the tent is so crowded, visitors faint with the heat. Some people,' glaring at Barry, 'have no understanding of these things. The flowers will wilt and the vegetables will be dried to a crisp. I had such plans . . . But as we are democratic and it's gone to the vote, then so be it.'

Caroline intercepted the look Sheila gave Barry as she

spoke. She could tell the matter wasn't really closed as far as Sheila was concerned.

'The next item on the agenda is the stalls,' Louise announced. 'Barry, would you like a word about your plans? I understand Mr Fitch has spoken to you about them.'

Barry stood up, took a piece of folded paper from his trouser pocket, and after examining it closely he began to speak. 'Yes, I've had a consultation with Mr Fitch and he says I've to go ahead with my own ideas and he'll fall in with whatever I've planned, keeping in mind a certain amount of restraint regarding cost. Which really means I've to account to him for every penny *before* I spend it. The idea I've come up with is that all the stalls shall be the same size—'

Sheila interrupted him. 'Oh no, that would look boring. They want to be all different.'

'Just let me finish, please. As I was saying, the stalls will all be the same size and will all be done up as if it was a mediaeval Show. They'll have small roofs over them and be decorated with crêpe paper all the same colours and quite close together. *Not* spread out all over the field. If yer spread 'em out, people won't bother to walk to some of 'em and those ones won't take much money, but if they're together in, say, three sides of a square they'll look more effective. We'll have flags flying on top of the stalls and that. The estate will make them all and then store them somewhere for next time. I'm recruiting some boys from the village to help put them up during the week before, so there's no need to worry about that.' Barry sat down and waited for some response.

Sheila spoke first. 'Well, I'm sorry but no. It won't do. All the charity people running the stalls will want to do their own thing . . .'

Barry interrupted. 'And a right mess they'll be, too. The only thing I intend letting them do is providing a sign across the front to say who they are – and even that'll have to be to my measurements. Believe me, they'll be glad to be relieved of the job of decorating them.'

Jimbo came down on Barry's side. 'Frankly I'm in wholehearted agreement with Barry, and my marquee shall be just how you want. Tell me the colours you're using for the stalls and I'll do the same with a bit of variation here and there.'

'Boring, boring, boring.' Sheila tugged indignantly at her skirt, pulling herself more upright in her chair. 'You must be mad, Barry.'

'Yer only getting back at me because I balked you from having a bigger marquee than Jimbo here. You know it makes sense.'

Louise called the meeting to order and Michael Palmer in his most conciliatory voice said quietly, 'I've been to lots of Shows of this kind over the years, and the standard of decoration on the stalls has been quite appalling. They've just no idea. If Mr Fitch is willing to pay for all this, then I suggest we fall in with Barry's plans. It will look very stylish.'

Hastily Louise said, 'All those in favour?' It was passed unanimously with the exception of Sheila who folded her arms and looked everywhere but at the other members of the committee.

Bryn broke the silence by saying, 'What about my beer-tent? Nobody's mentioned that.'

Sheila indignantly came to life. '*Beer*-tent? Who said anything about a beer-tent? Common, that's what that is. We need to keep some standards!'

Jeremy tut-tutted his impatience. 'Mr Fitch *wants* a beer-tent, and if it's a hot day it'll be a necessity. That doesn't trespass as far as you're concerned, does it, Jimbo?' Jimbo shook his head and Jeremy continued by saying, 'Could you minute that, Madam Chair, please? A smaller marquee for Bryn for a beer-tent.'

In a quiet voice Linda said, 'I've a friend in Culworth who runs a hot-dog stall by the station in the evenings. Would it be an idea if I asked him to come for the afternoon? He could park his van by the beer-tent and the two things would kind of work together, wouldn't they?'

Startled by Linda's thoughtless treachery, Jimbo protested loudly: 'Linda! Kindly remember who employs you. *I'm* paying for the food concession. I do not want a hot-dog van taking my trade. If I have the food concession, then I have it and no one else. If the committee would allow it, I would provide a separate ice-cream outlet or even perhaps two if the weather's hot. How about that?'

Sheila rushed to support him. 'What a good idea, Jimbo. Much more tasteful than a hot-dog stand.' Linda shrank back into herself and vowed not to say another word. For two pins she'd give up her job in the blasted post office – that would show Mr Charter-Plackett he couldn't ride roughshod over her just because he employed her – but what with the wedding and things and jobs being so scarce she really couldn't afford to resign. She'd just have to swallow her pride.

Louise took the lead again. 'Right, I've noted all that and will let you have a copy of the minutes as soon as I've typed them up. What I should like is a list from Barry of how many stalls he's proposing to construct . . .'

'Twenty.'

' . . . Oh right, and which charities he's contacted . . .'

'Don't know about that, 'cos I'm better with my hands, I am. You'll have to do all that asking people if they want a stall . . .'

'Oh, right then, I will. I'll ask the Scouts, Guides, Red Cross, et cetera – any charities I can think of. If you know any who might want to participate, please let me know. I also need to know things like classes for the competitions, food available, a list of the entertainments like the tug of war that we're putting on in the arena, and the timings,' she nodded to Bryn and he gave her the thumbs-up, 'what displays the children from the school are doing,' Michael raised his hand and acknowledged what she said, 'and anything else we can mention in the publicity. I'm sure Peter will let me use the rectory computer for doing the advertising, it's so much more powerful than mine,' she looked at Caroline for confirmation and got it, 'and all we have to do now is arrange the date of the next meeting, by which time we shall all have a lot more input.'

Jimbo raised his hand. 'I say, just a minute, I've had an idea. Don't you think we need more in the way of entertainments? Something to keep people really interested in staying at the Show and spending until they've no more money left.'

'How about a firework display?' Linda said, hoping to get back into his good books.

There was a chorus of, 'What a good idea!'

Jimbo shook his head. 'Sorry, but that would mean going on until dark and the whole project would take far too long. In any case, we might have reached saturation point with my fireworks; time I gave them a rest. My idea is – what about trips in a hot-air balloon? I have friends who are real enthusiasts. They'd come, I'm sure, when they know it's for charity. What do you think?'

Everyone's faces lit up with enthusiasm as they took the idea on board. Louise was highly delighted at his innovative idea. 'Brilliant, but we should have to be specifically insured for it. Mr Fitch is taking out insurance obviously but hot-air balloon trips are a whole new ball-game. I'll have a word with him about it, and I'm certain his insurers will come up with something. It's a wonderful idea though Jimbo. They'll be a really big attrac—'

The door opened abruptly. Peter was standing there looking at Caroline, his face as white as the snow outside. He didn't need to speak; they could all tell by his demeanour that something had happened which none of them would want to hear. Caroline studied his face, the colour draining away from her cheeks even before he spoke. 'Darling, I'm afraid you'll have to come home. There's . . . there's been an accident. You must come.'

Chapter 2

Caroline went towards him walking stiffly, her muscles paralysed by fear. He held out his hands, clasped firmly hold of hers and led her outside into the snow. The ice-cold wind took away her breath and she gasped for air.

'Peter, for God's sake – what is it?'

Still holding her closely to him, he said quietly, 'I'm afraid it's your mother and father. They were driving—'

'Are they all right? I mean, are they injured or . . . is it worse than that?' She pulled away from his arms and put her head back so she could see his face. In it she read the message she dreaded to hear.

'Oh God, please God, no?'

'Not dead, darling, no. Badly . . . badly injured. I don't know what to say. I really don't. Come home, please, out of the cold.'

He helped her walk back to the rectory. When they got there, Sylvia was waiting with the brandy bottle and a glass on the table beside the sofa. Peter sat her down and poured her a glass. 'Here, darling, drink this. It'll help.'

'No, I shan't, not till I hear what you have to say. Tell me now. Right now!' She shook his arm as she spoke, to emphasise her urgency to face the truth. 'Go on, tell me. No matter how hard it is. *Tell me.*'

'Well, it was Ginny who rang – she telephoned from a hospital in Newcastle. Apparently they were about twenty miles from home, and with the snow and the driving conditions being so bad, I'm afraid they came off the road and went smack into a tree, and rolled down an embankment. The car turned over several times, I understand. They're both still unconscious.'

Caroline sat without speaking, quite still, quite silent, stupid silly little memories flooding into her head. Memories of seeing her mother standing by the river watching them swimming and desperately disguising how anxious she was about them all. Her mother on prize-giving days, trying hard not to look superior to everyone else when her girls won prizes. Her pride when she, Caroline, had qualified as a doctor. Her father, respected and loved by all his patients, his dark hair always tousled, his suit baggy, his tie askew. She wouldn't cry. No, she wouldn't. She absolutely wouldn't cry. There were things to be done, like phoning the hospital, and arrangements to make so she could go up to see them. Yes, of course. She, more than any of the other three, would know the score.

'Peter, I'll have to go home, won't I?'

'Of course, my darling, of course. Drink your brandy. Please. That's an order.'

Caroline sipped it slowly, her mind racing with chaotic thoughts. Someone appeared in the doorway and Caroline couldn't think who on earth she was. Peter seemed to know her because he said, 'That's fine, Sylvia, thanks for your help. We'll make some plans tomorrow first thing. Yes, fine. Thank you. OK. Good night.'

The person came right into the room, and taking her

hand she said gently, 'Don't you worry about a thing. The rector and Willie and I will see to everything here. We'll make sure the children are well cared for, so don't you fret. I'm so sorry.'

She realised it was Sylvia. 'Thank you, thank you, I know I can rely on you. I'm so grateful to have you.' When Sylvia had gone Caroline said quietly, 'Peter, did Ginny say what injuries they had?'

'No, they hadn't told her when she rang. All she knows is that it's serious, very serious.'

'I'm ringing the hospital. Right now. Use my influence. Yes, that's what I'll do.'

Peter nodded. 'Right.'

At three o'clock in the morning, she had told him she would drive herself home, but Peter had said no. 'If I'm to stay here with the children, then you're certainly not driving yourself and most definitely not in this weather.'

'Peter, *I can drive*. I've not lost my senses.'

'Not in this state you can't. All that way to Northumberland? No, absolutely not. I cannot allow it.'

'I'm not a fool.'

'I know. But it would be a foolhardy thing to attempt. You've got to think of the children, darling. They need you. You must not take stupid risks, not now you have children.'

'Oh yes, of course, Alex and Beth.' She got up out of bed. 'I'll go and check they're all right.' She padded away into the nursery. Beth was sleeping on her back, her right thumb close to her mouth, the blankets pushed to one side, her nightgown round her waist. Caroline made her comfortable and tucked the blankets around her firmly. Alex was sleeping on his side, well tucked in. She really would have to see about him going into a bed. He was so much taller than Beth and the cot was definitely on the brink of being uncomfortable for him. She stroked his head, expressing with her hand all the love she had for him. As she did it, she half-remembered the touch of her own mother's hand in the night, once when she had a temperature and her mother felt concerned for her. The caring bond was never broken, and now it was her turn to care. She returned to bed, snuggled into Peter's protecting arms and fell into a troubled sleep.

It was Malcolm the milkman who spread the news round the village about where Caroline had gone. 'Just leaving the milk when they came out of the rectory. Sylvia Biggs was holding on to them twins and the rector and her, that is Dr Harris, was getting into the car. He's taking her to the station, yer see. Can't drive all that way in that state. It's 'er parents – them what went 'ome yesterday. Bad crash on their way back. Terrible it is.'

Pat Duckett, hurrying to get ready to go over to the school and open up, said: 'I didn't know – I'd no idea. How awful! She will be upset. They were so nice; I met them out with the twins when they were here. Such nice people. Just like her, no edge.'

'Yer right, 'er mother is lovely. I cut mi hand last week on a broken bottle, and I'd wrapped it up with a bit of rag till I finished the round. But she came to the door with the weekly money, saw the rag and made me go in the rectory where she cleaned it up and put a proper dressing on it. And she was waiting for me next morning to 'ave another look, make sure it was going on all right. Really kind, just like Dr Harris.'

'Them poor little kids, they will miss their mum.'

'She'll miss 'em too – devoted to 'em, she is.' Malcolm put down the crate he had in his hand and propped his shoulder against the doorframe, preparing for a long chat. 'Sylvia Biggs was saying she won't have no swearing, no talking about guns an' killing an' that. Right particler she is.'

'Quite right, too. I'll go round when I've done the school, see if they need a hand. Thanks, Malcolm.'

'How yer liking it here then, Pat? Big move up for you, ain't it? Four bedrooms and all mod cons. Bet your dad's pleased to 'ave got a job like this. Gardener and a house thrown in. Liking it, are yer?'

'Lovely. Just lovely. Never been as well off in my life.'

'All yer need now is a man to keep yer warm at nights!'

'You offering your services, are yer?'

Malcolm backed off the step. 'No, no. Not me. I'm well fixed-up.'

'Over the brush, I understand.'

'None of your business.'

'No, and my private life is none of yours.'

'Saw Barry Jones with yer at the Bonfire Party. You could do worse.'

'Marriage bureau your latest sideline, is it? The scams you get up to would fill a book.'

Malcolm chuckled and tapped the side of his nose. 'No. No. I'll be off then.'

'Yes, get off.' She punched his arm playfully. 'Mind 'ow yer go, Malcolm, take care.'

Michelle and Dean eating their breakfast right behind her in the kitchen contemplated an aspect of their mother's life they had never thought of before.

Michelle swallowed her mouthful of Corn Pops and said, 'Mum, are you really thinking of marrying Barry?'

'Of course not. Three drinks last November doesn't mean wedding bells, does it?'

'I like Barry.'

Dean pushed back his chair; he'd noticed the time and needed to be off. 'I like him too. He's a great bloke. If you married him he'd make us some nice cupboards and that. Yer keep saying you could do with some.'

'Yer don't marry for the sake of some nice cupboards, our Dean. And would you want his mother for a grandmother? I ask yer!' Dean pulled a face, laughed and disappeared upstairs.

Rather wistfully Michelle said, 'Mum, I'd quite like having a dad.'

Pat smiled indulgently at Michelle. 'It would be nice for yer, love, with not remembering yer own dad, but that's not the right reason for getting married, is it?'

'No. I expect yer've got to marry for L-O-V-E. I can hear Grandad coming down. He'll need a fresh pot, you know what he's like.'

'Yes – demanding, like all men.'

Pat called at the rectory as soon as she'd finished at the school. Peter hadn't yet returned so it was Sylvia who answered the door on her way back from the study where she'd been taking a coffee in to Louise.

'Good morning, Sylvia. Just heard about Dr Harris's mum and dad. Thought you might need a bit of 'elp and that, in the circumstances. Come to offer my services, I thought.'

Sylvia caught Alex just as he was about to leap over the threshold into the road. 'Come back, Alex, there's a good boy. Thanks for calling in, Pat, we've got everything organised for now but if I do need any help then definitely

I'll give you a call. Louise is here today so she's answering the telephone.' Sylvia pulled a face and then carried on saying, 'Perhaps you could sit in one night if the rector needs to go out?'

'That would be great. Glad to be of help. I've always been fond of the twins. Any news from Northumberland this morning?'

'Dr Harris called the hospital before she left. Still critical, I'm afraid. They've got terrible injuries. They're both being operated on today. Look, come in or I shall be losing these two before the morning's out.' They stood in the hall while Sylvia listed their injuries. 'So all told, they've broken bones, internal injuries and serious head injuries. So I don't know when things will be back to normal.'

'Still, once they've turned the corner she'll come home, won't she? These two'll miss her; 'spect they'll be playing up no end, poor little things.'

Sounds of a furious argument in the kitchen made Sylvia terminate the conversation. 'Must get on, Pat. Thanks for calling and I'll let you know.'

Pat stepped out into the road, waved and left, calling out from the lane, 'Don't forget to ring! I'm on the phone now since we moved.'

Sylvia nodded her thanks and raced back into the kitchen. 'No, Beth, that is Alex's car; this one is yours. Here you are. Now no more shouting, please.'

But the children wouldn't be pacified and Sylvia was relieved to hear Peter's key in the lock.

'Now, Rector, caught the train all right?'

'Yes, we did. Caroline's promised to ring as soon as she has any further news. It's been a terrible shock for her. She's the eldest, you see – she's always felt responsible for them all, so they lean on her.' He turned to the children. 'Now my little ones, what's all this noise?'

'They're very upset, Rector. They're not used to her leaving them and they're missing her already.'

'So am I.' He stooped down to pick up the children, one on each arm, and he kissed them both soundly. 'No more arguing, you've both to be good. Daddy misses Mummy too, and I'm not shouting and being cross, am I?'

Louise stood in the doorway, her coffee cup in her hand. She strode forward and placing her hand on Peter's, said, 'Don't worry, Peter, I'll do the best I can to help. Anything, anything at all. I'll come in every day if need be.'

Peter thanked her and said he thought that between Willie, Sylvia and himself they'd manage. 'But if we do have a crisis, I shall know who to call on.'

Sylvia said, 'Pat Duckett's been already. I expect she'll be the first of many. As soon as everyone knows, we'll be inundated with offers of help, so don't worry yourself, Louise. You confine your efforts to the computer – after all that's what you're best at.' And Sylvia went to unload the washing machine, leaving Peter surprised by the sharpness of her tone.

'Right then, children, down you go. Louise and I have a lot to do this morning. Be good.'

Caroline rang that night to say both her parents had come through their major operations that day, and although they still weren't out of the woods, things were looking a little more hopeful. She described the operations in so much detail she made Peter almost wish he hadn't married a doctor. She knew far too much for his liking. 'Mother's opened her eyes and spoken to me, but Dad's only looked round and then fallen asleep again. He didn't know me really.'

'Well, he always has been a bit vague, hasn't he?'

'Peter!'

'Well, he has. Remember that time when we came back from our honeymoon and he mistook me for a patient? I mean! His own son-in-law.'

'He'd been on call all night and he was exhausted, OK? Darling, how are the children?'

'Noisy and fractious. Missing their mother, like I'm missing my wife. Loads of parishioners have called to offer their services. Sylvia's got so many promises of walks and minding and things, she's having to keep a roster. I probably shan't see the children at all. Louise has promised to come in every day . . .'

'Naturally.'

'Caroline, please! What she does is out of kindness. After all, she's not getting paid.'

'I know. I know. However, I've got something better to talk about than her. Like how much I love you, and I wish you were here.'

'Look, would you like me to come up?'

'Absolutely no. You're better to be at home giving the children security. There's nothing you can do anyway. Just pray for them, darling, please.'

'I have been.'

'Thank you.' There was a pause. 'Thank you for that. I'm exhausted, I've just got to get to bed.'

'Of course. Take care, my darling, and good night. My love to Mum and Dad tomorrow when they can talk. Have the girls got there?'

'Oh yes. Peter, I'm so worried! There's nothing I can do and I wish there was.' There was a moment's silence and then she said shakily, 'My love to you. I'll ring tomorrow night.'

'Good night, darling. Sleep tight. God bless you.'

Peter put down the receiver and went to look out of his study window. He'd always admired his parents-in-law. Stout-hearted Northerners, down-to-earth, tough, humorous, compassionate and latterly so forgiving of him. He hoped more than anything that they would pull through.

Just before he fell asleep that night it occurred to him to be careful where Louise was concerned while Caroline was away. He'd have to watch his step. The parish wouldn't stand for any more nonsense from him; one foot wrong and that would be it. He couldn't think of any possible reason to stop her helping with the parish work and she'd been a boon, no doubt about that. But helping with the children, no, definitely not. God's work, yes, but not his. He thought about Caroline sleeping in Northumberland in her old bed and wished she was home in Turnham Malpas in his.

Chapter 3

'Mother, have you seen that file for the Show? You know, the red one. It's got a blue label with "Show" written on it?'

'No, dear, I haven't.' Sheila emerged from the kitchen, her stocky figure swathed in her latest negligée, pale pink with little bouquets of white flowers on it. Ron thought it too thin for decency, but he was no expert. Underneath she wore a matching nightie. Since she and Ron had restored, to use Ron's words, 'diplomatic relations', she'd endeavoured to bring a touch of excitement to his life by wearing tempting nightdresses. 'I'll look in your room, dear. It can't have gone far.'

Louise, head down in the bottom drawer of her desk, shouted triumphantly: 'Eureka!'

Sheila flinched. 'I don't think that's a word suitable for the drawing room, dear, do you?'

'Mother, for heaven's sake! Thank goodness I've found it. I can't think why I put it down there in the bottom drawer when it's so urgent. I'll just put these lists in the right place and then I'll be off.'

'How they managed before you came I shall never know. Peter must be really grateful for your help.'

'He is. She isn't.'

'Don't say that. I've a very soft spot for Caroline Harris.'

'Can't think why. I can feel she doesn't like me every time I see her. And those clothes! Who does she think she is?'

'Well, she was a doctor before the twins arrived, so she would be earning good money and then I have heard on the village grapevine that Peter has a private income, so he doesn't have to rely on his stipend, you see.'

Louise pretended disinterest. 'Oh well, that accounts for it then. Now, where does this go? Oh there. Gilbert Johns says he knows some Morris Dancers. I've wondered about asking them to come to the Show.'

'Oh, that would be *so* colourful! We've been in Turnham Malpas five years now and there's never been Morris Dancers here, not even on Stocks Day. That would be a real draw! I thought you weren't speaking to Gilbert since he's being so awkward about having you in the choir?'

'I'm not, but he doesn't seem to have noticed. In any case I haven't given up the idea at all. Just letting it lie dormant for a while till I get another chance. It's perfectly ridiculous to refuse to have a woman in the choir. But then what else can you expect?'

Sheila, who had been busy spraying leaf-shine on her rubber plant while she talked, stopped and looked at Louise. 'What do you mean?'

'Well, he's always so mild and kind of soft, he wouldn't know how to cope with having a woman in the choir.'

'He's always been very much the gentleman as far as I've been concerned.'

'It doesn't mean because he doesn't make waves that he can't be a gentleman as well, Mother.'

'No, I suppose not. He never socialises at all, does he? Never stays for coffee after the service or anything. You never get to know him any better however many times you talk to him.' She glanced at the clock under its glass dome, its little brass weights steadily rocking back and forth. 'Look at the time, Louise, you're going to be late at the rectory. How are they managing without Caroline?'

'Pretty well. The children are being farmed out all over the place. They're very naughty at the moment, you can't leave them for a minute.'

'Missing their mother, I expect. Well, she's not really their mother, but you know what I mean.'

Louise swung round from the mirror, her top lip lipsticked and the bottom still awaiting her ministrations.

'Not their mother?'

'I thought you knew. They're his but not hers.'

'Haven't they been married long, then?'

'Oh yes. A good long time like seven years or something. But those twins are his by someone who used to live here. It was quite a scandal at the time, but the village closed ranks and no one let on. She left immediately the twins were born. We never mention it now. I thought you knew.'

'You mean he was unfaithful to her and they then adopted the twins?'

'Yes.'

'God! I didn't think he could be tempted away. They're so lovey-dovey with each other. Kiss here. Hug there. Darling this, darling that. Well, well! This puts a whole new light on the matter.'

'On what matter?'

Louise turned back to the mirror. 'Oh, nothing. Just a figure of speech.' Her hand trembled ever so slightly and she had to wipe away the lipstick on her bottom lip and apply it again.

Louise studied her reflection in the mirror. She'd tried to soften her strong features, so like her father's, by lightening her hair to a kind of ash-blonde, and she'd had it cut short in a severe bob to give her a more youthful look. She wore mascara to enhance her eyes but sometimes wondered if they were her best feature, after all. Fancy Peter Harris doing that . . . She could understand completely how someone could be attracted to him, but imagine a man of the cloth allowing such a thing to happen! And twins too! That seemed to make it worse, somehow. So Caroline hadn't got as much of a hold over him as Louise had imagined. She pondered about how many times adultery had taken place; though she supposed it only needed once to conceive. She patted some powder over her lips. She hated shiny lips, they looked too aggressive. Then she imagined his arms around her, her hands caressing his wonderful red-gold hair, his strong athletic body pressed close to hers, inch for inch, his lips lingering in her hair, listening to him whispering . . .

'Good morning, Louise. You're up bright and early.'

It was Dad. 'Morning, Dad. I'm off – they need me at the rectory. You've promised to be the starter of the races at the Show, haven't you, Dad? The tug of war and the children's races? That's what I've put you down for, anyway. See you. Shan't be home for lunch, Mother. I've promised to give Sylvia a hand with the twins. They're wearing her out. Where's my briefcase? Oh, there it is. I'm off.'

'I shan't be here anyway. Dad and I have promised ourselves lunch at the pub.' As Louise slammed the cottage door, Sheila smiled indulgently. 'How Peter managed before she came I don't know. I've never seen her so enthusiastic, have you?'

'No. Where's my breakfast?'

'Won't be a minute.'

'I don't like you wearing that . . . thing about the house. It's all right for the bedroom but not downstairs.'

'All right, keep your hair on. I'm not walking down the street in it, am I, only sitting in my own drawing room.'

'And don't encourage Louise so much with all this voluntary work. She needs a proper job. Money doesn't grow on trees.'

Louise hastened on winged feet across the Green to the rectory. Fancy the twins not being Caroline's. She found it hard to believe. Amazing what you learned about people. Everything all wonderful on the surface but underneath . . . Today she had the opportunity to help him, to make herself indispensable – yes, that was it, indispensable while Caroline was away. She knocked impatiently on the door.

It was Peter who opened it. 'Good morning, Louise. Snow's going at last. I like it when it first comes but then after a while one wishes it anywhere but where one is.' He took her coat and hung it in the hall cupboard. Louise noticed that before he shut the door he smoothed the back of his hand down the sleeve of a coat of Caroline's. She could have burned that coat there and then. He opened the door to the study. 'I've dictated a lot of stuff but you'll soon whizz through it. If you've work to do for the Show, today could be the day.'

'Don't you worry about that, I'm staying for lunch to help Sylvia, we arranged it yesterday.'

'I really don't want to put on you any more than I have to. I thoroughly appreciate what you do for the parish and I'm sorry the church can't afford to pay you for doing it, but I really can't have you spending time looking after my children. It simply is not right. Thank you all the same.'

Louise blushed bright red. Partly with anger and partly with disappointment. 'But I've promised Sylvia. She has no chance to get her housework done now with Caroline being away.'

'The twins are going to Harriet Charter-Plackett this afternoon straight after lunch, so Sylvia will be able to catch up then. The twins love playing with baby Frances. They're staying there for tea.'

'When was this arranged?'

'Sylvia organised it yesterday afternoon, why?'

Louise left the study and went to find Sylvia. She was upstairs stripping the two cots and putting clean sheets on. Alex and Beth were playing with some old soft toys they'd found stored away in the nursery cupboard.

'Loo' Lulu, it BooBoo, Beth's BooBoo.' Beth held up a tatty well-worn rabbit with one ear missing for Louise to see, but she hadn't time for her.

'Look here, Sylvia,' she burst out, 'we had it all planned. I was going to stay for lunch and look after the twins this afternoon. You knew all about it. Now I hear they're going to Harriet for the afternoon.'

Sylvia picked up Beth's counterpane from the carpet and without pausing in her work to look at her said, 'I know, but Mrs Charter-Plackett offered and it was the most convenient day for her so I said yes.' Sylvia finished smoothing the counterpane on Beth's cot and turned to look at Louise. 'Let's face it, you really much prefer the computer to children. I know exactly why you want to take care of the twins, don't I?' Sylvia stared meaningfully at Louise, who glared back.

'What exactly do you mean by that remark? Speak plainly, I don't like innuendos.'

'Very well then. I know you want to look after the twins to usurp Dr Harris's place here while she's away . . .'

'Well, really! You're being ridiculous! Why should I want to do that?'

'I can't put it plainer than that, and I won't have it. Come, children, help Sylvie put these toys away and then we'll go to the Store. Mr Charter-Plackett says he'll have that *Jungle Book* video in he promised.'

Louise protested. 'All I'm doing is trying to help while this family is in difficulties. I can't think what can be wrong with that.'

Alex slammed the toy-cupboard door shut and shouted, 'Sylvie, done. Come on, Sylvie. Bimbo's Bimbo's.'

Sylvia bent down to pick him up. 'In future the only domestic thing you may do is make your own coffee and that's that. I'm sorry.' She called Beth and the three of them went off down the stairs.

Louise took a deep breath and followed them down. She found Peter keeping a low profile in his study.

'Peter! Sylvia has deliberately arranged for Harriet Charter-Plackett to have the children later today when she knew we'd arranged for me to help her look after them. I'm very hurt. They know me, and they'd be quite happy with me. I'm only trying to help.'

'I know you are, and I'm grateful for all you do, but the house and the children are Sylvia's responsibility whilst Caroline is away, and well . . . that's how it must stay.' He looked pleadingly at her and her heart melted. The poor dear man, dominated by two bossy women. What some men have to put up with. If he was hers he'd have the last word on everything. If he was hers . . .

In his gentlest voice, Peter said, 'So shall we get on with what we know you do best, which is relieving me of having to plod slowly along for hours with my two-finger typing?'

'Yes, of course. I'm here to help you in any way I can – and you mustn't hold back from asking me for anything, however difficult.' Louise smiled sweetly at him, and switched on the computer.

While she sorted out the work he'd done for her to type he worried about how to broach the subject of her joining the church choir. Gilbert Johns had spoken to him about her on Sunday evening after the service.

'You see, Peter, she persuaded me to give her an audition. Fine. I didn't mind, not at all. Didn't take long.' He sighed. 'I hate to cause pain to anyone and I'm telling you and only you because I know I can rely on you not to gossip, but you see although Louise has a powerful contralto voice, and can read music perfectly, her singing is ever so slightly, and I mean ever so slightly, out of tune. A mere soupçon, that is all. But to someone with an ear like mine it is discernible and makes me wince. So even if I had females in the choir I wouldn't have her. Can you tell her for me, discreetly, please? And not mention she's out of tune?' Gilbert had begged so charmingly that Peter had agreed to do it. But how? Better tackle it now. Clear the air.

'By the way, Gilbert Johns spoke to me on Sunday evening. I'm afraid the answer to your being in the choir is still no. He's absolutely adamant. He's had another discussion with the men in the choir and they wish to stick to tradition and keep it all-male. So I'm afraid there's nothing more to be said.'

'Oh, did he really consult them? I bet! It's ridiculous that in this day and age they won't have women in.'

'Well, I'm sorry but there it is. You see, he has a waiting list of boys wanting to join, a position most village choirs would be exceedingly glad to find themselves in, so . . .'

The telephone rang and saved him from having to pursue the matter with Louise. By the time he put down the receiver Louise was immersed in her typing. Just as he had become absorbed in his own work, the computer fell silent and he realised Louise was crying.

For a few minutes he ignored her, hoping the crying would stop and he could pretend he hadn't noticed. But it didn't. He put down his pen and said quietly, 'Can I help?'

His gentle inquiry made her sob.

'Please tell me, it may help.'

Louise wiped her eyes and said, 'It's always the same. I'm all right for typing and administration and office work, but when it comes to something personal no one wants to know.'

Peter perceived there was more to the problem than what had happened that morning with Sylvia and Gilbert's refusal. 'I don't think it's just this morning, is it, that's made you say this.'

Louise shook her head. 'No, it isn't. I . . . I . . . that's why I'm here.'

'In Turnham Malpas, you mean?'

'Yes. If I tell you, can I rely on your confidentiality?'

'Of course. Absolute secrecy, I promise.' He turned his chair to face her and waited.

'I worked at a bank, as you know, and I was in charge of helping people who were starting up new businesses. I listened to what they had to say, saw their business plan and commented on it. If it wasn't right I helped them to put it right, decided if it was viable, talked to them about a loan and the conditions of repayment, took the whole thing to my manager, thrashed it out with him and with his approval agreed it, then kept a watching brief through the first critical years. I was doing well, really well till one day . . . till one day this man came in. He was utterly charming. Polished upper-class accent, like yours,' Louise smiled at him, 'well-mannered, not good-looking but . . . Anyway, he had a good business plan – well-presented, not on a scrap of paper like some of them did – and I worked on it, though there wasn't much to do. The manager was on holiday and I should have waited until he got back, but somehow it all seemed so genuine and the client was so keen, and so open and friendly. If I shilly-shallied, he'd lose the opportunity so I contacted the area manager instead. Of course, to him the sum involved was peanuts in comparison to the figures he dealt with every day, and because he had confidence in me he gave the go-ahead.'

'And it didn't work out?'

Louise shook her head. 'I was completely taken in. We started having our business discussions while taking lunch together, then it became dinner, then I . . . began to fall in love with him. After that, I was no longer behaving rationally where his loan was concerned. Anyone else and I would have been alerted, but in the circumstances . . . Look you don't want to hear all this. Sorry.' Louise turned back to the keyboard.

'If it makes you feel any better, I am here to listen – that's fifty per cent of the job for a clergyman.' She looked at him. He smiled.

Louise almost choked with gratitude. 'Well, I gave my notice in at the bank at his suggestion and was going to join him. General factotum, secretarial work, learning the business so that I should become his partner and not just in the business. I couldn't resist his charm. I began helping weekends and evenings while I worked out my notice, and I have to admit I could think of nothing else but him. Then I'd a day's holiday to come so I thought I'd take the

34

opportunity to get ahead with the spread-sheets I was doing for him, so I'd be free at the weekend. I walked in the office early and there was this blonde, all legs and . . .' She paused. 'It wouldn't have been so bad if he hadn't been so cruel. Searingly cruel. I couldn't for the life of me tell you what he said.'

'I'm so sorry. It must have been dreadful.'

His sympathy made her tremble. 'I . . . I'm not telling anyone, not even you, what he said. It was staggeringly hurtful. I stormed out and drove like a maniac. I don't know to this day why I didn't have an accident, I really don't.' She wiped her eyes. 'I spent an horrendous weekend and on the Monday went to the bank and straight to his file and began working through it. Of course his references turned out to be forged; the whole story had been a complete fabrication. I had to go to the manager and tell him. If I hadn't already given in my notice I would have been sacked on the spot. You see, I should have delayed authorising the loan until my manager had come back from holiday, and what was worse I had involved myself with the man. Should have kept it entirely on a business footing. I, who thought I had a head for business, had ignored all my training. He had me absolutely fooled.'

'I'm so sorry.'

'So not only had he made me lose my job, he'd also broken my heart. I can't forgive myself for being so taken in. How could I have been such a fool? I loved him, you see. He behaved like a gentleman, said he valued me too much to anticipate our marriage.' Louise stopped while she regained control over her sobs. 'Said he wanted our relationship to be on the right footing, and I admired him for that; it made me feel cherished as well as loved. But it was all a sham. A total sham. It was because he didn't want *me*. I was all right, you see, for getting the loan and doing the work, but not for a relationship. That's how it always is. Good old Louise. My parents think I was made redundant, so please don't tell them, will you? I couldn't bear for them to know the whole story.'

'Of course I shan't tell them. You know, when something like this happens, one has to pick up the pieces and plod on and eventually one gets through the maze.'

'You're so kind. So understanding. Thank you. I really do appreciate you listening to me. I feel so much better now, having confided in you. It's wonderful to have you to talk to, just wonderful and you're such a sympathetic listener. You have this gift, you know, of helping people to speak the truth and—'

To his relief there came a knock at the door. It was Sylvia back from the Store with the video clutched in her hand.

'Only me, Rector. I need a word. Is it convenient?'

'Of course, come in.'

Sylvia nodded her head in the direction of the kitchen. So Peter stood up and followed her in there.

'Rector, I've told Louise she's not to interfere with our domestic arrangements. I won't have it. Yesterday she coerced me into agreeing that she could look after the children, and you've no idea how relieved I was when Mrs Charter-Plackett rang up offering to have them both. I won't have it and I know Dr Harris wouldn't want it either. So that's it. I won't desert my post in her absence, but if I have any more interference then as soon as Dr Harris returns I shall give in my notice. She and I work beautifully together and I would regret doing it – I've never had a job I've enjoyed so much – but the sooner that woman finds herself a proper job, the better it will be for us all.'

Peter said, 'Now see here, Sylvia, I know that you're under pressure without Caroline, but please don't allow yourself to get so upset. Louise is no threat to you; in fact, it's all rather sad and I feel rather sorry for her. But I have told her myself she must confine her help to the parish and that our domestic arrangements are off-limits. So we are both on the same side. Please don't even contemplate giving in your notice, because if you do Caroline will have me hanging from the highest branch of the royal oak for all to see.'

Sylvia laughed. 'Oh sir, I'm sure she wouldn't, oh no. So long as you and I have an understanding then we shall both act accordingly. She mustn't be encouraged. Right, children, drink and biscuit-time, I think, while we watch *Jungle Book*. Your Sylvie needs her coffee, and I expect Daddy does too.' Sylvia went to put on the kettle, shaking her head in amusement.

Friday lunchtime in The Royal Oak dining room was always busy. There was a hint of the freedom of the weekend coming up, and besides retired people enjoying their well-earned pleasures, there were plenty of villagers intent on enjoying themselves too. As they had already promised, Ron and Sheila had arrived for lunch, breathlessly later than they had intended so they were having to wait in the bar while a table became free. Ron was standing talking to Bryn with one foot on the bar rail and in his hand a pint of Bryn's homebrewed ale. Sheila was sitting at one of the small round tables in the window sipping her gin and tonic. She was scrutinising Ron and comparing him with other older men in the bar. He'd weathered quite well really, considering. Now he'd lost weight his stomach had been reduced to more manageable proportions and the fat around his throat, which had wobbled when he spoke, had disappeared.

The door opened and in came Sir Ralph with Muriel. She never could get used to calling her Lady Templeton. After all, Muriel had only been a solicitor's secretary before she married Sir Ralph. My, but he was handsome. All that thick white hair and his tanned skin and that aristocratic haughty nose. Class. Yes, definitely class. Sheila waved eagerly to Muriel and she came across.

'There's room for the four of us if I move my handbag. Here, do sit down. It's so busy in here today, isn't it?'

Muriel sat down, eager to be friendly. 'Hello, Sheila. It's a little warmer today, isn't it? I'm so glad the snow has almost gone. How's Louise? Has she got a job yet?'

Sheila laughed. 'No, not yet. She's looking round though. Wants the kind of job she can get her teeth into. Though how she's going to find the time I don't know. She's so busy at the rectory now, especially with Dr Harris being away.'

'Of course. I haven't heard today. Do you know how things are?'

'Well, they've both had their operations and it's simply a question of waiting to see. Six hours in the operating theatre, they say. Of course, at their age it must have been the most tremendous shock.' Ralph brought Muriel's drink across and then went to rejoin Ron and Bryn. 'Louise's helping all she can. She's having lunch there today and looking after the twins for Sylvia this afternoon.'

'She's certainly keeping very busy. I understand she was hoping to join the choir. Has she done anything about that at all?'

'Well, yes.' Sheila drew closer to Muriel and quietly said, 'She persuaded Gilbert Johns to give her an audition, which of course she passed, but he's said no way will he have women in the choir. She's very upset about it, but she's not given up on him yet – oh no, not my Louise.'

'Well, if Gilbert Johns has said no I don't see how she will change that. He's a very quiet man but very determined where his choir is concerned. We're really very lucky to have him, you know. He's made it such a wonderful choir and when you think about it, for so small a village we are very privileged.'

Ralph came across, glass in hand. 'Hello, Sheila. Everything all right with you and yours?'

'Yes, thank you, Sir Ralph. Everything's hunky dory. I hear Mr Fitch is opening the Village Show. Pity it couldn't be you.'

Muriel saw Ralph's lips press together with annoyance but his answer came out cordially enough. 'We shall be abroad when the Show is taking place, Sheila, so the matter doesn't arise.'

Muriel quickly decided she needed her lunch. Anything to stop Sheila putting her foot in it any more than she already had done. Sheila was renowned for annoying Ralph.

'I think we'll go in for lunch, Ralph. We booked for half-past one, didn't we? If you're ready, that is.'

'Of course, dear. Of course. Will you excuse us, Sheila?'

To Muriel's distress, Sheila and Ron followed them into the dining room and asked if they could share their table as it looked as if all the other diners had become glued to their chairs.

'Would it be a bother?' Sheila asked.

Ralph stood up, pulled out a chair for her and said, 'Certainly not. We shall be glad of your company.' When they had got seated they discussed the menu. Ralph said,

'I'll order, this is on me.' Under the table Sheila tapped Ron's knee with a newly lacquered bright red fingernail and he agreed to Ralph's suggestion and thanked him for his offer. Ralph went to the food hatch and placed their orders.

They chatted about village affairs and the Show and the annual Stocks Day and how nice it was having somewhere decent in the village to eat lunch. When Ralph returned to his seat, Ron mentioned the houses Ralph was having built. 'So glad you got permission for them. The price of houses around here is astronomical. Renting out your properties will inject new life into the place – encourage families and such. This snow has held things up though, hasn't it?'

'Unfortunately it has, but with luck they'll all be completed by the middle of the summer.'

'Have you got any tenants yet?'

Muriel eagerly explained the situation. 'Alan here,' she nodded her head in the direction of the barman, 'and Linda are having one, though it won't be ready in time for their wedding, and three of the others are already promised. So that leaves us with four tenants to find, but we've had lots of enquiries, haven't we, Ralph?'

'Yes, we have. I'm being a bit particular about the tenants. I don't want the houses being rented by people who don't actually *need* housing in the village. None of this business of using them as weekend hideaways. The houses must serve a definite purpose. I haven't, or rather *we* haven't had them built just to make money.'

Sheila, impressed by Ralph's good intentions, said, 'Well, I think it's wonderful. The village needs those houses – we're losing so many young people because they can't afford to buy. I hear Mr Fitch is trying to snap up any cottages going spare. He's bought Pat's and he's put in a bid for one of the weekenders' cottages, but I don't suppose he'll be as high-minded as you are, Sir Ralph.'

Just as Ralph was about to thank Sheila for her compliment, the dining-room door burst open and Louise stood on the threshold looking around. She spotted Sheila and Ron, smiled sweetly when she saw with whom they were dining and went to join them. Ralph stood up, and belatedly Ron did too after another dig from Sheila's sharp fingernail.

As Sheila moved her chair closer to Ralph's to make room for Louise, she asked, 'Why aren't you having lunch at the rectory? You said you were.'

Teetering between tears of disappointment and an outburst of temper, Louise said between gritted teeth: 'They're going to Harriet's straight after lunch for the afternoon. Sylvia arranged it. I'll go and order my food.' She pushed her chair back so roughly that it almost fell over, but Ron caught it adroitly and stood it up for her.

'Well, really! She does seem annoyed,' Sheila whispered. 'I wonder what made Sylvia decide to do that? It seems awfully rude.'

Trying to pour oil on troubled waters, Muriel suggested that maybe Sylvia had got her plans confused. 'She must have so much to do with Caroline being away and the telephone to answer and things, I expect she's got mixed up. And the children will be missing their mother, so I suppose they'll be more difficult than usual, which won't help. They are such dear little things but so . . . inventive!'

Ralph wholeheartedly agreed with Muriel, and Ron said, 'Yes, I expect so. One at a time was enough for us. Two must be murder!'

'Looks to me as if our Louise could commit murder. That

Sylvia is getting too big for her boots, you know. But still, Louise loves working for Peter and he's so appreciative of what she does. She's completely reorganising the quarterly magazine, and of course you'll have got your copy of the parish telephone directory?'

Muriel nodded her agreement. 'Oh yes, we have. A very good idea, that. I didn't realise we had so many people connected with the church. I just wish they all . . .'

Louise returned, and as she sat down again she said, 'I've been told I'm to keep to the secretarial side and have nothing to do with the children or the house. I'm permitted – *permitted*, mind – to make myself a coffee when I want as Sylvia has too much to do to be waiting on me, she says.'

Muriel grew increasingly uncomfortable at Louise's outburst. When she'd finished speaking, Muriel said quietly, 'I think Sylvia is overwhelmed with the responsibility and all the work, and—'

'Oh no, Lady Templeton, it's because Caroline has told her not to let me have anything to do with the children.'

Ralph decided to intervene. 'Louise, I'm quite sure you're mistaken. Caroline's not like that.'

Louise retorted sharply, 'Peter would be delighted for me to help with the twins, but Sylvia's put her foot down and he's got to go along with it, or he'll catch it in the neck from Caroline if Madam Sylvia gives her notice in.' Louise said how sorry she felt for Peter with two women dominating him; it wasn't fair to him, not fair at all. He certainly didn't deserve all the harassment he got. So engrossed was she in her sympathy for Peter, she didn't realise that her eyes and her face glowed with love.

Muriel read the signs only too well. So did Ralph. So too did Ron. But Sheila blundered on with, 'Well, of course he's so lovely, so kind, he'll let them ride roughshod over him. You're so perceptive, Louise, trust you to put your finger on the problem. You ask him again, he's bound to let you help.'

Ron cleared his throat and firmly intervened. 'Louise, you'll not meddle in other people's affairs. Accept the situation. After all, since when have you enjoyed children's company? You're better with computers and things. That's the best way for you to help.'

'Please don't be telling me what to do, Dad. Haven't you noticed I'm a grown woman now?'

'In that case then, you should have more sense and behave like one. Finished, Sheila?'

'Well, yes, but I want . . .'

'Thank you, Ralph and you too, Muriel, for a very nice lunch. We'll do the same for you sometime. Come along, Sheila, we've lots to do.'

'Lots to do? What have we got to do then?' But Ron took her by the elbow and hurried her out. Louise gulped down the remains of her meal and after a quick, 'Goodbye,' she too left.

Ralph finished the last drops of his coffee, put down his cup and said, 'I'm afraid there's a big problem there. Let's hope Peter knows how to deal with it.'

'I'm sure he does.'

'Well, we'll see. "A woman scorned" you know . . .'

Chapter 4

Jimbo was unable to attend the next meeting of the Show committee, due to a severe cold. He'd been determined to go, but Harriet had insisted that he go to bed. 'Next week is absolutely hectic, so if you don't take care *this* week then it's a sure thing you'll be too ill to do anything *next* week. Ask Pat to go instead. After all, she's in charge that day.'

'Brilliant! Of course – ring her up. She'll enjoy all the gossip. Tell her she'll need to call round for my file with all my notes in.'

When Pat called Jimbo was in bed so Harriet gave her the notes and wished her good luck. Pat asked if there was any more news from Northumberland.

'I babysat for them last night and Peter said Caroline's parents were beginning to come round though they were still not out of the woods, obviously. Slight improvement, I understand. Caroline's hoping to come home next week. She's missing the children, to say nothing of Peter.'

'Oh well, that's good news. Them children are missing her and not 'alf.'

'They are. If you don't mind me saying, you're looking very smart tonight. I love your suit.'

'I saw this in a closing-down sale and it fitted. Glad you like it. I didn't really want to dress in the Oxfam shop but I'd no alternative before. I'll make notes of anything important and let Jimbo have these back.' She waved goodbye with the file and pushed her bike up Stocks Row.

There was plenty of laughter coming from The Royal Oak. A while since she'd been in there. If the meeting finished in good time she'd call in. See if Vera and Jimmy were in. She missed her chats over the garden wall with Vera. Pat glanced across to her old cottage as she crossed Church Lane. They'd put new windows in now. Double glazed, too – now that would have been nice. Still, not nearly as nice as where she lived now. She wouldn't change, not for a king's ransom. She wheeled her bike to the dark side of the church hall and put the lock on it. Yer never knew these days, not even in Turnham Malpas. The lights were on and Louise was making the coffee.

'Hi there! Milk and sugar?'

'Yes, please. One sugar.'

'I'm doing the coffee with Caroline being away.'

'She's hoping to be back next week.'

Louise swung round quickly, almost spilling the coffee she was handing to Pat. 'Is she? How do you know?'

'Harriet told me.'

'I see.'

Barry was the next to arrive. 'Two sugars, Louise, and plenty of milk. Make it strong. A man needs something to give him stamina!' He accepted his cup and went across to sit next to Pat. 'Hello, Pat. You're looking great tonight.'

'Thanks, you don't look so bad yourself. New jumper?'

'Yes, Mum bought it me for Christmas. Haven't seen you around.'

'No, well, I've been busy getting the house straight.'

45

'Any problems, ring for Barry. I shall be only too pleased to pop round and have a coffee in that nice kitchen of yours.' He put his arm around her shoulders and gave her a good squeeze.

'Barry!'

'Go on, give us a kiss!'

Pat pushed him off though at the same time she was quite enjoying his attentions. 'Give over! For goodness sake, what yer thinking of?'

'A kiss, that's what. A kiss from the best girl in the world.'

'Barry!'

'Go on! It'd liven up the meeting, wouldn't it, Louise?'

'I don't know about that.'

Pat chuckled. 'You've kissed the blarney stone, you 'ave.'

'There's not a drop of Irish blood in my veins. It's you, yer get me going.'

'Well, you're not getting going with me, Barry Jones. Just you watch your step.' It was a long time since any man had paid attention to Pat in that kind of way, and though she wouldn't have admitted it for the world she quite enjoyed his banter. His arm still lying nonchalantly across the back of her chair felt comfortable. She hitched ever so slightly closer to him and he squeezed her shoulder in recognition.

'Coming for a drink in the pub if we finish in time?'

Pat hesitated, then shook her head. She made the excuse that it would be late when they finished and she didn't like cycling up the drive in the dark when it got late.

'Tell yer what, I'll put yer bike in the back of the van and drive you home. How about that? That's worth a drink, isn't it?'

'You still driving that disgusting old van?'

'My Ferrari's being serviced.' He grinned and at such close quarters she could see his beautiful white teeth, evenly spaced and shining, and she sniffed the antiseptic smell of mouthwash on his breath with pleasure.

Pat dug him in the ribs. 'You daft thing.'

'Well?'

'All right then. One drink, that's all.'

Barry held out his empty cup to Louise. 'Here you are, thanks. Let's get this meeting speeded up tonight, I've other fish to fry.'

'Hmmmph!' Pat retorted. 'First time I've been likened to a cod.'

Barry laughed loudly and she could see he hadn't a single filling in his mouth. Somehow that seemed to put him in a class of his own. There weren't many men so careful of themselves that they hadn't got a single filling by the time they reached forty.

Louise called the meeting to order. She tapped the end of her pen on her saucer and said loudly, 'Can we begin, please? There's a lot to get through. Thank you. Good evening, everybody. Firstly, apologies via Peter for Caroline's absence. I understand her parents are showing some improvement at last, though they are still very ill and will be in hospital for some time yet. Also from Jimbo, who has a severe cold. Pat has come in his stead. Give him our best wishes, Pat, please, when you see him. Now, you've all received a copy of the minutes of the last meeting. Are there any matters arising?'

Bryn asked about the hot-air balloon situation. Had anything been done?

Pat nervously spoke up. 'In 'is notes Jimbo says the friends of 'is who 'ave the balloon are willing to come. They'll charge £5 a head for a turn. It sounds an awful lot of

47

money, doesn't it, but the cash they take will be donated to a charity.'

Michael Palmer thought that seemed very reasonable. 'I'd give £5 for a turn. Never tried it, but I'd like to. I wonder how many passengers they can take at once?'

Pat studied Jimbo's notes. 'Don't know – it doesn't say. He's given me a list of the food and the prices he'll be charging. There's a copy for everyone.' She passed the pile around the circle and they each took one.

Sheila Bissett was horrified. 'Fifty pence for a cup of tea? At our flower-arranging society we only charge twenty-five pence. That's outrageous. You can see what he's done. Paid a small amount for the concession and then he's charging prices like this. Shameful. It is for charity, after all.' She scanned further down the list. 'And look at this – fifty pence for a sausage roll!'

Pat leapt to his defence. 'Yes, and if you went into one of them posh cafés in Culworth, what would you pay there? Ninety-five pence for a small pot of tea. Nearly a pound for a scone with butter and jam. I think his prices are quite reasonable in the circumstances.'

'And what circumstances are those, pray?'

'Proper tables and chairs to sit at. Proper cups, not those blasted paper things that burn yer 'ands and make the tea taste like cardboard. Nice knives and spoons, not them blessed plastic things, and serviettes. And you've got to take into account the losses he stands from people nicking the cutlery. I reckon someone took enough for a whole set when we did the catering for a company "do" in Culworth. Six of each. Just wish I'd caught 'em at it. Besides which, you have nice smart pleasant waitresses serving at the counter and clearing the tables. I know 'cos I shall be organising 'em.'

'And what do you, with your education, know about arranging such matters?'

Barry, who had been slowly coming to the boil during this attack on Pat, now rose to his feet, crossed the circle of chairs and stood feet apart, pointing his finger in Sheila's face.

'Any more lip from you and we'll start talking about *your* education and *your* past, shall we?'

Michael quickly intervened. 'I say let's cool it, this isn't right.'

Jeremy tut-tutted and suggested Barry sat down.

Bryn shook his head and Linda blushed.

'I will when she's apologised. I'm waiting.'

Pat, embarrassed at his defence of her when she was quite capable of defending herself, muttered. 'It really doesn't matter, you know. I don't care.'

'No, but I do. Well? I'm still waiting.'

Louise quietly said to her mother, 'There's no call for that.'

Linda, who had never liked Sheila because in her opinion Sheila always treated her like something that had crawled out from under a stone, piped up with, 'I don't know what education has to do with it. If Mr Charter-Plackett has asked Pat to be in charge then he must think she's capable, and I myself think the prices are very reasonable.'

'So do I,' Bryn said, having grown weary of Sheila challenging every decision. 'Sit down, Barry, do and let's get on.'

Remembering that he wanted the meeting to finish in reasonable time so he could take Pat for a drink, Barry reluctantly agreed and sat down, putting his arm across the back of Pat's chair again as though that was where it belonged. Pat shuffled away from him a bit and he removed his arm and looked glum for the rest of the meeting.

Bryn said, 'Well, we've organised the food and the hot-air balloon rides, now I'm going to talk about the events in this arena Mr Fitch wants. I've scheduled things to happen so they don't clash, and so we don't get similar events following on after each other. First there's the fancy-dress parade, then the tug of war between the two pubs – I've put that early so they can compete before they've all had too much to drink. I'm donating a barrel of beer for the winners, as you know.'

There was a general murmur of thanks for his generosity which he acknowledged with a nod of his head. 'I understand that Sir Ronald,' he nodded his head in the direction of Sheila, 'will be starting them off. Best of three, I think. After that there's the school display, then the Morris Dancing.' He nodded enquiringly at Louise who agreed it was all in hand. 'Then the police motorcycle display team have agreed to come on. Oh – and to finish, there'll be the children's races. Thought that would keep the kids and their parents there all afternoon. I think that about sums it up.'

'Excellent! Well done!' Jeremy complimented Bryn.

'Absolutely, Bryn, that's great! Thank you very much indeed. What a lot of hard work.' Briskly consulting her list, Louise suggested they got on with the business in hand.

Bryn nodded and said, 'By the way, I'll leave *all* the children's fancy-dress competition to you, Michael – classes, prize, age groups, et cetera?'

'Of course.'

'We'll definitely have that as the first event in the arena then. Otherwise the costumes will be ruined if they have to wait. We'll do a grand procession round the Show, finishing in the arena. Could you sort some judges out, Michael?'

Briskly Louise pushed on through the agenda, and much to Barry's delight it closed within another half an hour, leaving him plenty of time to take Pat for a drink.

'Good night, everybody. See you on the twelfth of next month.'

'Not the twelfth, Barry. It's Friday the thirteenth!'

'Oh yes, that's right.'

While Barry was putting her bike in his van, he said, 'I could have strangled that Sheila.'

'Oh, don't worry, she's always like that. Oh Gawd, me bell's dropped off. Did yer hear it? Just a minute while I look for it. Here it is – rusted away it has, I'll have to get a new one.'

Barry put it in his pocket. 'I'll fix it for yer, Pat, leave it to me. Come on, hop in and we'll drive round.'

They parked the van in the car park behind the pub and walked round to the saloon door. Barry held it open for Pat and she popped in under his arm. As she straightened up she saw, sitting at her favourite table, Sylvia and Willie and opposite them Jimmy, whom she hadn't spoken to in a long while.

'What will yer 'ave?'

Pat hesitated and decided she'd get more trendy than in the past. 'I'll have a gin and tonic, please. Shall we go and sit with Jimmy and them?'

Barry didn't want to, but on the other hand he might be pushing things along too fast if he insisted they sat alone. Make too much of a point of his intentions in front of everyone.

'Yes, fine, I'll get the drinks.'

When Sylvia saw Pat coming across she slid further along the settle to make room for her.

Jimmy grinned at her. 'Well, Pat, long time no see. Too posh are yer nowadays then?'

'Enough of your cheek, Jimmy Glover. I've been far too busy getting straight as you well know. Just because I'm living in the Garden House doesn't mean I've given up on me friends. Hello Sylvia, hello Willie.'

She plumped down on the settle making sure she wasn't creasing her skirt.

'Must say you're looking smart, where've you been?' Jimmy commented.

'To the Show committee meeting in place of Jimbo, he's got a shocking cold and Harriet wouldn't let him go. Right meeting we've 'ad and not 'alf.'

Jimmy, always ready for a bit of gossip, said, 'Let's get your drink in and then yer can tell us.'

'That's all right, thanks, Barry's getting mine. Will yer mind if he sits with us?'

There was a chorus of, 'Of course not,' just as Barry came to the table with the drinks.

Jimmy greeted him with, 'Evenin', Barry. Don't see you in here much.'

'No.' Sylvia moved up a little further and Barry squeezed in beside Pat. 'I'm a Jug and Bottle man myself, but this was the nearest tonight. It's quite nice in here, isn't it? I might change my allegiance.' He smiled at Pat, showing those lovely white teeth again, and she smelt the mouthwash. She'd never known before that mouthwash could be so . . . so . . .

Willie urged Pat to tell them what had happened at the meeting.

'Sheila Bissett's put her foot in it again.'

Barry banged down his glass and said, 'Bloody woman! Needs her brains examining, saying Pat couldn't run the refreshment marquee! For two pins I'd have throttled her.'

Pat chuckled. Jimmy, unable to resist making a comment about Pat's escort, gave Barry a sly look and then said, 'It'll be a long way up that drive this time o' night on yer bike, Pat.'

'Mind yer own business, Jimmy.'

'It *is* my business. Me and Willie 'ere have been guarding your interests for a long time. We don't want you cycling up there in the dark, do we, Willie?' Willie agreed. 'Can I offer yer a lift in me taxi?' Jimmy asked.

Pat felt a fool. She blushed.

Barry laughed. 'Yer can stop digging for clues – *I'm* taking her home. Her bike's in my van right now.'

'Oh well then, I'm relieved. I know she'll be in capable 'ands with you, Barry. Oh yes, very capable hands. Very capable . . . hands.'

There was something about the twinkle in Jimmy's eye and the smirk on Willie's face which made Pat question what Jimmy had said. 'What do you mean by that?'

Jimmy jerked his thumb in Barry's direction. 'Ask 'im.'

'Well?'

'I don't know what he's talking about. Take no notice, Pat.'

'Why have you gone red then?'

'I haven't.' But he had. Bright red and very embarrassed.

Willie chuckled. 'Casanova. That's what he is. Casanova.'

'He's had more girls in the last twenty years than I've had hot dinners,' Jimmy sniggered.

'That wouldn't be difficult, seeing as it's mostly pork pie and a bag of crisps for yer dinner,' Pat retorted. Oddly she

53

felt quite pleased Barry was inclined that way. It would make life more exciting. Her Doug had been about as sexually active as a monk. She never did quite understand how she had ever managed to conceive twice.

'Come on then, Barry, if yer've finished yer drink. I've an early start in the morning, and it was already beginning to freeze when we left the meeting.' Barry squeezed out from the settle followed by Pat. Behind Barry's back Jimmy gave her the thumbs-up and Sylvia flashed her a wink.

Barry shouted, 'Night all,' as they both left.

As he helped her climb up into the van, he said, 'Take no notice of what they were saying in there.'

'Doesn't matter to me. You're only giving me a lift 'ome. Why should I worry?'

'Oh I see.' She was glad when he shut the doors. The air was freezing cold. In the short time they'd been outside her nose had gone cold and she was shivering.

'No heater in this old wagon, I expect?'

'No. I'm a hot-blooded man meself, don't need no heating.'

'Hot, are yer? So it *is* true?'

'Look! They were only pulling yer leg. OK, I haven't reached forty without having been around a bit. You wouldn't have it otherwise, would you?'

'No, I suppose not. I like a man to be a man. Anyway, it doesn't matter to me.' The slush of the last few days had now become treacherous ice. The wheels made crisp crunching sounds on the hardened ruts and ridges of the road surface. As they turned into the drive gates the van slewed across the road and almost slid into the stone pillars.

'Mind out, Barry! Watch it!'

'OK. OK. Keep yer hair on!'

Barry parked the van close to the estate tractors and the two motor mowers. Across the yard Pat saw Grandad's light was still on. She could pick out the pattern on his curtains. My, they were lovely. They were Michelle's choice, she had a good eye for colour she had. She saw Dean's light go off. Time she was in bed too.

'Thanks for the lift, Barry. How d'yer open this door?'

'Yer can't from the inside. There's something the matter with the lock.'

'Is that your idea of a joke?'

'Certainly not. Try it for yerself.'

She did and it wouldn't open.

'There's a price to pay. Give me a kiss and then I'll open it.'

'I should cocoa. I'm out of practice. Seven years since my Doug died, and I 'aven't kissed a man since. Not that I kissed him all that much when he was here. He wasn't the kissing kind.'

'I am. There's nothing like kissing a good woman, specially one who's nicely rounded like you. I prefer something to get hold of. Don't fancy stick-insect women. Come on, let's have a go.'

The idea was more tempting than he would ever know. Inside her, there welled up feelings she'd been ignoring for years. The touch of someone who appreciated her, her as she was, simply her. Pat. Pat Stubbs that was. 'You are daft. Go on then. Just a little peck and then I'm off in.'

'I've got you in my clutches and besides, I've also got yer bike. There's no escape, Pat Duckett. Come 'ere.'

Her handbag was in the way, and Jimbo's file dug relentlessly into her thigh. It must have dug into Barry's too because he thrust it impatiently onto the floor amongst the oily rags and toffee papers and the sawdusty bits around her feet. She opened her mouth to protest but he closed his lips on her open mouth and kissed her like she'd never been kissed before. She didn't respond, didn't eagerly give back what he was giving her, but she liked it. Oh yes, she liked it. She couldn't release her feelings but they were there, they had surfaced. A few more tries and she might give as good as she got. His hands began wandering . . .

'That'll do, Barry Jones. You've had yer kiss now let me out.'

As she waited for him to lift her bike out, she looked at the house and thought she saw Dean's curtain flick back into place.

'Good night, Pat. By jove, we could be good together, I can feel it. I'll be round for coffee tomorrow morning. See yer.'

Chapter 5

Barry turned up for coffee the morning after the Show committee meeting, just as he'd promised. Pat hadn't believed he would but she'd made sure when she got back from school that her hair was brushed – she was growing out her frizzled perm so it was difficult to make it look good, but she did her best. She'd changed from her school trousers and jumper and was wearing a skirt and sweater she'd spent a fortune on in M & S. It wasn't really meant to be for every day, but just in case he meant what he said she'd put it on. There was a pile of ironing to do so that seemed to be the easiest rather than him finding her sweating over cleaning the windows or something.

She snapped the board open, banged the iron on it and plugged it in. Now she'd two men to iron shirts for, the weekly ironing seemed to take an age. Barry didn't seem to wear shirts – well, not proper shirts, just T-shirts and things under thick sweaters. She thought about his abundant black hair, nearly like an Arab's, and those laughing brown eyes. Doug had been gloomy, Barry was jolly. Barry oozed sex; Doug had oozed sweat. When she thought about it, in her darker moments she'd often wondered why on earth she'd married him in the first place. Liked the idea of a wedding day, she supposed. The excitement of showing off an engagement ring. The thrill of walking arm in arm with a man, and it had seemed a good escape from that dreary job in the café . . . She was just finishing the last of her father's handkerchiefs, when she heard Barry's van skidding into the yard.

Pat tried to remain unconcerned, but her heart skipped a beat and that strange feeling she'd experienced when he'd kissed her surfaced again.

The back door shot open.

'Morning, Pat. Got the kettle on? I've only got fifteen minutes.' He was standing in the doorway laughing at her. Pat bent down to unplug the iron.

'Not for you I haven't, but I'm having one.'

'Aw now, Pat. You promised.'

'No, I didn't. You said you were coming, I didn't promise anything.'

'Come on, Pat, do a fella a good turn. I've been working since just after seven, and it's half-past ten, OK?'

Pat grinned. 'OK. Just this once, but don't make a habit of it.'

They sat at the kitchen table where Barry had already envisaged he'd be having his bowl of porridge one day. 'Nice kitchen this. Very nice.' He looked round appreciatively. 'I told you this was the right spot for the table, didn't I?'

'You did.'

'Pat!'

'Yes?'

'There's a new theme park opened, have the kids been to it?'

'No. Got no transport.'

'How about it then?'

'Well, I can't go, can I? There's no bus, and what's more I can't afford it.'

'I mean, shall I take you all?'

Pat took a deep breath and said, 'I don't know about that.'

'We'd go in my car, not the old van. Yer dad can come as well. I like yer dad. He's a skilled craftsman and I've a lot of time for people like him.'

'So are you. He'd never come. By the time he's done a week's hard graft gardening up at the Big House he's ready for his chair and the racing weekends. I'll ask the kids, see what they say. Dean's getting a bit old for gallivanting with his mother.'

Barry drank the last drops of his coffee, put down his cup and said, 'There's a chance, then?'

'Perhaps.'

'Saturday, I thought. I'm a real kid at those sort of things. I have a go on everything that moves, every blessed thing there is.'

'OK. We'll see.'

'I'll call tomorrow and you can tell me what you think.'

'OK.' For the first time since he'd entered the house Pat looked directly at him. She'd never noticed how long his eyelashes were, nor how strong his hands looked, resting tensely on the table, locked tightly finger to finger. This morning there was a faint smell of aftershave. He stood up, leaned across and kissed her. He tasted of sweetness, and kindness, and security today.

'Any coffee going, Pat?' It was Dad calling from the back door, as he stopped to pull off his boots.

'I'll be off. Persuade Michelle to come. Morning, Greenwood.'

'Morning, Barry. Jeremy's looking for you. Old Fitch is on the warpath, been on the phone from London for nearly half an hour. If I were you I'd look busy and be quick about it.'

'Right. Bye, Pat!'

'Bye.' Pat went to the cupboard to get a mug. 'How's things, Dad? You don't usually come in for coffee.'

'No, well, I saw his van, and I knew Jeremy was looking for 'im. They're getting him a mobile then he won't be able to sneak off. Got in the habit of calling to see 'er at Home Farm, before that the Nightingales.'

'The Nightingales? God! As if she isn't busy enough with that brood of hers.'

Greenwood looked wise. 'Ah, well. Yer'd better watch out, if he's started calling here. My coffee ready? I 'aven't got all day.'

After Dad had gone Pat went back to the ironing. She was in two minds. Furious with herself for not knowing what Barry got up to, but at the same time captivated by him. Well, blow it. So long as he didn't get her into bed why shouldn't she have a fling? Someone to take her out in his car, someone to laugh with – and heaven alone knew, there'd been little enough of *that* these last years. She'd browbeat Michelle into going to the theme park come Saturday – she'd *pay* her to go, anything so long as Barry took them out. Why shouldn't she have some fun? Why-ever not? Right, Barry Jones, you're on. Oh no! Half-past eleven. She unplugged the iron again, threw on her coat and wool hat, grabbed her bike and fled down the drive to the school.

After the school dinner was finished and the children were out at play, Mr Palmer left Mrs Hardaker in charge and disappeared into his house for half an hour's break. Pat, needing some more cleaning materials, went across to the schoolhouse to interrupt his rest and ask for some petty cash.

'Hello-o-o, Mr Palmer! Hello! Anyone at home?' She knocked on the door but getting no reply, pushed it open and called down the passage: 'Hello! It's only me!' The sitting-room door was partly open so Pat pushed it wider and saw Mr Palmer standing by his sideboard with a silver photo frame in his hand and what appeared to her to be a daft expression on his face. She cleared her throat. 'Excuse me – I did knock.'

Mr Palmer jumped and hastily put away the frame in the open sideboard drawer and slammed it shut. 'You made me jump, Mrs Duckett. What can I do for you?'

'Well, Mr Palmer, I'm needing petty cash for cleaning materials. I'm a bit short this week otherwise I would have got them and then asked for a refund. Sorry to disturb you. I did shout but you didn't hear me.'

'No, no. Sorry. Right. I'll get the petty cash out. Ten-pound note be enough?'

'Oh, yes. I'll bring the change back. It's bleach for the lavatories and the kitchen sink, and polish and window cleaner.'

Mr Palmer disappeared into the kitchen. Pat knew he'd be a few minutes, he kept the petty cash well locked up. She tiptoed across to the sideboard and after one quick check at the kitchen door, slipped the drawer open and found herself staring at Suzy Meadows. She swiftly shut the drawer and went back to where she'd been standing, her head racing with thoughts. He'd kept *that* quiet. Who'd have thought . . . Mr Palmer came back.

'Oh thanks, Mr Palmer. I'll be back with the bill and the change.'

'I'll be in school when you get back, so bring it to me in my office.'

'Right-ho.'

Suzy Meadows. Well! She wouldn't believe it. No one had heard a thing about her since the rector and Dr Harris had adopted the twins. Just fancy if the rector knew! Or more so, if Dr Harris knew! The crafty monkey, he must have been in contact with her all this time. Over two years since she'd left. Must be, 'cos the twins were born beginning of December and they were over two now. Wait till she told Jimmy and them, they'd be amazed. Then she thought about how kind Mr Palmer had always been to her, and how much she'd liked Suzy Meadows when she'd lived in the village, and how lovely Suzy's three girls had been. Stupid names – Daisy, Pansy and Rosie. Beautiful girls, though.

The bell on the door of the Store pinged joyously as Pat pushed it open.

'Hello, Jimbo! Am I glad to get inside. It's still so cold. Hope this blessed slush will be gone soon. Can't be soon enough for me. Cold better?'

'Not much, but thanks for asking. Meeting go all right?'

'Yes, thanks. Usual arguing and gossiping. I've brought you up to date in your file. Here it is.'

'Oh good! Must press on. I'll look at it later.'

The Store was busy. People who'd put off coming out shopping while the snow was at its worst, had now decided they couldn't wait any longer and were busy stocking up. Barry's mother was the centre of a small group exchanging news, thankful of an outlet at last after being incarcerated by the snow.

Barry's mother had to move to allow Pat to reach for the bottle of bleach. Pat made a pretence of studying the different brands on offer to give herself an opportunity to find out what they were talking about.

Barry's mother put down her wire basket, and folding her arms said, 'So, he's been seen with 'er by our Terry *and* our Kenny when they went there to the races at New Year.'

'No!'

'True as I'm 'ere. With 'er *and* 'er girls. Course, I'm saying nothing. I'm drawing no conclusions.' She drew herself up self-righteously and looked round the attentive group. 'It doesn't do to gossip, does it? But really! She's third-hand and not half. Bet the rector, God bless him, 'ud be surprised if he knew!'

By mistake, Pat knocked Barry's mother's arm as she reached for the bleach.

'Oh sorry, Mrs Jones.'

'Hello there, Pat. We're just talking about your Mr Palmer. Right sly old fox he is, don't yer think?'

'It so happens I have the greatest respect for Mr Palmer. He's a very nice person to work with. And if you're gossiping about 'im then I don't want to hear.'

Barry's mother gave her arm a nudge. 'Oh come on, Pat, don't tell us you don't know. You must. He's seeing Suzy Meadows. Thick as thieves they are. It's all round the village. Bet you could tell us a thing or two.'

'I couldn't and I wouldn't. You should watch your tongue. One day you'll get sued for what you say, you will.'

'Listen who's talking! Whiter than white are we? Huh! You've passed on some rare bits of gossip in your time, Pat Duckett. Gone all hoity toity now, have yer, since yer've gone to live at the Garden House.'

'No, I haven't, but I don't pass scandal on about someone who doesn't deserve it.'

'That's cheek, that is, Pat. Accusing me of stirring it. Don't come to me when you want to know the latest. Giving yerself airs!'

Pat shrugged her shoulders and went to the till. 'Give me a bill, will yer, Jimbo? It's for the school.'

Over the shelves Pat heard Barry's mother say, 'Listen to 'er! Jimbo this and Jimbo that! Who does she think she is?'

Jimbo winked at her. Pat chuckled and left.

Mr Palmer was in his little office when she got back to the school. Everyone called it his office but all it really consisted of was a desk, a chair, and a wash basin, with a curtain across one corner for the teachers to put their coats behind. If a parent came to see him, they sat in his chair and he propped himself on the wash basin.

Pat put her head round the door. 'There you are! Here's the change and the bill. I'll be off now. See yer later, Mr Palmer. Snow'll soon be gone, thank goodness.'

As she mounted her bike out in Jacks Lane, Barry passed in his van. He pulled up with a shriek of brakes and the slush in the road sprayed wildly about, catching Pat's boots and bike wheels. She jumped to one side as best she could.

'Eh, Barry! What yer doing? Watch out!'

Barry leaned out of the window. 'Sorry! It was the shock of seeing you – got my blood racing. How's things?'

'Same as they were when I saw yer last. Middling!'

'Don't forget to ask your Michelle, will you? I'm looking forward to it. One whole day in your company!'

'I'm looking forward to it as well.' She put her hand on the edge of the open window. 'I haven't asked our Michelle, not in school-time. I'll ask her tonight. I'm sure she'll say yes.'

He leaned out of the window and tried to kiss her, but Pat dodged away. Barry laughed, bunched his fingers, kissed them with a flourish, put the van into gear and drove away, taking the corner into Church Lane with more speed than sense. Neither Pat nor Barry had seen his mother standing at the corner of Shepherds Hill and Jacks Lane watching them. Neither of them saw her lips press firmly together in annoyance. As everyone in the village knew to their cost, Barry's mother's displeasure was something to be taken seriously.

Chapter 6

Peter took the children with him when he went to pick up Caroline from the station. They'd been awake since six. Having no one at home to care for them while he said his early-morning prayers in the church, Peter had had to abandon his half-hour prayers and his three-mile morning run with Jimbo until Caroline got back, so he'd been containing them and entertaining them that morning for what seemed like half a year. The need for re-establishing his life pattern was growing; his routine of having Caroline around him, of breathing her scent, of holding her, of knowing she was there picking up the pieces. God, he'd be glad to have her back. He'd taken to touching her coat in the hall cupboard whenever he had to open it and sometimes when he didn't need to. He just deliberately held the door open and absorbed the feeling of Caroline by holding her coat. It was the longest time they'd been apart since their wedding day.

At the very least her return would sort out the problems with Louise and Sylvia. What a fortnight it had been! Placating one, confiding in the other. He couldn't manage without either of them, with Caroline away. But he had to finish with Louise, even if she did make his life easier and free him for the parish. Caroline would see to everything, that was for sure.

In his rearview mirror he spotted Alex trying to undo the fastening on his safety seat. 'Alex, no! Leave that, please. We shan't be long, the station's only five minutes away.'

Peter found a place in the station car park, and with a twin firmly gripped in either hand, he marched to the station entrance. Beth took fright at the size of the station concourse and had to be picked up. She clung to him, her soft cheek against his own, her eyes closed, her breath fluttering rapidly on his neck. He checked the arrival screen and mercifully he'd got there on time. 'Platform seven it says, children. We've got to go over the bridge. Come along, Alex. Hurry. Big steps. Up! One, two, three.' Beth struggled to get down. 'Me, me.' She climbed the steps too, her sturdy little legs trying to keep pace with Peter's.

As they reached the platform on the other side, Caroline's train drew in. Passengers came pouring off. For a moment Peter couldn't see Caroline and then he did. His heart bounded with joy. 'Look! There she is, children! There she is! There's Mummy!'

As she walked towards them, Peter rejoiced in her strong determined walk, her dark hair blowing in the wind which swirled so cruelly along the platform, her sparkling eyes, the sheer joy the sight of her gave him. Caroline put down her cases. The children clung to her legs with cries of delight, Peter kissed her, she kissed him, she kissed the children and then Peter again, then hugged the children close. 'Darlings! I'm so glad to be home. I'm sure you've grown. Alex, you've had your hair cut!'

'Yes, he has. It kept falling into his eyes and annoying him and I knew you wouldn't like that. And, yes, I think they *have* grown. Are we glad to see you. You take the children, I'll carry your cases. How's things at the hospital?'

'Well, both Mother and Dad are improving every day. Mother's got this mad idea she's going to discharge herself. Which of course is ridiculous as she has both legs in plaster and a fractured skull and three broken ribs and terrible bruising. She's making their lives hell in there. Dad keeps trying to calm her down and constantly reminds her that she's the patient and not the doctor at the moment, but it's no good, she won't behave herself. In some ways I'm quite glad I've come away, she's so embarrassing!'

'Sounds as though she's on the mend.'

'She is. Oh yes, she is. I may go back up there when they both come out, just for a few days. But that won't be for some time yet. Hurry up, I'm longing to get back home and catch up on all the news.'

When Peter unlocked the front door of the rectory, he called out; 'Sylvia, we're back!' Alex and Beth ran straight to the kitchen, shouting 'Sylvie, Sylvie, Mummy come. Mummy come on train.' But there was no reply.

On the kitchen table was a note.

Welcome home. Glad you're back. Thought it would be nice for you to have the place to yourselves for a while. Casserole and jacket potatoes in oven. Fruit pie in fridge. Kettle just boiled. Cake in cake box. Messages in study. See you 8 a.m. tomorrow.

Yours, Sylvia

'Isn't that lovely of her? She's so thoughtful. I don't know what we'd do without her.'

It wasn't until they were in bed that night that Peter confessed how close they'd come to losing her.

'Her notice? I don't believe this. How could you let it happen?'

'I didn't let it happen. It just nearly did.'

'If she goes, then I've had it. I won't cope.'

'We'd get someone else.'

'There's no one like Sylvia. She and I understand one another. She can't be replaced.'

'Don't worry, darling. She's still here. You mustn't fret.'

'It was Louise interfering, wasn't it?'

'Well, yes.'

'I knew it. The woman's a menace.'

'She's a tremendous help to me. She's so efficient and full of bright ideas. I don't know how I managed before she came.'

'I see. Has she got a proper job yet?'

'No.'

'I see. Has she been for any interviews?'

'No.'

'I see.'

'You keep saying "I see". You must have a very clear picture in your mind by now.'

'Oh, I have. I always have had about her. The way she feels about you is there in her face whenever she looks at you.'

'What *do* you mean?'

'Peter, you are an absolute darling! You never notice, do you, that Louise actually glows when she looks at you. She tries hard to disguise it, but she can't – not from *me* anyhow. However, there's one thing I'm sure of – it isn't *she* who's in bed with the handsomest man there ever was, but *me*, so we're going to enjoy ourselves. It's been such a long time . . .'

*

69

Over breakfast, Caroline told Peter he should tell Louise she was not needed any more. 'After all, losing Sylvia would be a greater loss than Louise going, believe you me.'

'In my own time, Caroline, in my own time. I have absolutely no justification for asking her to stop working for me. She's in the middle of the quarterly magazine and saving me hours of typing time. I'm sorry, I can't dismiss her out of hand. Just allow me to do it gradually. Please. This is my area, after all.'

'Agreed. It is. Sorry, I forgot. But I won't brook any interference in my domain. What's sauce for the . . .'

'Right.' He looked at her, enjoying her early-morning look, and the dampness of her hair fresh from the shower. 'Love you. Last night . . .'

Caroline put her hand on his as he reached out to her across the kitchen table. 'I know. Love you.' Their brief moment together was split apart by Beth, who had crammed her mouth with toast and was quietly choking. 'Oh, heavens above!'

They were in his study going over the notices for the following Sunday so Caroline would be up to date, when Peter couldn't resist holding her tight and kissing her. Neither of them noticed that Sylvia had been to the front door to let Louise in. The first they knew was the study door opening and Louise saying, 'Good morning, Peter . . . Oh, sorry!'

Caroline was furious with herself for allowing Louise to catch them embracing, but on the other hand perhaps it would serve to emphasise that there were no grounds for thinking she might make progress with Peter.

'Good morning, Louise. How's things?' Caroline said.

'Very well, thanks. Nice to have you back. We've managed to keep things going, haven't we, Peter?'

He nodded in reply. Louise asked after her parents and then Caroline excused herself and went to attend to the children.

'Now let's get down to work.' Peter smiled his devastating smile and Louise's insides flipped. Oh God, he was gorgeous. She felt a powerful jealousy of Caroline and her intimacy with him.

'The magazine is nearly ready for putting together. Just needs my letter for the inside page and then you can finish laying it out. After that there'll be the photocopying and the collating and stapling. From then on I can't take advantage of you any longer. You must have time to concentrate on getting a new position.'

'Are you saying you don't want me to come any more?'

'Not that, no. I'm merely being considerate to you. No one can manage nowadays without a regular income, and I'm trying to give you the time to attend to that.'

'But I *want* to help. I can go for interviews any time. Who'll do the weekly *Parish News*? Who'll collect the material for the magazine? Who'll type all the parish correspondence? You can't, you've enough to do.'

'Somehow or other I'll manage. There must be lots of people who would be glad to assist. Your help has been invaluable, but my conscience won't allow me to let you do it any longer.'

'Don't let your conscience worry you.' Louise turned swiftly in her chair and staring straight at him with an angry face said, 'Is this because of Sylvia? Has she said something?'

'No. Certainly not. I make my own decisions.' Louise was tempted to ask if it was Caroline who had queered her pitch, but quickly changed her mind. That would alienate him and she couldn't face that. The sun was coming in through the study window, catching the red-gold glints in his hair, making, as she saw it, a halo around his head. He looked so handsome, so . . . charismatic. She could feel his strong vibes reaching her from across the room. Perhaps one day she would be stroking that wonderful head of hair and . . . Then she remembered someone saying that Peter had looked so penetratingly at them, they genuinely believed he'd read their thoughts. What if he was reading hers right now?

Swamped by her emotions and quite unable to control her feelings for Peter, Louise burst into tears and fled from the study. Startled by her reaction Peter called for Caroline.

She appeared at the study door, her arms full of clean laundry. 'Yes?'

'It's Louise, have you seen her just now?'

'No.'

'She's burst into tears and run out.'

'Run where?'

'I don't know. Somewhere. You go and find her – please. I mustn't.'

'Right. What have you been doing to her, I ask myself.'

'Absolutely nothing. As you well know.'

Caroline grinned, put down the laundry on the hall table and went in search of her. She noticed the front door slightly ajar. Panicking, she shouted, 'Sylvia! Have you got the children?'

'They're both here with me, cleaning your bathroom.'

'OK, thanks. Peter, she must have gone home. She's left the front door open. Has she taken her bag and things?'

'Her bag's here.'

'Give it to me.' Her coat had gone from the hall cupboard, so Caroline put her own coat on and taking Louise's bag set off for the Bissetts' cottage.

The snow had gone completely now and the sun had broken through the clouds. The sight of the cottages ranged round the village green, the pond and Jimmy's geese, brought joy to Caroline's heart. How she loved living here. Timeless, beautiful, welcoming, enriching . . . she couldn't find enough words to describe how much it all meant to her. You could keep all your big impersonal cities, with their high-rise flats and their smoke and their traffic. There might not be much happening hereabouts, but it nourished her soul.

She tapped briskly on the door of the Bissetts' cottage. No one came. She tapped again and then after a moment the door opened. It was Sheila, looking upset.

'Good morning, Sheila.'

'Good morning, Caroline. Come in.' She opened the door wider and Caroline stepped in. It was the first time she'd been in Sheila's cottage, and somehow the décor didn't take her by surprise. It was just how she had imagined Sheila would have decorated it. Sweetly pretty, overdone with frills and furbelows, pretty, non-controversial water-colour prints lined up on the walls and artificial flower arrangements placed in every conceivable spot.

'Terribly sorry, Sheila, but Louise seems to be upset. Has she come home?'

Sheila nodded.

'She's left her bag and things. Here they are. We don't know . . .'

'She won't tell me.'

'Should I see her?'

'If you like.' They'd conducted their conversation in stage whispers, but now Sheila said in a voice slightly louder than normal, 'Do come in, Dr Harris. I'm sure Louise will be pleased to see you.'

She was sitting scrunched up in a corner of Sheila's sofa, desperately trying to look as though nothing was the matter. But her eyes were red, her cheeks blotchy. When she saw Caroline she straightened herself up and attempted to give herself more presence.

'Louise! I'm so sorry. Can you possibly tell me what has upset you? Peter's distraught that it might be something he's said.'

Louise swallowed hard. 'Oh no, it's nothing he's said – no, not at all. He's too kind to say anything to upset *me*. Well, not intentionally anyway.'

'So what's caused all this? It's not like you. Is it the time of the month? If so, Peter will understand.'

Sheila froze with embarrassment; she was scandalised. Rectors shouldn't know about private things like that.

Louise flushed and said, 'Oh no, it's nothing like that. It's just that Peter said after the magazine was finished he wouldn't be needing me any more. He only said it out of kindness, I know, because he's anxious I have time to get a job. But I do so love coming across to the rectory and helping. It feels really worthwhile. Such a lovely atmosphere to work in. A real home. A truly welcoming place to be, and I would miss it.'

She looked up and gave Caroline a trembling smile. The compliment about her home won Caroline over despite all her wariness of Louise, and before she realised it she was saying, 'Look, if you like working for Peter, well, that's fine by me. After all, you only come three mornings. That gives you plenty of time for interviews and things, doesn't it? Peter does appreciate your help. He's so slow at typing and I'm worse than him, so it's no good me trying to help. I'm just sorry the church can't afford to pay you, but it can't. Don't let what's happened upset you too much,

Louise. Stay at home this morning and we'll start with a clean slate on Wednesday. How about that?'

'Thank you very much. I do appreciate you asking me. You're really kind. I'll be in on Wednesday then. A clean slate, like you said.'

'Good. I'll be off then.'

Sheila asked if she'd like to stay for coffee. 'No, thanks, I've a lot to do this morning – just got back, you see. Another time, perhaps. I'll let myself out.'

Caroline went home to the rectory unable to believe that she'd agreed to, no actually *invited* Louise to continue working there. She considered herself to be either the biggest fool this side of the Cul, or the very best kind of Christian ever.

In the Bissetts' cottage Louise couldn't believe her good luck. She kept dabbing her eyes so her mother wouldn't realise how pleased she was at the turn of events. Underneath, her triumph made her want to burst out laughing. Out of the ashes of her disastrous, ridiculous exit she had got exactly what she wanted. Caroline, not Peter, but *Caroline* asking her to go back to the rectory. What she'd said to make it happen she didn't know, but it had.

'Well, there you are, dear. You see? I told you how lovely Dr Harris is. She *must* like you going there. I heard the rector saying what a great help you are to him. I did tell you how nice they both are.'

'Indeed you did, Mother, indeed you did.'

Chapter 7

Pat went to get her bike out from under the shed where her father kept the mowers. If she didn't watch out she'd be late for opening up the school. Thank Gawd the last of the snow was gone. A bright winter sun was striking through the trees, and Pat felt a certain lift to her spirits. Truth to tell, she'd felt full of good spirits ever since Saturday. What a brilliant day they'd had. Barry certainly knew how to have a good time. Him going with them had persuaded Dean to go too and they'd had a lovely family day out. Michelle went on everything Barry and Dean went on, and Pat had to admit it was all wonderful: Michelle hand in hand with Barry, Dean opening up and talking more than he'd done for years. He needed a man, did Dean.

Where the blazes was her bike? It was no great prize, but it was all she had. Blast it! Someone had pinched it. She'd have to walk. She turned away cursing the light fingers of someone who could find her old bike worth stealing. Then she noticed propped against one of the mowers a bike which didn't belong to her. There was a luggage label tied to the handlebars. It said:

Dear Pat,
Have mended your bell. Here it is attached to your new bike.
With love, Barry.
P.S. Hope you like it.

It wasn't absolutely brand new, but near enough. And there, neatly fastened to the handlebars, was her old bell, well-oiled and cleaned up. Shining as all bicycle bells should. Pat couldn't believe it. It was no good, she'd have to give it back. She'd use it today and then . . . yes, and then give him it back. Let's hope he hadn't thrown her old bike away.

The saddle needed a bit of adjustment; her feet wouldn't reach the ground.

'Dad! Come here a minute.'

'I'm having my breakfast.'

'Never mind yer breakfast, come here and sharp.'

Grandad came grumbling out of the back door. 'What's so urgent I can't fini— Aye Aye! What's all this then? I didn't know you'd got a new bike.'

'Neither did I. I'm using it today and then it's going back.'

'Who's it from?'

'Guess who?'

'Not Barry?' Pat nodded. 'I warned you about 'im, didn't I?'

'Look, I need it right now to go to school on, then he's getting it back, believe me. Lower the saddle, will yer, Dad? It's getting late. I don't want to let Mr Palmer down. Be sharp.'

'All right. Hold yer horses.'

Michelle came out. 'Oh Mum, a new bike! Where did yer get it from?'

'Barry, and it's going back.'

Michelle was horrified. 'Mum, yer can't give presents back. He'll be ever so upset.'

'I don't care, he's got a cheek.'

'No, he hasn't, Mum, it's your present. He's only being kind. Please don't hurt his feelings.'

'Well, I shall.' Michelle burst into tears and ran inside.

'That it then, Dad? That's better. Thanks. Be nice to her, tell her I can't accept presents from him, no matter what.'

'OK. Off yer go, then.'

She'd be going to the Show committee tonight; she'd tell him then. They weren't at the stage for giving big presents. He'd ruined it all. She whirled along down the drive amazed at how far the bike went with such a small amount of effort. It definitely put her old bike in the shade and not half.

As she swung round into the schoolyard, Mr Palmer was coming back from the Store with his newspaper.

'Morning, Mrs Duckett. New bike, I see.'

'Not for long. It's going back.'

'Why? It looks great.'

'It is. It's the giver who isn't great. However, nice morning, isn't it? See yer later.'

When she'd finished her morning efforts at the school she went to the Store to pick up a few things she needed. A card for Dad for his birthday, some meat for tonight, four pints of milk and a couple of nice bread rolls for Dad at lunch-time. She propped her bike in the stand Jimbo had provided and wandered in.

Linda was concentrating on her accounts behind the post-office grille and Harriet was by the till.

'Hello, Pat. All right?'

'Yes thanks, Harriet. Jimbo's away at the conference today?'

'That's right. Back tomorrow night. Don't let on but Fran's in the back with Mother. Our part-timer's got the flu so I'm having to fill in. Jimbo would explode if he knew.' Pat tapped the side of her nose with her forefinger and promised not to tell.

She went between the shelves looking for the things she needed. She was just choosing her Dad's card when the little brass bell jangled angrily and the door slammed shut with a loud bang. Pat heard Barry's mother's voice. 'Would you mind telling me whose bike that is outside?'

Harriet said, 'Well I don't know really. Lots of people put their bikes there, sometimes even when they're not coming in here.'

Pat popped her head round the end of the card display. 'Someone wanting me?'

'Me.' Barry's mother tapped the lapel of her old brown anorak with a sharp finger as she marched towards Pat. 'Me, that's who. It's yours, is it?'

'Well, in a manner of speaking, yes.'

'I'll have you know that was *my* bike. What are you doing with it?'

Pat fumbled in the bottom of her bag and brought out the luggage label Barry had tied to it. Barry's mother snatched it from her but didn't have her reading glasses.

'I'll read it for you.' Pat took it back and read the words out loud. Harriet turned her back, to hide her laughter. Barry's mother all but exploded.

'He bought that bike from me for a song. I'd no idea he was giving it to *you*.' She became red in the face and for once was speechless.

'Don't you worry, you'll be able to give him his money back, if you haven't already spent it, 'cos he's getting it back tonight. I'm not having him giving me presents.'

'Well, at least you're showing more common sense than I gave you credit for; even so, our Barry's too good for the likes of you.' Harriet gasped. Linda pressed her handkerchief to her mouth in horror. But Barry's mother didn't realise she'd met her match.

Pat went white as a sheet. 'Considering your Barry's past history, I think it's me who's too good for him.'

'Past history?'

'Yes. If all I've heard is true, I'm the one who's in the position to be picking and choosing, not Barry.'

'Well, I never. Not one of my sons . . .'

It was Pat's turn to tap the brown anorak. 'Just a minute, what about your Kenny and that dodgy car? The police couldn't prove it but we all knew. And what about your Barry and his trips up to Nightingale Farm, eh? Or your Terry and that barmaid from The Jug and Bottle – it was her husband who blacked his eyes and broke his nose that time, wasn't it? Don't start denying it or I might remember some more juicy bits about the three of 'em.'

Unable to deny what Pat had said, Mrs Jones tried another method of attack. 'And what have you had to do to get that bike?' she sneered.

At this Pat drew herself up, turned her back on her and stalked out of the store.

Harriet was appalled. So rude. So hurtful. She felt proud of Pat, though; she was the first person she'd ever heard stand up to Mrs Jones. Jimbo would have given his right arm to have been here and heard all that.

'Anything I can get for you, Mrs Jones?' Harriet asked in her sweetest tones.

'No.' And she marched from the store, earrings swinging, breathing fire and intending to give Pat further lashings with her tongue. But she was too late to catch Pat, she was already disappearing up Stocks Row, pedalling furiously. If Mrs Jones could have seen her face she would have seen tears – and Pat hadn't cried in a long time.

It was a cold crisp night, and Pat was well wrapped up for her cycle-ride down the drive to the meeting. She'd debated all day as to whether she should keep the bike to spite Mrs Jones or hand it back like she'd first intended. Michelle was so upset. And Dean had put his pennyworth in, coming down on Michelle's side. 'Mum! He gave us a lovely day out, did Barry, he's really kind. I liked him. Don't be nasty to him.'

'Look, our Dean. You're old enough to understand about grown-ups. I don't want to encourage him. When you get to my age you need to take things steady. It's not like it is with these young things who hop into bed the first night they meet.'

'They're not all like that, Mum.'

'Well, I know, but I need to go steady, and giving me a nearly new bike is rushing his fences.'

'Tell yer what, Mum, I wish I'd seen his mother on it. That'd be a right laugh.' Pat couldn't help smiling at the thought.

By the time she reached the church hall she still hadn't decided what to do, but left the bike in the dark behind the hall well locked up.

Louise was making the coffee tonight, and Pat was the first again.

'Hello, Louise.'

'Hello, Pat. You take sugar, don't you?'

'Yes, please, but only half. I'm trying to lose a bit of weight.'

'It's a slow process, isn't it? I keep trying but it's such hard work when you've got a sweet tooth.'

Pat covertly eyed Louise's figure and secretly agreed she did need to lose weight. 'Chocaholic, that's me.'

'Me too.'

Barry was the next to arrive, his face alight with the anticipation of hearing Pat's gratitude.

'Evening, Pat.' He stood, legs apart, arms folded directly in front of her, waiting expectantly. 'Well then, what d'yer think to it?' His handsome vigorous face was so appealing in its childlike eagerness that Pat couldn't ask him to take it back.

'Well, Barry, I . . .'

'Go on then.'

'I owe you a big thank you. It's the best present I've had in years.'

'Aw Pat, that's great. 'Ere, give us a kiss.' He reached out with both arms, gave her a hug and kissed her cheek in front of the rest of the committee just arriving together.

'Barry!'

'Never mind them, they won't mind. D'yer like it really?'

'It's lovely. It goes so fast. One turn of the pedals and I'm halfway down the drive. It's wonderful. What have yer done with my old one?'

'It's still in the back of the van. Daren't throw it away in case you wouldn't keep yer new one.'

'Our Michelle's dead impressed.'

'Does she need a new bike?'

'No, no, I've bought her one already.'

Barry looked disappointed. 'Anyway, so long as your bike pleases you, that's what counts. Couldn't let you go on any longer with that old thing of yours.'

Linda, sitting on a chair drinking her coffee, put down her cup and said, 'After what went on in the Store today,

I'm surprised Pat hasn't thrown it in the beck.' Barry spun round to face her. Pat tried to shut her up, but she was too intent on her story to notice. 'The way your mother treated her, it's a wonder Pat's still speaking to you, Barry Jones. It was a disgrace.'

'What's this all about?' Barry asked Pat.

'Look, I'll tell yer later, all right? Not now. Give me a lift 'ome and then.'

Louise called the meeting to order. 'Can we begin, please? Are we all seated? Right. You have the minutes of the last meeting; are we all agreed to take them as read?' She looked round the circle and they all nodded their assent. 'Right then, matters arising.'

'I'm short of men for the tug-of-war team for The Royal Oak.'

'I need help with the competitions in the flower tent. It's impossible to do it all by myself, much as I try.'

'What are we doing about prizes for the fancy dress?'

'I've got far too many people wanting to have stalls. I'll never get them made in time.'

'Who's going to find all the money for everything? We have no advance funds, only what comes in at the gate on the day.'

'Who's opening it – Sir Ralph?'

'No, he's away all that month.'

'I'm planning for the children's display to last ten minutes. Is that long enough, do you think?'

The problems and queries seemed to last an age and Barry, who was so upset that his lovely idea had apparently been spoiled, scarcely noticed the progress of the meeting.

He only came to life when Louise gave them the date for the next meeting. He stood up. 'Right, that it then? We're off.'

He put Pat's bike in the van alongside her old one, and helped her in. They drove to the Garden House without saying a word. He never even offered her a drink in the pub. When he'd switched off the ignition, he turned towards her and said, 'Well?'

'She was annoyed, very angry in fact, that you'd given her bike to me.'

'I paid her for it.'

'She said you'd got it "for a song".'

'That's not true. I'll tell you something, Pat. I've realised just lately that all I ever do is go after women who are already well-married. That way, you see, they're unobtainable. That way, there's no chance I shall be in a position to commit myself to anything at all. And do you know why?'

'You don't like the idea of being tied down?'

'Well, I suppose it's partly that, but in truth it's because of my mother.'

Pat laughed. 'Come on, Barry, if yer under her thumb that much you can drive off into the sunset right now. We'll call it a day.'

'Our Kenny and our Terry, we're all the same. She rules our house with a rod of iron. Nobody would think we were grown men. Dad's given up, he can't fight any longer. She rules him too. She's no intention of any of us getting married and leaving home. Good money coming in and a purpose in life, that's what it is, and she thinks no one's good enough for us. I'm sorry. I expect she was a complete bitch. But the reason is, you see, you're available, aren't you?'

'Don't know about that.'

'Well, yer know, able to get married if you choose.'

'Avril Nightingale and her at Home Farm certainly weren't available.'

84

'If you've heard tales about me and Avril you can forget it. Right?'

'Right.'

'Just a bit of fun. Livens up the day.'

'Now we've got that straightened out, I'll be off in.'

'Friends again, then?'

'OK.'

'Take you out Saturday night. Just you and me?'

'Not Saturday, I'm working for Jimbo.'

'Give you a lift there and back?'

'Jimbo takes me. Another night.'

'OK. Coffee next week? Your kitchen?'

'Yes, if yer want. Thanks again for the bike. It's lovely. Good night.'

'That's all right, Pat. Glad I could be of service. I'll get it out for you. Next time my mother picks on you, ignore her. She's a jealous old bitch.'

'Thanks. Good night.'

Dad was waiting up. 'Did yer give him yer bike back then?'

Pat flung her coat and bag on a chair and flopped down beside her dad on the sofa.

'No, I didn't. He was so delighted with himself I couldn't disappoint him.'

'Michelle'll be glad. A dad would be nice for her, and for Dean too.'

'I know. I know. But yer don't marry just to give yer kids a father, do yer?'

'No, but it is a plus, isn't it? And bringing up Dean isn't easy. A good dad would be a help. He'd fit in here. Me with me own room and that.'

'You wouldn't mind then?'

'No. We're two of a kind, Barry and me. Craftsmen,

85

who take pride in our work. Yer could do worse. He has a generous nature.' Dad laughed.

'That story about Avril Nightingale isn't true, right?'

'OK. OK. Right, I'm off to bed.'

'Good night, Dad.' She sat ten more minutes before the fire watching the dying embers. It was no good. She wasn't having all that again. Bed and that. She'd got used to being on her own. No point in upsetting the applecart.

Chapter 8

The quarterly magazine had reached the stage when several hours had to be spent photocopying all the pages. The copier was squeezed into a spare corner of the choir vestry so Louise, having been forewarned by Peter, always so thoughtful, put on her warmest trousers and sweater and was getting organised for heading off to the vestry one cold Saturday morning.

'Look, take a flask.'

'Mother, please. I'm not a child. If I get cold or thirsty I'll pop into the rectory for a drink. I don't like Thermos coffee, as you well know.'

'All right, dear, I'm only trying to help. You know your Dad's sorry you haven't been getting any interviews. Aren't you beginning to worry?'

Louise put the finishing touches to her face powder before she replied. 'No, not yet. A job will come in its own good time.'

'Yes, dear, but all your savings will be disappearing, won't they?'

Louise patted her mother's arm. 'Don't fret yourself, I'm all right. It's not your problem.'

'Well, I know, but Dad and I haven't got a bottomless pit. He gets a generous pension from the union, and there's his TV and speaking fees and that, but it'll only stretch so far.'

'Tell Dad not to worry. I know what I'm doing.' She bundled some papers into her briefcase and hurried away across the Green.

She knew for a fact that Caroline and the children were visiting a friend's house for the day, which left Peter in the rectory all by himself. Sylvia didn't go in at the weekend, unless it was an emergency, and as it was supposed to be Peter's day off, she had high hopes of a quiet hour with him all to herself.

The choir vestry was empty so Louise set about the copying. She needed to be methodical, because she was copying on both sides of the paper and she wanted it to be absolutely perfect. That was her way. Whatever she did had to be perfect. Sometimes she wished she wasn't like that, wished she was more laid back, gentler, more appealing – softer, more casual. But always people relied on her for perfection, always expected it of her and she'd come to want it herself more than anything.

The front cover had come out really well. That friend of Caroline's had done an excellent design job on it. It was ten o'clock. She decided she needed coffee. She took a copy of the front cover to show Peter. He answered the door as she knew he would.

'Oh, hello. How's it going?'

'Just fine. Look, I've brought you the front cover hot off the press, so to speak. What do you think?'

'Come in. Why, it's brilliant. Really good. Your idea of the yellow paper for the spring edition has worked out beautifully, hasn't it? However did we manage before you came? I'm just making coffee – would you like some?'

'Well, I didn't really expect it, but yes I will. That's most kind. It's so cold in that vestry.'

'Not for long. They start work next week on the central heating.'

'Really? Where have you found the money for it?'

'Mr Fitch at the Big House gave it to us.'

Louise whistled. 'My word. How generous.'

'It certainly was.'

Louise spent a blissful half-hour sitting with Peter in the kitchen, talking about this and that. There were no interruptions, no children calling for Daddy, no wife looking askance at her, no housekeeper looking daggers, no telephone ringing. Just the meeting of two beautiful people.

He looked different in his casual clothes; jeans, the collar of a checked shirt showing at the neck of his black sweater. She admired his big strong hands wrapped round his mug of coffee. All of six feet five, but gentle and vulnerable. Broad-shouldered but needing support. Physically powerful but such a sensitive man. Louise swallowed hard. Her excitement at being alone with him almost overwhelmed the tight rein she had on her emotions; she mustn't let her feelings ruin this wonderful opportunity.

'You must be glad of a day by yourself. The children can be very trying, can't they?'

'I wouldn't be without them for the world. Until one has children of one's own, one doesn't remotely understand how deep the bond between parent and child goes.'

'Caroline does wonderfully with them, doesn't she, considering they're not . . . her . . . own.' She could have bitten her tongue out. The moment he'd realised what she was going to say, a shutter had come down over his face and he'd immediately withdrawn to some place she couldn't follow.

Desperate to retrieve the situation, she hastily added, 'Please forgive me.' She reached across the kitchen table and took his hand. 'I'd no business to say that. I'm so sorry. I have such respect for her, and for you. If I've given offence, please forgive me.'

Still holding his hand, her feelings for him surfaced and her eyes glowed with love, which she quickly veiled when his eyes opened and he said, 'You only spoke the truth. But never, never, *ever* mention the matter again.' He smiled sadly at her as though apologising for his curtness. Her heart went out to him.

Peter stood up and said, 'I promised myself some study-time today while the house is quiet. Would you mind if I got on with that now?'

Louise stood up also. 'Of course. I'll wash up the mugs and then I'll be off. There's still a lot to do.'

She might have overstepped the mark with her choice of subject, but she knew they'd moved closer together through having experienced that delicate moment. She'd certainly touched a raw spot.

The vestry was occupied when she got back. Gilbert Johns was there. He was kneeling down in front of the choir cupboard sorting through his sheet music.

He looked up as she came in. 'Hello, there. Will it be annoying if I look through my choir music while you do that?'

'Of course it won't. Just hope you're warmly dressed for it, though. It doesn't get any warmer in here.'

'The sun never gets round to these windows, does it? I've put an extra sweater on under my jacket.'

Still excited by her half-hour alone with Peter, Louise's hand trembled as she set the copier zinging again; the sound of its rythmic pulsations filled the vestry. She stood silently watching the sheets filing steadily from the machine, trying to bring common sense to the situation in the rectory kitchen. It wasn't the time for letting him know how she felt. Not yet. Instinct would tell her the right moment.

Gilbert carried on sorting through his music without speaking. He had little social chitchat, she knew, but he could at least say *something*. Without any warning, just then a whole shelf-ful of music fell from the cupboard, scattering all over the floor as far as Louise's feet and under the machine.

'Damn and blast! Oh, sorry. I do beg your pardon.'

'Here, let me help you pick it up. This lot could well do with cataloguing, couldn't it?'

'How right you are. It's one of those jobs I've kept promising to do for almost five years and haven't got round to.'

'I can't bear things not to be organised. Wouldn't it make life easier if it was all put in order?'

'Well, it would. I promise faithfully I shall do it this very next weekend.'

'Look, Gilbert. As you know, I'm not working at the moment . . .'

'So I heard.'

'If I sorted it all out, would I be doing you a good turn?'

He stood up, hands full of music, and looked intently at her. 'Do you mean that?'

'I wouldn't say it if I didn't.'

'You must be one of life's angels.'

Taken aback by his compliment, Louise didn't reply for a moment. Then: 'Not really, just someone who can't stand mess.'

'I don't wish to be impertinent, but would you know how to do it?'

'Well, as you are aware, I *am* a singer,' Gilbert looked embarrassed – and so he should, she thought, 'so I would have some idea. Though there may be a query or two.'

'I would be glad to advise.' He bowed graciously. 'I've never actually got to the bottom of all this music. One tends to have favourites, so I never have had all the stuff out. It could prove quite interesting.'

The copier interrupted them. It had ground to a halt from lack of paper. Gilbert stacked the piles of music he and Louise had collected on to the shelf, brushed his hands together to get rid of the dust, and with a brief, 'Thank you,' and a quiet, 'Good morning,' he put a sheaf of music in his music case and left the vestry.

She'd done it again; let her organising ability be made use of once more. If she kept on like this, when would anyone see her as anything other than a person obsessed by tidiness? She'd organised the rectory files, redesigned the quarterly magazine, put the parish directory together, revamped the weekly *Parish News*, done all the lists and the minutes for the Show, and now she'd be tackling a job someone had left undone for five years. After she'd completed cataloguing the music, that would be it. She wouldn't volunteer ever again to organise anything at all. Then perhaps people would see her as she wanted to be seen. In fact, as she really was. Passionate, loving, spirited, artistic.

She caught a glimpse of herself in the mirror, which for centuries rectors and choirmen had used to check their appearance before going into the church for a service. What she saw was strong, almost masculine features, with a straight, sharply cut hairstyle that did nothing to flatter her face. Though its colour was softer than it had been, she knew in her heart of hearts that Peter would prefer a more natural look. Even her grey sweater, neat and restrained, its polo neck covering her right up to her jaw, was merely serviceable but not alluring. There was nothing about her to tempt any man, least of all someone like Peter. Perhaps if she dressed more gently, in softer colours with more feminine styling, he would notice her. Yes, that was it! Forget the power dressing and the practical clothes. She'd re-vamp herself. *That was it!* She'd finish the copying and then she'd rush into Culworth and do something positive. This was where she'd been going wrong all these years, and like a stupid fool had never realised it. Yes, she'd dress more like . . .

Willie came in, a huge bunch of keys in his hand. 'Wanting to lock up if that's possible. You nearly done?'

'Oh yes, I have. In fact, I'll stop now and do the rest on Monday morning.'

'Sorry to rush yer but we can't leave the vestry unlocked with the church open to the public. Me and my Sylvia are going out for a couple of hours, so I want to lock the vestry up. Specially with the copier being in 'ere. You're doing a grand job with the Show and all this typing for the rector. You're good at your job, Louise, I'll give you that.'

What Willie said put fire into Louise's decision. She stopped only long enough to make everything tidy and then rushed away across the Green.

'Mother! I'm off into town.'

'Oh, good! Can I come too?'

'Sorry. Another day. I shall be ages.'

Sheila was disappointed. 'Oh well, all right then, but collect your father's suit from the cleaners. I'll give you the ticket before you go.'

'I might not have time.'

'Take it just in case.'

'I'll not wait for lunch.'

Curls, yes, restrained curls and waves. Not sculptured, like it was now. Yes, that's what she'd have. Coloured brown like her hair really was, but curly.

Chapter 9

That Saturday night, Pat and Barry went for a drink in The Royal Oak. They'd taken Michelle to the cinema in Culworth earlier in the evening, dropped her off at the Garden House and left her sitting in Grandad's room having a drink of tea and biscuits with him before she went to bed.

'Nice kid is Michelle.'

'She thinks you're the best thing since sliced bread.'

'Does she? That true?'

'It's true.'

'And Dean?'

'Oh, he's quite keen 'cos he'd like some cupboards in his room and he thinks you'd build them for him if . . .' She looked away, embarrassed by what she'd nearly said.

'I'll build them anyway.'

'It's not my house, you know. You'll only be improving it for Mr Fitch.'

'I dare say, but you'd have the use of 'em. I've plenty of wood I can scrounge. Nobody'll miss it. Cost next to nothing. I'll start next weekend.'

'Barry! Your mother already thinks there's something going on.'

'She'll be wrong then. Another gin?'

'Oh thanks. Let me pay for this.'

'When I need financial help I'll let you know.' He stood up and went across to the bar. Bryn was serving.

'Evening, Bryn. Where's that charming blonde bomb-shell of a wife of yours tonight then?'

'Wedding bells. Alan and Linda got married this morning and Georgie's been up there. We couldn't both go, and Georgie does like a good wedding, so she's representing The Royal Oak as yer might say.'

'I'd forgotten that. Funny chap.'

'He has his good points. First-rate cellarman.'

'Well, that's what you need in this business. Same again, please. You'll have heard the news about the sewers?'

'Sewers?'

'Yes. They've got to put sewer pipes in at the Big House. Been using septic tanks all these years and they're no longer adequate. All those people living there all week long's causing havoc with the plumbing, and the health people say there's to be a proper sewage system put in. Got to connect the house to the main system. And guess where they're going? Straight across the front lawns and then across Home Farm field and into the main road. There's been a long holdup because they've to be very careful where they dig, you see. County Hall has plans of the area all round here and there's ancient sites that the trench for the sewers will have to avoid. So they've been backwards and forwards with detailed plans making sure nothing's disturbed that shouldn't be disturbed. Course, that's what's taken the time and made the starting date so late.'

'God! How long will all that take?'

'Old Fitch says it's to be done like yesterday. Could be weeks, he's blazing mad. The phone-lines and the fax have been buzzing like nobody's business. He's kept fending them off but the day of reckoning has arrived.'

'But what about the Show? What are we going to do?'

'Exactly. With a bit of luck and a following wind, if you get my meaning, they might be finished in time. They start on Monday. Let's pray for fine weather, then they won't get held up.'

'All the effort we've put in . . . I can't believe it.'

'Neither can Mr Fitch. The Show was one way for him to get back at Sir Ralph. Yer know, all this Lord of the Manor stuff. But they can't put it off. Things is really serious, not to say disgusting, in the plumbing department up there.'

'Does Louise know?'

'Not yet. They only agreed it yesterday. Thought she might be in here tonight. Old Fitch is going mad about the damage to the lawns. They're his pride and joy. Spent pounds on bringing 'em up to scratch. Like bowling greens they are. "Manicured" I think is the word. Anyways, they'll be a right mess when they've finished digging. He tried to persuade them to take a different route and go out the other side of the estate, but that would be twice the distance and twice the cost so that's not on.'

'Serious for once, are you?'

'I'm not pulling yer leg, it's true.'

'No-o-o-o, I mean . . .' Bryn nodded his head in Pat's direction.

Barry looked across at Pat. She was wearing her new suit – a dark blue with a lovely soft flowered scarf in the neck. Her new haircut suited her, and the half-stone she'd lost had revealed the bone structure in her face. He liked what he saw. She caught him watching her, grinned and waved.

'Could be, Bryn, could be.'

'Since she started going out with you she's knocked ten years off her age. Could be moving to the Garden House has helped too.'

'Perhaps.'

'You're playing your cards close to your chest tonight.'

Barry laid his hand on his heart, grinned from ear to ear and said, 'There are some things lay too close to the heart for words. See yer.'

As he handed Pat her drink she said, 'What was Bryn saying?'

'What a glamorous beauty I was escorting tonight.'

'Don't be daft. I'm no beauty.'

'It's amazing what love can do.' He toasted her with his glass and then took a long drink of his beer.

'Yes, like a good thump round the head, and that's what you'll be getting before you're much older.'

'Be serious, Pat.'

'I am.'

'No, yer not. You pretend to be tough, but inside you're all marshmallow. Being tough's kept you going all this time – well, now you can stop the pretence.'

'It isn't a pretence. I am tough.'

'I'm going to find the marshmallow bit in you.' Barry took her hand in his and holding it firmly took it up to his lips, then he grinned and said, 'Oh God, disinfectant. Pat – for goodness sake!' He pushed her hand away and pretended to cough. Playfully she slapped him round his ear.

'I'll give you disinfectant! It's my new handcream. I'm fed up having hands that look as if they've been scrubbing floors with carbolic all week. Anyways, it doesn't look good to be serving food with chapped hands and broken nails.'

'You like working for Jimbo, don't you?'

'I do. It's like a new world opening up for me. For the first time in my life I'm becoming somebody. Not just a skivvy but *somebody*. I've never really thanked you for the bike. I do love it, Barry. Thanks ever so much. It's made such a difference.'

'I'm glad. Pat I've been thinking how about if . . . oh, there's Louise.' Barry waved to catch her eye, and beckoned her over. 'Come here, Louise. Got something to tell you.'

Louise gave him the thumbs-up and went to the bar to buy herself a dirnk.

Pat whispered to Barry, 'What in heaven's name has she done with herself? She's dyed her hair again. And she's changed the style.'

'Must say she looks different.'

'Different! That's to put it mildly. And new clothes. What the heck.'

Louise came across to their table. She put her drink down and seated herself next to Pat.

'Hello, thanks for asking me across. I'm supposed to be meeting someone but they haven't turned up yet. You wanted to tell me something?' The brown hair certainly suited her skin tone better, more like her own possibly, thought Pat, and the pale crushed-strawberry sweater with the soft neckline was certainly a more feminine style compared to the one she usually wore, but it was the cut of the black trousers which Pat had noticed as Louise walked across to them. They must have cost a bomb. Louise took a sip of her Cinzano and lemonade and looked enquiringly at Barry.

'Yes. Bad news, I'm afraid. On Monday they're starting digging to put the new sewer pipes in at the Big House. Right across the lawns, over Home Farm field and out into the main road.'

'*What?* Are you kidding me?'

'God's truth. Old Fitch has been trying to play for time, but the Health say do it now or we close you down. So he's got no alternative.'

'But they won't be finished in time, will they?'

'Good summer, let's hope so.'

'What a mess. All the work we've put in. The Morris Dancers, the police team, the hot-air balloon, the competitions.' She took a sip of her drink and then something else occurred to her. She sat bolt upright and for once spoke without considering every word she said. 'The printing – we've had the printing done! All that money. I'm expecting all the leaflets and posters to arrive this week. It's far too far advanced to cancel that. What are we going to do?' Some of the customers sitting close to their table heard Louise's raised voice and the news passed round the bar in a trice.

'Show cancelled, you say?'

'Never!'

'Well!'

'New sewers? Not before time. Our Melanie works in the kitchens, says them lavatories is a disgrace. They gurgles and don't flush properly, according to her.'

'Health have too much power. Shut 'em down, indeed! What business is it of theirs, I say?'

'Exactly. It's like living in a police state.'

'It is, yer right.'

'Time this government got their comeuppance.'

'Exactly. Give me yer glass, I'll get 'em in this time.'

Louise recovering from the first shock-waves, said, 'Still, two and a half months . . . that's a long time with these modern diggers and things, isn't it? We shall be all right, shan't we?' There was a request for reassurance in the tone of her voice.

'I expect so. Well, I hope so.'

'I shall go up to the Big House on Monday and have a word with Mr Fitch in my capacity as Show secretary.'

'Won't do much good. He's in Toronto and won't be back till next weekend.'

Pat, who hadn't spoken a word since Louise joined them, said how much she liked Louise's new hairstyle.

Louise looked pleased. 'Oh, thank you. I had it done this afternoon. Not had curly hair before.'

'New clothes too.'

'Yes. Not before time.'

Pat was puzzled at the back of her mind. There seemed to be something familiar about the clothes, and she couldn't think why.

They talked for a while longer and then Pat pushed back the cuff of Barry's jacket and looked at his watch. 'Time I went home, Barry. We'll love you and leave you, Louise. Hope yer friend turns up.'

'Friend? Oh yes. Right. Good night. Let's hope the sewers get done in time. I think I'll still go up there on Monday and have a word with the men. Chivvy them along a bit.'

'Good idea. Good night.'

Barry and Pat left the saloon, and after they'd gone heads got together and they became the subject of speculation.

'Just 'ope she knows what she be doin'.'

'All alike, them Joneses. Sex mad.'

'Talk about spreading it about.'

'Remember that time . . .'

'She wants to watch her step. Just got herself nicely sorted with that big house and that, and then he turns his sparkling eyes on her.'

'Cor, he's got something though, hasn't he? Those thighs! Gawd! Wouldn't mind a bit of it meself.'

'You devil you.'

'He's a bit of all right, is Barry.'

'Can't think what he sees in '*er*.'

There was no friend coming to join Louise, and she sat alone until her drink was finished and then she left.

'Before you go up to bed, Dean, I'll have a look to see where you want your cupboards putting.'

Dean leaped off the sofa. 'Do yer mean that? Are you going to make me some?'

'Your mother says I can. If that's all right with you.'

'Come up. I'll be your apprentice if you like.'

'OK.'

Pat put the kettle on and got out the cups and saucers. She found a crumpled tray cloth at the back of the tablecloth drawer and smoothed it out on the tray, anchoring it with the teapot and the sugar basin. Somehow she wanted to give a good impression. She didn't know why, but she did. She found some chocolate biscuits which Dean had missed and laid them out on a plate.

Barry came down, he was scribbling on a piece of paper he'd torn from the pad Dean used for his essays.

'There, that's it. I'll have it done in no time at all.'

'You're too kind. Don't do it if you're too busy.'

'Nonsense! He wants cupboards and cupboards he'll get. He could do with encouraging. Boys need a man about.'

He sat beside her on the sofa. She poured the tea, giving him a heaped teaspoon of sugar, the way she remembered he liked it.

'He's going to do well at school, isn't he?'

'Yes, but I don't know where he gets it from. Used to be a tearaway and now he's working all hours. School says when he's done his GCSEs, which isn't for a bit yet, he should stay on and do A-Levels and go to University. Doug would have been that proud.'

'Still miss him, Pat?'

'No.' She offered him the biscuits.

'Thanks. Once bitten, twice shy?'

'Don't know.'

'Come here. Give us a kiss.'

'Dad'll be in.'

'I've paid him to stay in his room.'

'You haven't, have you?'

'No. But he was young once.' Barry kissed her and this time she kissed him. She'd taken her jacket off when she'd come in the house, and as he kissed her Barry smoothed his hands up and down her bare arm to where her sleeve began, and then more adventurously he slipped his hand inside her blouse and was caressing her collar bone as they kissed. Then her neck and then he slid her bra strap from her shoulder and began kissing the hollows at the base of her neck.

'Mmmm . . . you smell good.'

'Barry, that's enough. Please.'

'Come on. Come on. You know you're beginning to enjoy it . . .'

And she was, but she was afraid. Afraid of wanting him to go on. Afraid of enjoying it too much. Afraid of going too far, from which there would be no stepping back. And anyways, Pat Duckett didn't do things like this and *enjoy* them. There wasn't room in Pat Duckett's life for enjoyment. All the same, it did feel . . .

'That's enough, you two. Anybody'd think you were teenagers. Is that tea still hot?'

It was her dad. Pat struggled to sit upright, hooking her bra strap back up and straightening her hair. Barry laughed. 'Come on, Greenwood. You're a spoilsport.'

'Spoilsport my foot,' Greenwood said. 'Your reputation goes before you, Barry. You're not spreading it about round here. I want her treated with respect, and your past record doesn't lead me to believe that's what you'll do.'

'Come off it! That's the first time we've really had a go.'

Humiliated, Pat snapped, 'Dad, be quiet. I'll get you a cup.' She disappeared into the kitchen.

'And I'll tell you something else, Barry. You don't mess her about and then float off to pastures new. She's had a rotten life with that fool she married. I'm not having her hurt again.'

'Cross my heart and hope to die, I'm not messing about. Honest.'

Pat came back.

'Oh, I see. Cup and saucer tonight. Usually it's a mug. Thanks, Pat. I'll say good night.' He nodded curtly to Barry, took his cup of tea from Pat and left.

'You'd better go. Thanks for the drink tonight.'

'That's all right, my pleasure. I've been thinking, Pat. I know someone who has a big residential caravan. I did some jobs for 'im a while back and he said any time I wanted to borrow it, so long as he wasn't needing it, I could. A week, he said. It's quite close to the sea and there's a river with trout fishing. I could take my rods and Dean could fish. There's places to visit. I know Michelle likes to look round gardens . . .'

Pat put up her hand to stop him. 'Oh no! I'm sorry, but no. I've got too much respect for my kids to have them knowing I'm . . .'

'Pat! Let me finish. There's three bedrooms. It's huge.

Dean and me could have one, you and Michelle the other and Greenwood could be on his own. How about that?'

'I'm sorry, beg yer pardon for misunderstanding. It's a wonderful idea, but I'd have to talk to them about it. I'll let you know. We'll have a family conference and see. It would have to be when the schools break up. Our Dean can't miss school at the moment, and our Michelle will want to be there, seeing as it's her last term.'

'Of course. I understand that. I'll make enquiries then, just in case. Say yes, please. Goodnight, Pat.' He left without giving her a kiss and she felt quite let down.

Before she went to sleep, Pat thought about the evening and how much she'd enjoyed it. A week by the sea would do them all good. But she couldn't understand the game Barry was playing. What with Avril Nightingale and the woman from Home Farm, and all the tales she'd heard, 'cos Jimmy and Willie knew what he was like, it didn't fit in that he wanted a holiday with two kids and a grandad. Still, she liked the bedroom arrangements and with Dad there he couldn't, could he?

As she was falling asleep she found the answer. It sprang into her mind in a flash, just when she was thinking about Barry's lips on her collar bone. Of course. *That was it*. It was as plain as the nose on yer face. *Louise was trying to look like Caroline*.

Chapter 10

On the Monday morning, instead of heading straight for the rectory, Louise went up to the Big House to see what was going on. Quite by chance she met Jeremy Mayer out on the front lawns. He was standing with his bulky legs apart, his pocket watch in his hand.

'Good morning, Jeremy. Nice day.'

'Good morning, Louise. To what do I owe this pleasure?'

'Sewers.'

'Ah, yes. They should be here by now, but they're not. Eight o'clock start they said, and it's now half-past nine.'

'It's all very well you know, but what about the Show? We can hardly run it if there's diggers and trenches in the way.'

'My very thoughts. Mr Fitch is steaming over there in Toronto. In fact, I'm amazed he hasn't been on the buzzer yet.'

'The leaflets and the posters are being delivered this week. I don't know what to do.'

'My dear young lady — and you're looking dashed handsome this morning, I must say — if Mr Fitch has anything to do with it, we shall *all* have spades in our hands before long, me included.'

He patted the sleeve of her new suede jacket with his white podgy hand. She adjusted the Jaeger scarf at her neck and said, 'Do you mean that?'

'He hasn't got where he is today without making things happen. But this time he seems to have come up against something even he can't fix. Believe me, if paying everyone to get behind a spade will speed things up, he'll do it. This Show's important, you see. It's all part of establishing himself in the village. Shouldn't be saying that but it's true and they all know it, but he doesn't realise they all know it.'

'So basically the committee have to keep their fingers crossed?'

'Exactly. But things don't augur well, do they, when the men haven't even turned up. Try not to worry.'

'We've arranged so many events,' Louise fretted. 'I haven't the courage to confirm things, but I'll have to pretend it's going ahead and keep my fingers crossed.'

The receptionist came out of the front door. 'Mr Mayer — it's Toronto!'

'Oh God! Pray for me. Coming, Fenella.' As fast as he could, considering his bulk, Jeremy scurried back inside.

Louise drove back along the drive, feeling in two minds about the Show. One half of her wanted to take the gamble that it would go ahead, the other cringed at the thought and wanted to cancel the whole thing. Peter might have a few ideas — she'd consult him. While she waited at the drive gates for an opportunity to get out into Church Lane, she looked at herself in her rearview mirror and liked what she saw. Minimum of make-up, brown curls, the Jaeger scarf adding a touch of colour to the dark, dark brown of her suede jacket. She'd spent a fortune. Thank heavens for little plastic cards. But the day of reckoning would surely come, she knew that. In fact, the idea of getting a job began to loom in the furthest corners of her mind. As Mother said, and she didn't say much of significance very often, money didn't last for ever. But she looked good. Oh yes. Depending on the atmosphere at the rectory, today could be *the day*. She was brought down from the clouds by a loud tooting behind her. It was Barry Jones wanting to get out of the gates.

She twinkled her fingers at him through the open window and with a quick check turned right into Church Lane. Barry Jones . . . He gave off that extra bit of something she couldn't quite define. A kind of manly vibrance. A sexuality which excited. Still, Pat was welcome to him – though what he saw in *her* she couldn't imagine. She, Louise Bissett, had her sights on higher targets than an estate carpenter.

She put on the handbrake, picked up her new leather handbag and her briefcase and leaped out ready for what could be the best day of her life so far. Because today things would happen. She was vague about exactly what, but today she was taking a big step forward of some kind.

When she opened the door in response to Louise's knock, Caroline was taken aback but strove not to show it.

'Good morning. Isn't it lovely today? Like the hair. What a transformation. Makes you look completely different!'

Louise hung her suede coat, with the new scarf tucked down the sleeve, in the cupboard and smiled. 'Thought it was time I smartened up, seeing as I shall be going for interviews soon. Don't want to look like a country bumpkin.'

'Absolutely not. They couldn't think that about you before and certainly not now. You've got interviews then?'

She couldn't downright lie so she said, 'In the pipeline, thank goodness. I'll do an hour and then go and finish the photocopying. Has Peter shown you the front cover?'

'Yes, I'm so pleased with it. When the magazine's finished I'd like a copy to send to my friend.'

'Of course. That design on yellow paper has worked really well. We make a good team, don't we, Peter and I?'

Tongue in cheek Caroline agreed and said, 'Sylvia's making coffee. I'll ask her to bring it in.'

Caroline was constructing a tent for the children with a couple of blankets and the kitchen table when Sylvia returned from taking Peter and Louise their coffee.

When Caroline emerged from under the table Sylvia said, 'There's your coffee, Dr Harris, on the corner by your rocking chair. I'll sit in the other one, otherwise we'll spoil the tent.'

Usually Caroline and Sylvia chatted while they had their morning break but today Sylvia was silent. The only sound in the kitchen was the slight creaking of Caroline's chair as she rocked and the chattering of the children having their own drink and biscuit in their makeshift tent.

'Is there something the matter, Sylvia? Have I upset you or something? You're awfully quiet today.'

'You haven't upset me, no.'

'Well, then are you not well? I'm sure we can manage if you'd rather be at home.'

'I'm quite well, thank you.'

'I see.' Caroline looked at her over the rim of her mug and pondered on the cause of Sylvia's silence. She'd come to rely on her for bits of information about the village that she ought to be aware of, and drinking their morning coffee was one of the best times for talking.

'Has someone else upset you then?'

'Nothing no one's said, if that's what you mean.'

'What then? Come on, you can tell me. I'm the soul of discretion.'

Sylvia reached across and placed her mug on the corner of the Aga. 'If I tell you I could upset several people. But I can't keep quiet. For your sake I can't keep quiet.'

'Well, then spit it out.'

Sylvia cleared her throat, hesitated for a moment while she found the right words and then said, 'Since the first day she walked in here, into this rectory, it's been as if a time bomb's been waiting to go off. I can't put it more strongly than that. A time bomb. You know it. I know it. The only one who doesn't is the rector, bless 'im. And now this.'

'This what?'

'Haven't you noticed anything different this morning with Louise?'

'She's had her hair done and bought some new clothes. I thought she looked quite good.'

'That's right – she does. But have you realised what she's doing? I noticed it in church yesterday.'

'Brightening herself up, I suppose. Ready for going to interviews.'

'No, Dr Harris, she's copying you.'

Caroline was astounded. 'Copying *me*? Really, Sylvia, I know you've never liked her but this is ridiculous.'

'Is it? Dark brown suede jacket, expensive scarf, Jaeger skirt and blouse not exactly like yours, but the same colours. Saw her in church, wearing a pale pink jumper and black trousers very, very similar to yours – and her hair has now gone brown and curly. Believe me, I'm right.'

'I never realised that, but you could be right . . . They *are* similar, aren't they?' Sylvia nodded. 'But what would she want to do that for?' Caroline said slowly.

'Think about it. It's not because she admires *you*, is it?'

Caroline put her mug down on the table and sat deep in thought. Then she said, 'I'll leave the children with you for a while, if I may.' She stood up and left the kitchen by the back door. Sylvia could see her walking in the garden; to outward appearances she was checking her plants but Sylvia, who knew her well, guessed rightly that she was searching in her mind for an answer to the problem.

Louise came in with the empty coffee mugs from the study before she left to finish the photocopying.

'Thanks for the coffee, I'm off now. Caroline not about?'

'No. She's not.'

'I wanted a word.'

'You can leave a message.'

'Tell her . . . tell her . . . Never mind, I'll see her next time I come.' As Louise went towards the door into the hall she half-turned and smiled oddly at Sylvia. The back door opened and in came Caroline.

'Louise! I'm glad I've caught you. I wanted a word.'

She returned to the kitchen. 'Oh right. Yes?'

'Flattering though it is for me to find that you have chosen to copy the way I dress, I don't like it.'

'The way you dress? What *do* you mean?'

'What you're wearing today. It's tantamount to a complete copy of my clothes.'

'You're being ridiculous. Why on earth should *I* want to copy *you*?'

'I don't know – you tell me.'

'You're totally mistaken. That was never my intent at all.'

'I don't like it, I'm afraid. However, I've said how I feel – I can't do any more.'

'You certainly can't. I repeat, you're quite mistaken. These clothes are my choice and nothing whatsoever to do with your taste in fashion. If I wanted to copy anyone, it would be Harriet Charter-Plackett, not you.'

Angry beyond belief at the manner in which Louise was speaking to Caroline, Sylvia interrupted: 'You know full well why you're doing it. We're not idiots in this village, though I know you think we are. You're doing it to get a response from the rector – and don't deny it!'

'Who do you think you are, speaking to me in that tone?'

'Someone who sees more clearly than you would like. If you're trying to win him for yourself, you're barking up the wrong tree. The rector wouldn't even *look* at you, even though you're dressed like Dr Harris. He only has you here to work and for nothing else.'

Louise turned to Caroline. 'Are you going to stand by and allow a . . . *servant* to shout at me? How can anyone possibly think I see Peter as anything other than my spiritual advisor? When have I ever done anything to make anyone think otherwise?'

Sylvia didn't allow Caroline time to answer. 'Dressing like you are today, and when I saw you yesterday in church. If you never came back in this house again it would be too soon. I know exactly what you're up to. The rector, bless him, can't see it, because he never thinks ill of anyone, ever. But I can see straight through you, oh yes! Now buzz off and don't come back.'

By now the children, sensing that their mother and their beloved Sylvie were upset, had crawled out of the tent and had become very agitated, crying, 'Mummy, Mummy!' They clung to Caroline's legs, begging to be lifted up.

Caroline, in an attempt to calm the situation said, 'Sylvia! This won't do. Please leave it to me.'

'I can't, because you won't say what has to be said. I saw clean through her the first day she came here. I knew her little game. Well, it's to be stopped before it goes any further. I won't see this family broken up and stand by and say nothing. So, off you go.'

Not one of them noticed that Peter had heard the arguing and come from his study and was now standing in the kitchen doorway. Louise, seething and fast losing control of the situation, said the one thing she knew cut right to the heart of her intention. 'Broken up? This family broken up? As if I would do such a thing to these two little children.' She looked lovingly at the twins as they stood clinging to their mother.

'"These two little children?". You don't care *that* much for 'em.' Sylvia clicked her fingers as close to Louise's face as she could. 'You only pretend to care to keep in the rector's good books. They're his and Dr Harris's and don't you forget it.'

Louise finally lost her self-control. 'Hers and Peter's? Oh yes?' There was a scornful note in her voice which stabbed straight at Caroline's heart. She went ashen, and her hands began to shake. The children fell silent.

Sylvia stepped forward as though she would strangle Louise. 'Get out! Go on, get out. Never *ever* come back here. Do you hear me? Never!'

Peter's voice at its loudest would have stilled a storm and he used it now, overriding Sylvia's shouting, every word couched in cold implacable anger. 'I will not have this arguing in my home. Your behaviour is disgraceful. Both of you should be ashamed. Absolutely ashamed. Not another word. Sylvia, please leave. And you too, Louise. Out! Your behaviour in front of my wife and our children has been quite unforgivable.' Neither of them moved. 'I'm waiting.' His face was deathly white with temper, and he smashed a fist against the palm of his other hand as he repeated, 'I'm waiting!'

Louise suppressed the urge to speak to him, recognising that she had gone far too far, and would probably never retrieve the status quo again. Sylvia, fearful of his anger, quietly went into the hall, took her coat from the cupboard and rushed home to the comfort of Willie's arms. Louise had no such arms in which to shelter; she went home to weep alone.

Peter stood quite still for a moment breathing heavily and attempting to regain his self-control. Alex and Beth were still crying, so he picked them both up and sat each of them on a kitchen chair. He opened the cake tin and gave them each a piece of flapjack, and with shaking hands poured some juice into their beakers. Having spoken reassuringly to them, he turned his attention to Caroline. She was standing apart, tears silently pouring down her cheeks, one hand pressed to her forehead shielding her eyes, the other gripping the back of the nearest chair.

'Caroline, come.' Peter opened wide his arms and she went to him. A safe anchorage was what she needed and that was what she got.

'My darling girl. I'm so sorry. So very sorry. I'd no idea things had gone that far.'

'But Peter, I did say.'

'Yes, and I was easing her out but you invited her back.'

'I know. I know.'

Peter wiped her eyes for her and kissed her eyelids. 'No more crying. The matter is finished or it will be when I've dealt with it.'

'She said how much she loved coming to our house because it was so welcoming and warm, and of course that won me over. I couldn't believe it when I heard myself saying she could come back.'

Peter groaned. 'I was even so blind that I complimented her on her clothes this morning.'

'You're too kind. I couldn't stop Sylvia; she was so wild she wouldn't listen to sense. She was like a terrier.' Caroline took out her handkerchief and wiped her eyes again. 'She's no fool, she saw through Louise from the word go. Peter, what are we going to do? You've lost your secretary and I've lost my housekeeper.'

'Come and sit on my knee.' He seated himself in Caroline's rocking chair and she perched on his knee. With her head on his shoulder and his hand caressing her arm, he said, 'I shall deal with Madam Sylvia after lunch when tempers have cooled. Don't worry, Willie and I will sort it out. We've a good understanding, him and me.'

'Will you sort Louise too?'

Peter gave her a grim smile. 'I'll have to work at that. She's harder to solve than Sylvia. Can't leave it as it is now, though.'

'There's going to be no end to the pain, is there? I think the answer is for us to leave here and make a fresh start somewhere else, where no one knows. But it would break my heart to do that. I love it here.'

Peter gripped her tightly and gently shook her. 'So do I. So do I. But, I promise you faithfully here and now, if things get too bad for you, Caroline, then move we shall. The decision is entirely yours.'

'Oh Peter, I wish I was a million miles from here, right now, just for a while.'

'I wish you were too. Well, I mean all of us together a million miles away. Never mind, not long now and we *shall* be away. For two blissful weeks.'

'Devon, here we come. I won't have Louise back. I'm sorry, I know I'm trespassing, but I won't.'

'Neither will I. That's it – finished. I must have been a complete fool not to have noticed the way things were going. Sorry.'

'I'm sorry for her at bottom. She must be desperate.'

Peter kissed her. 'You're so kind, Dr Harris.'

'So are you. What a mess. I feel drained. Such a scene in my own kitchen. It will be a while before I get over this, and the children too, they were so upset. I'm glad they're still too young to understand. However, must get on. I'll start lunch. Finished, my little ones? Come on, then, down you get.'

'They are your little ones, Caroline, they truly are.'

'I think so myself sometimes.'

'Don't doubt it. They went into shock when you were away. So difficult to handle. Sylvia did wonders but they wanted you.'

'Whilst I make the lunch, you'd better occupy your mind with how we'll get Sylvia back. That's the phone – will you take it or shall I?'

He tipped her off his knee and went to answer it.

After he'd eaten lunch, Peter went next door to apologise to Sylvia. He knocked at their cottage door and Willie answered it.

'Ahh, Rector. Just having a bite of lunch with my Sylvia. In need of some company, she was.' His look held an element of disapproval.

'Good afternoon, Willie. Come to make sure you've found the details for the grave that has to be dug. I left them in your tray. It's an old one, not been opened for more than fifty years.'

'I know that one, sir. My father was the last one to open it. It's nearer sixty years. Leave it to me. Now the weather's warmed up, 'spect we shall have a few more graves to dig. It always 'appens. Freezing weather, they all stay alive. Warms up and Bob's yer uncle, they drop like flies.'

Peter whispered, 'Can I speak to Sylvia?'

'She's very upset and so am I. She was only defending Dr Harris.'

'I know, it's all such a mess. But can I speak to her – to apologise?'

'I'll ask.' Willie went back inside and Peter thought he could hear some agitated whispering. He strained to listen but couldn't make out the words.

After a few moments Willie came back. 'Yes, sir, Sylvia's in.' He gave Peter the thumbs-down sign, which he acknowledged with a rueful grin. 'I'll be off then, Rector, and leave you to it.'

Peter bent his head and went in. The ceilings in Willie's cottage were much lower than in the rectory, and he had to keep his head bent. He found Sylvia in the sitting room, in an armchair, twisting her handkerchief round and round her fingers.

'May I sit down? It's so uncomfortable for me to stand.'

'Of course. Yes, of course.'

Simultaneously they both said, 'I want to apologise for—'

Peter raised his hand to stop her speaking. 'No, Sylvia, I've come to apologise. You were only guilty of putting up a spirited defence of my wife and our children. I was so angry at the whole situation and even more angry with myself for not having realised the way the wind blew. You didn't deserve what I said. So I'm here to apologise most sincerely to you and to ask if we can let bygones be bygones and, please, will you possibly be able to consider coming back to the rectory?'

'I don't even have to consider it. Of course I'll come back. Working for Dr Harris is so . . . well so . . . She's a lovely person to work for and I love your children, I really do. They help to make up for not having any of my own, even if they are little devils!'

'Which they are, I have to confess.'

'But – and it's a big "but".'

'Go on.'

'I won't come back unless I have your absolute firm promise that Louise doesn't come near the rectory. If she does, I shall probably throttle her. Please, sir, if you value your family, don't have her back. I know I've no business talking to a clergyman like this, you're much too clever to need advice from me, but I've got to say it. She's trouble.'

'You have my solemn promise.'

'In that case then I'll be back. I'll just get my coat.'

'No, don't do that. Leave it until tomorrow. Have the rest of the day to yourself. And thank you for accepting my apology. I can't bear for Caroline to be hurt, and she was hurt, badly hurt.'

'I know. And I'm sorry. Very sorry for the way I behaved, but I was so angry.' Sylvia stood up. 'I won't keep you. So long as we have an understanding, that's all that matters.' She smiled at him. 'I didn't know you had such a temper. It was quite a revelation.'

'Sorry.'

'Thank you for coming round.'

Peter came out of the cottage and went to stand by the pond on the Green. Jimmy's geese came hustling forward in the hope that he would be feeding them.

'Sorry chaps, no bread today. I envy you your uncomplicated lives. How I envy you. Still, with a brain the size of a walnut, or it could even be the size of a pea, I suppose I can't expect you to solve problems like mine. I've solved one and now I'm off to sort out another. Do you have any advice to offer?' They honked busily. 'No, I didn't think you would have. I shall have to leave it to the Lord to help me find the right words.'

The door of the Bissetts' cottage was slightly ajar when Peter knocked. 'Hellooo! Peter here, from the rectory. May I come in?'

Chapter 11

The story of Peter turning Louise and Sylvia out of the rectory was round the village in no time at all. By the middle of the afternoon, the main topic of conversation in The Royal Oak was what on earth had taken place to make him do such a thing. A peace-loving man like him, chucking the two of them out? Well, they knew he had a temper. Look at the time he confronted them all when they were stoning Beryl and Gwen's house. Or that time they turned against Alan Crimble when he ran Flick Charter-Plackett down and she was laid almost lifeless in Church Lane. But even so . . .

Most likely it was to do with Sylvia running the cake-stall at the Show for the Red Cross. That Louise wasn't half bossy if she took a mind.

Jimmy Glover knew different. 'I reckon that Louise has gone crackers. When she rushed across home after she'd been turned out she was wearing Dr Harris's clothes.'

'Don't be daft. How could she be?'

'Well, I saw 'er and she was. True as I'm 'ere, or if they wasn't Dr Harris's they was a dead spit.'

'Well, we all know she 'as her eye on the rector. Perhaps

fancied looking like Dr Harris to tempt him.'

'Take a lot more than looking like Dr Harris to make anyone be tempted with her!' The speaker chuckled into his beer.

'I reckon that's why she volunteered to help him, 'cos she fancies him.'

'Anyways, let's face it, he wouldn't be tempted by *'er!*'

'No, course he wouldn't. It's her doing the running, that's what. Desperate for a bit of that there 'ere and she fancies him, made her feelings plain and Sylvia's 'ad a row with her.'

'Good at her job though. Made a right improvement to the weekly church newsletter, and I hear the magazine's been hyped-up no end.'

'Not saying she isn't good at her job, but she's no business stirring it at the rectory.'

'Wonder what he said to her when he went across there this afternoon?'

'Didn't know he'd been.'

'Oh, he has. He went to Willie and Sylvia's then across to see her. There quite a while he was.'

'What you been doing then all afternoon? Sat looking out the window?'

'Day off. Felt like a rest, but it's been that busy with the comings an' goings I might as well 'ave been working.'

The conversation turned to the Show and who would win the prizes in the vegetable section. They plumped for Willie winning the beans and Barry's mother the Victoria sponge and the cut flowers like usual.

Peter was in his study thinking over what he'd said to Louise.

When he'd first gone there and called through the open

door, it was Sheila who'd come to speak to him.

'Good afternoon, Sheila. I was hoping for a word with Louise. Is she in? I see her car's outside.'

'Oh, good afternoon, Rector.' Peter knew he was in trouble if Sheila Bissett called him 'Rector'. 'Coming to make things straight with her, are you?'

'I'd like to talk, yes.'

'She's very upset and she won't tell me what's happened – except she keeps blaming you. After all she's done for you and not a penny piece in return, all voluntary and she comes home in that state! It wasn't right.'

'Is she in? Can I have a word?'

'I'll go and see. I think she's in bed. Wait there.' She left him standing in the little hall, while she went upstairs. After a few minutes, she came back down and said, 'Louise won't come down, but she says will you go up?'

'I don't think so. If she wants me to wait while she dresses then I will, but it's imperative I speak with her.'

Sheila climbed the stairs again. After a few minutes she returned, followed by Louise who was wearing the clothes she'd had on earlier in the day. Her hair was well-brushed and combed, her make-up meticulous and she was looking subdued and cautious as though afraid of saying the wrong thing yet again.

'Good afternoon, Louise. Can we sit down somewhere?'

'Of course, how nice of you to come to apologise.' She led the way into the sitting room and pointed to the largest and most comfortable chair in the room. 'Sit here, it'll be better for you with your long legs.'

Louise seated herself in a smaller chair quite close to his own and waited. Peter had realised instantly that this could prove to be the most difficult conversation of his life.

'Firstly, Louise, I have not come to apologise. Not for losing my temper, not for turning you out, not for anything at all. I *have* come to say that I am afraid I cannot permit you to come to the rectory any more. What you said this morning – well, the bit I heard – was the truth. What was unforgivable was for you to say it in the manner you did and in front of Caroline and our children.'

'Just a moment. Have I got this right? What I said was true but it had to be left unsaid?'

'Yes. Positively yes. Caroline and I shall decide when the time is ripe to tell the children. Also, this business of dressing like my wife . . .'

'That was not my intention at all. It was pure coincidence, but of course *I* shan't be believed. You prefer to believe someone who is only a servant.'

'Sylvia is not a servant, nor is she a fool. Even I, when it was pointed out to me, recognised that this was what you had done. It's just not on, Louise. Someone in my position has to be very circumspect . . .'

'Of course you have. I wouldn't want it otherwise. I know a clergyman must be very careful not to compromise himself in any way, so I have never given you one moment's cause for concern.'

'No, I suppose that is true. You haven't, but there is this feeling . . .'

'Don't worry, Peter. I know how difficult it must be for you, sandwiched as you are between two domineering women. It must be very hard for such a gentle person like yourself. You need to keep the peace with Caroline, and if that means hanging on to Sylvia then that is what you must do.' Peter tried to protest, but Louise rushed on with what she had to say. 'You and I will sort it out. First, I have a word-processor here in my room which I could quite easily use for doing the church typing. You leave the tapes here, with your little machine as you so charmingly call it, I'll do the work and you can collect it. How's that for an idea? Just because things are difficult at the rectory it shouldn't mean that you miss out on secretarial help.'

'If you get a job, then . . .'

'I can always do it in my spare time. Don't you worry about that.' As she spoke Louise allowed her hand to rest on his knee for a moment. Because his mind had been scrabbling around for reasons why this scheme wouldn't work, Peter hadn't drawn away immediately and through his cassock he'd felt the warm pressure of her hand. He'd sensed there was more to it than sympathy and he knew he had to make a stand.

He moved his leg away from her hand, but Louise continued speaking in the same vein. 'Two intelligent human beings like us, you see, have found a solution, haven't we? You and your family are very dear to me, Peter. I wouldn't dream of doing anything to disrupt your family life. Not at all. And I mean that. Let's try out our new scheme and see how it goes. A little adjustment on both sides and it should work splendidly.'

At this point Peter stood up. 'I'm afraid not. It won't do. I want to thank you for all you've done these last couple of months – no one has been more grateful than I for your efforts – but I have to call a halt. I'm sorry but there it is. I'll say good afternoon now. I sincerely hope that this little misunderstanding will not affect your coming to church. I would be very upset if it did. You have a splendid contribution to make to the life of this village and I hope you'll go from strength to strength. Thank you, Louise.' He proffered his hand for her to shake. She held it with both her own.

'I can't believe you're saying this to me. Not after all

we've meant to each other. I'm indispensable to you and well you know it. You're allowing Caroline, and Sylvia too, to dictate to you against your better judgement. It all stems from their jealousy of me. All I've ever wanted is to be useful to you in whatever capacity you need.'

Peter extracted his hand from her tight grip and said, 'There's nothing more to say. I'm going now. Perhaps when you've thought it over you'll realise I've made the best decision. Pray about it. That way you'll come to terms, and understand why I have said what I have, I'm sure you will.'

'I shan't. Not ever.'

Sheila was dusting her ornaments in the hall as Peter left.

'Good afternoon, Sheila. I think we've got the position clear now. See you in church on Sunday. Bye bye.'

'Bye bye, Peter.'

He walked home and went immediately to his study. He'd done all he could, but he had an uneasy feeling that this was not the end.

The moment he'd shut the door, Sheila raced into the sitting room to have a word with Louise.

'Well, what did he say?'

Louise stretched as though she hadn't a care in the world. She laid her head back against the cushion and smiled. 'Right now he's doing exactly as those two women have said he should. But I haven't worked closely with him all these weeks not to know him through and through. He doesn't want to do as they say. He wants me to stay working for him in his study. He relies on me, you see, Mother. Just wait another day or two, a week at most, and when the work starts piling up, he'll be back. The poor man, I feel desperately sorry for him.'

'Oh, I do too. He's such a lovely person. So charis . . . what's that word?'

'Charismatic.'

'That's it. Charismatic. You feel so drawn to him. He only has to hold your hand and look at you . . .'

'That's just what he did.'

'Did he really?'

'Yes. He looked really deeply into my eyes, you know like he can sometimes and you feel as if your soul is being stripped bare . . .'

'Oh yes, I know, it makes me do the right thing even when I don't want to. I can't help myself.'

'Well, he looked at me like that and said I had a great contribution to make to the life of the village and he hoped most sincerely that this little fracas wouldn't stop me from going to church. He would be very upset if it did.'

'Really?'

'Believe me, all I have to do is wait and I shall be back at the rectory before dear Caroline knows where she is.'

Suddenly Sheila felt things weren't quite right. There was something disquieting about Louise's attitude, almost as if she was seeking revenge on Caroline. Sheila decided to warn Louise about the unpredictability of the villagers if they decided things weren't as they should be.

'The whole village will know by now. You'd better be careful. They're not past stoning, you know. Quite med-iaeval, they can be. If they don't like what's happening, something comes over them and they all band together. I've seen it, I know.'

'Mother, you're going daft. Stoning – honestly!'

'It's true! It happened only two years ago – Peter had to come out and stop it. Terrifying it was, but he was wonderful.'

'He can be very masterful.' Louise sounded dreamy. 'He seems so gentle, but there's always that feeling of power there. Well, I shan't let stupid tales about stoning stop me. I shall go about my affairs as normal.'

'I'd stay at home for a day or two before you venture out. You could pretend to have a cold.'

'Sometimes, Mother, I wonder about your sanity, I really do. I need some chocolate.'

'I'll get it for you, dear. Let me go, I shan't be a moment. What would you like – fruit and nut?'

'No, I'm going myself. I want to choose.' Louise strolled up Stocks Row and into the Store. There was something very uplifting about the Store. It felt such a good place to be, as though going in and shopping there was a very fashionable and well-judged thing to do. She supposed Jimbo had deliberately planned it that way. The Store was very busy and the noise-level quite high, but as she walked in the hubbub died. She picked up a basket and began to wander round the shelves thinking that she'd buy herself some chocolates, she deserved a treat after all she'd been through. She might even purchase some of those special Belgian chocolates which Jimbo said were sold only in Harrods and in his store. That took a bit of swallowing but . . . then someone jerked her elbow quite savagely. The basket almost flew from her hand.

In an exaggeratedly polite voice Barry's mother apologised. 'Oh, I'm so sorry, *Dr Harris*. Oh, it's not Dr Harris – it's you, Miss Bissett. What a silly mistake to make. Did I catch your elbow? Are you keeping well?'

'Yes, thank you. I'm fine.'

'That's a good thing then. Busy at the rectory today, are you? Just popped out for something for their tea? We know how much they love you . . . popping in and out.'

Louise wanted to retort sharply but she quickly sensed the nature of the attack and sweetly smiled instead. A ripple of giggles followed her as she made for the glass counter where the continental chocolates were displayed. Harriet came to serve her.

'Hello there, can I help?'

'I'll have half a pound, please. Mainly hard centres and like pralines and some of those fresh cream ones, please. Oh, and I'd like a couple of marzipans too.'

While Harriet busied herself putting on plastic gloves and making up one of the gold cardboard boxes to put the chocolates in, Louise looked about her.

There was a knot of women gathered around Barry's mother. They kept glancing in her direction and smothering explosive laughter. She ignored them as best she could but their malicious interest in her became hurtful, so she watched Harriet tucking the chocolates into the box instead. Harriet, aware that Louise was being mocked, did her best to keep her attention. After all, Louise was spending money and it wasn't for Harriet to treat her badly just because she disapproved of what she did in her private life.

'There we are, Louise, I've put in a selection of the ones you asked for, and then filled up the odd corners with others. If it's a present, would you like me to gift-wrap it with ribbon et cetera, and a little card?'

It wasn't a present except to herself, but she nodded her assent. Perhaps by the time Harriet had finished, those women would have gone. But they hadn't and she had to run the gauntlet to the till.

'Prezzie for Dr Harris, is it?'

'Don't be silly. It's for the rector!'

'I hear you haven't got a job yet?'

'Devil finds work for idle hands!' A gale of laughter followed that remark and Louise fled from the Store with as much dignity as she could muster. Her mother for once was right – she'd stay at home for a few days. Then she remembered the Show committee meeting. Well, she'd go to that, but that was all. It was just a question of waiting for Peter to ask her to help him again. Peter the rock. Her rock, on which she would build her life. Quite how it would happen she wasn't sure, but it would. She'd see it did. Somehow.

Chapter 12

Caroline had decided that she must let bygones be bygones where Louise was concerned and turn up for the Show committee meeting as though nothing had happened. She wasn't exactly relishing the idea, but there was no alternative. If she gave her excuses, they'd all know the reason why and it would make them more determined than ever to ostracise Louise for what had happened at the rectory the previous day.

She decided to get there early to forestall any discussion of Louise's behaviour before it had a chance to start. Whether by design or not, Louise arrived early too.

'Hello there, Caroline. Making the coffee? Oh good! Just what I need.' Louise's tone was friendly but respectful, when Caroline had expected her to be belligerent.

'Yes, I promised I would,' she replied neutrally. 'Here you are – black, no milk, no sugar. Right?'

'How clever of you to remember! Jimbo's not here again tonight. Pat is not really a very good substitute; he's always so full of good ideas whereas she has none.'

'Pat's all right. I like her.'

'You've got to like people. Being the rector's wife, you've no alternative.'

'Oh, I do have an alternative. Believe me, I have.'

Louise dared to speak his name. 'Peter all right?'

'Shouldn't he be?'

'Oh no, I didn't mean anything by that, just wondering how he was coping.'

'I see. Well, he's fine, thank you.'

'Sitting in tonight?'

'Yes.' Caroline thought that with all her years' experience as a doctor she understood people pretty well, could sum them up, see beneath the surface, work out their motives . . . but Louise had her foxed. What was the woman up to?

They were saved from continuing this painful conversation by the arrival of Barry. 'Pat not here yet?'

'No, not yet.'

Louise archly remarked that they seemed to be an item nowadays.

'An item – what's that?'

'Well, I mean kind of pairing off, sort of.'

'Anything the matter with that? We are both free agents, and I'm not trying to steal her from anyone, which is more than can be said for some people not a million miles away from me.' He took his coffee from Caroline and went to sit on a chair, carefully putting his papers on the one next to him to make sure he could keep it for Pat. Louise sat down and avoided meeting anyone's eyes. Trust Barry Jones to be crude. People like him were so basic, they'd no subtlety at all. None. She sorted out her files and rehearsed in her head her opening speech. But what Barry had said kept coming between her and the words. Damn and blast him. Besmirching a beautiful relationship. Typical. He'd better not say anything in front of Mother when she came, or else . . .

Before the meeting, most of the members had been up to see the progress of the new sewer pipes over at the Big House. Jeremy and Barry saw it every day and so did Pat, but the others made separate journeys to see what hope there was of still being able to hold the Show.

Barry came down on the side of optimism. 'I've great hopes it'll all be completed. No problem. Don't you think so, Michael?'

'Oh yes, I'm quite sure. It'll be a close run thing but yes, I'm sure you're right.'

Sheila disagreed. 'I don't know about that. I think we should postpone it for two weeks, just to be on the safe side.' The others looked horrified.

Pat was appalled. 'Postpone it? How can we do that? All the printing's done and everything, and they're all timing their flowers and veg to come to their peak at the date we've fixed. If we delay for two weeks I don't know what they'll do. Willie Biggs has got some brilliant beans and you should see his roses – coming on a treat they are. Jimbo's sweetpeas are gorgeous too. I reckon he'll take the prize this year.'

'He'll have to go some to beat Mrs Beauchamp's. Saw hers last week – cor, the size of 'em! Asked her what she fed 'em on but she just tapped the side of her nose and refused to say. Special seed she got from a big specialist near London,' Linda put in sagely.

'Jimmy's entering some eggs. His are always the brownest ones you'll ever see.'

Sheila looked up surprised when Pat said that. 'Eggs? There'll be no classes for eggs.'

'No classes for eggs – whyever not? Proper shows always

132

have them – the biggest, the brownest, best-matched six all displayed on a doily in a basket . . . Course there's classes for eggs!'

'There aren't. Couldn't fit them in.'

'Well, Jimmy doesn't know.'

'He should. I distributed the advance lists weeks ago.'

'I wouldn't like to be in your shoes when he finds out. They always have eggs. Jimmy'll be real disappointed, he will.'

Louise checked the official printed list. 'No eggs. Sorry.'

''Ere, let me look at that.' Barry almost snatched the list from Louise. He ran his eye down both sides of it and said, 'She's right, there isn't. What yer playing at? Them at Nightingale Farm have them Welsummer hens, brilliant eggs they lay. They're planning to enter.'

Sheila drew herself up, patted her hair and answered firmly. 'Not this year they won't. It's all produce.'

Michael Palmer murmured, 'But what are eggs if they're not produce?'

'I mean growing produce like beans and flowers and things.'

It suddenly dawned on Linda what the reason was for the egg classes being omitted. 'Let me look at that schedule, Barry.' She scanned the list and quickly counted, as swiftly as she counted the stamps in the post office. 'I thought so. There's almost twice as many flower classes as produce classes. Well, I never. I wonder why?' She looked accusingly at Sheila. 'Obvious who's planned this.'

'You all saw the list before it went to the printers and you all approved it.'

'Yes, but you've added classes since we saw it, and crossed out others.'

133

'I never, Linda Crimble. I never have. Getting married's done you no good at all. You've developed a suspicious side to your nature.'

'Well, really . . . Just wait till my Alan hears what you've said.'

Louise, seeing her mother under siege, decided to interrupt. 'Now really, this won't do. My mother is guilty of no such thing. That's the list as you saw it before it went to the printers. Believe me.'

Pat decided to have her say. 'Oh yes? There weren't no class for flower arrangements with a seaside holiday theme. Definitely, 'cos I would've remembered that.'

Sheila triumphantly answered Pat's suspicion with, 'Seeing as you go away every year to the sea you'd be bound to remember.'

Caroline, who'd taken no part in all the wrangling, decided that things were getting far too personal. 'Shouldn't we deal with important matters like who's going to be in charge of keeping the money safe and who's going to be on the platform with Mr Fitch and who'll be at the gate to take the ticket money? Surely the eggs can be dealt with later.'

Sheila hurriedly agreed with this piece of sound common sense, mainly because she *was* guilty of adding flower classes after the schedule had been approved. These people had no idea what was style and what was not. Eggs indeed!

'You should have had a bigger marquee for the competitions. I did say so at the time, but I was overruled. If it had been bigger there would have been room for eggs.'

''Ere, just a minute. What's happened to the cake competitions? There's none for adults, they're all for children. My mum'll have something to say about this — she's a miracle with a Victoria sponge.' Barry glared at

Sheila. She swallowed hard. There seemed to be no end to the unpleasant discoveries tonight.

Pat looked down the schedule Barry was holding. 'Shortbread's my thing and there's no classes! There's always shortbread classes. Look 'ere, Sheila, you've overstepped the mark.'

Jeremy, who'd had to come to the meeting before he could have his supper, swore under his breath; hunger always made him short-tempered. 'I've something better to do than sit here listening to arguments about shortbread and eggs. Let's get on with it. Mr Fitch has suggested that I take charge of the money and lodge it in the office safe until we have time to count it. He'll make sure he's here to open the Show and he wants room on the dais for three guests; he suggests we choose three of us to represent the committee. So that'll be seven in all – quite enough. Two of his guests will be ladies and he would like them to be presented with bouquets. Large ones.'

Michael proposed that Caroline, Louise and Pat should sit on the dais.

Caroline declined. Louise agreed and Pat agreed and then realised she'd be too busy at that juncture and she'd look a fool in her waitress uniform anyway. She'd have to propose someone fast, anyone to stop Sheila preening herself up there in front of everybody. 'I can't accept as I shall be too busy then in the food marquee. Don't you think we should have a man on the platform, otherwise Mr Fitch will be the only one. What about Louise, Bryn and Mr Palmer?'

Bryn nodded his agreement. 'That's settled then. Louise, write down me, you and Michael.'

Sheila protested at the unfairness of this. 'But what about me? I've done a lot for this Show! It's not right. I ought to be on the platform.'

A deathly hush fell. Faint hearts looked at their shoes, stronger ones at a point somewhere west of Sheila's shoulders. As no one backed her up she said, 'Oh right. That's how it is, is it? You can organise your blasted Show as best you can. I'm having nothing more to do with it.' She picked up her bag and began stuffing her papers into it.

Jeremy said, 'Now see here, Sheila, we never meant to upset you.'

Pat muttered, 'Didn't we?'

'This little contretemps can soon be resolved, can't it?' Jeremy looked meaningfully round the circle of members. Michael took it upon himself to volunteer not to be on the platform.

'Seeing as the fancy-dress parade is the first in the arena I shall really be too busy supervising the children to have time to sit on the platform, so please, Lady Bissett, have my place. I'm sure you'll grace the platform far more decoratively than I shall.'

Wryly Pat whispered to Barry, 'He's right there. Her outfit will be Buckingham-Palace-Garden-Party-here-I-come standard, you'll see.'

Sheila, with her back to everyone as she zipped up her bag, stopped midway, beamed triumphantly and then, changing her face into an excellent impression of a woebegone spaniel, sat down again and said, 'Well, all right then. Seeing as you've asked me so nicely, I will sit on the platform – though how I shall find the time I really don't know, I shall be so busy.'

Pat jumped in quickly at this hint of doubt. 'In that case then we'll ask Dr Harris again, shall we? You'd do it, wouldn't you?'

'No, thank you.'

Louise said, 'That's settled then. Bryn, me and Mother

on the platform. I've made a note about the bouquets, Jeremy – I'll order those. Now, shall we continue? Who's going to be on the gate?'

Jeremy solved that by offering two estate-workers who'd been pressganged by Mr Fitch into giving a hand. 'They're both big and beefy so you'll have no trouble with gatecrashers trying to get in for nothing.'

After they'd cleared up several more points Louise was just arranging the date of the next meeting when Barry said, 'Before the meeting closes I think we should sort out this question of the classes which have been scrubbed. No good sweeping it under the carpet. Can we have an extra sheet printed, or something, so that the egg classes and that are back in?'

Sheila took a deep breath intending to enter the fray before things got out of hand but she felt a sharp dig in her ribs from Louise, so she kept quiet.

Michael answered him. 'I think that would be a very good idea. After all, we are doing this for the sake of the village, profit is not our prime motive, and if that's what the village expects then that's what they must have. A few eggs are not the stuff of crises, are they? Nor indeed are some more cake classes. Can we ask Lady Bissett to amend her lists please, before it causes trouble? We can blame it on a printing error.'

Linda agreed with him. 'I second that.'

'So do I. I've done two lots of shortbread to make sure I get me hand in before the day, and I think I'm on a winning streak. What do you say, Louise?' Pat looked hard at Louise as she said this. 'Well?'

'OK then. I'll type an amendment, photocopy it and slip it in each programme. Won't bother the printer – he'll only charge the earth.'

Michael stood up. 'May I offer a word of thanks to Louise for all this unpaid work she is doing for us? We all go away with a few jobs to complete but she has to keep her hands on everything that's going on. We're really most grateful to you for your wonderful organisation. All your lists and meticulous attention to detail, we're very lucky to have your services. You're doing an excellent job. Thank you.' He looked round the circle and putting his hands together, waited for the others to do the same. They all began clapping. Louise looked embarrassed.

Pat muttered, 'If only she'd stick to her lists we'd all do better.'

'What did you say, Pat?' Sheila broke off from clapping. She'd heard what had been said, and still smarting from Pat's victory over the cake classes was determined to show Pat up for what she was.

'I said it's good she sticks to her lists, that way nothing gets missed, does it?'

'That's not what you said.'

'If you knew what I said, why did you ask me to repeat it?'

'It was a nasty remark you made. It's not fair, she's working really hard.'

'All depends what she's working *at*, doesn't it?'

Caroline stood up and said, 'We've arranged the date for the next meeting, so shall we all go? Willie will be wanting to lock up.'

Ignoring Caroline's calming remark, Sheila stood up and said with a threatening look on her face, 'And what do you mean by that?'

'She knows what I mean only too well.'

Caroline said, 'Pat, please,' in a pleading tone.

'It has to be said, Dr Harris.' Pat looked directly at

Louise. 'We each of us know what you've been up to – well, you'd better put a stop to it right now, 'cos we won't stand for it.'

Louise stood up and looking directly at Pat said, '*I* have done nothing to be ashamed of. Nothing.'

Pat stood up and hands on hips said belligerently: 'You're not suggesting the rector *encouraged you*?'

Barry took her arm. 'Now Pat, be careful.'

'Careful? It needs saying. She's doing an excellent job with the Show, but heaven help us! She's causing trouble and it's got to stop.'

While Pat had been speaking, Sheila had been saying, 'What does she mean? I don't understand.'

Linda, seeing an opportunity to get back at Sheila, and indirectly at Louise for her condescending treatment of her at the post office counter, jumped in with support. 'No good trying to kid us that you've had *encouragement* at the rectory. That's enough to make a cat laugh.'

'Encouragement? What *are* you women talking about?' Jeremy had now finally run out of patience. 'If there are no more committee matters to discuss, then I for one am going home. I want my supper. Good night.' He marched for the door. Michael and Bryn wanted to do the same but both felt they should stay, just in case.

Caroline, normally so in control of herself and of events, tonight found herself quite unable to take command of the situation.

Barry said quietly to Pat, 'Leave it, leave it, there's going to be too much said that should be left unsaid.'

Pat ignored him and drove home her attack. 'Dressing like Dr Harris indeed! We all noticed. Think we're blind or something? Stick to what yer know best, lists and computers and things.'

'I don't have to put up with this kind of attack. All this malicious gossip, it's so unfair and quite unwarranted. Here,' she handed Pat her file and when Pat didn't take hold of it she dropped it on the floor, 'take that and you can be secretary seeing as you know so much. We'll see what kind of a good job you can make of it.' Louise picked up her bag and left, very close to tears because of Pat's attack. Wherever she went, whatever she did it always came back to the same theme. All she was fit for in other people's eyes was administration and organisation. Nothing else. Surely to God there was more to her than that . . . wasn't there?

Sir Ronald was at home watching the football in the sitting room. When the front door banged open he leapt guilty out of his chair. He called out, 'Kettle's boiled, the tea won't be a minute.' As he crossed the hall to the kitchen he realised Sheila was crying.

'Now then, old girl, what's the matter?'

'I don't know. Ask her.' She jerked her thumb at Louise and then burst into fresh storms of weeping.

'What have you been saying to her, eh?'

'Nothing, Dad, nothing. It's me who's been hurt, not Mother. There's nothing to blame me for.' Louise flung down her bag and made to go up the stairs.

'Just a minute, madam. You may be an adult but while you're under our roof you owe me an explanation of why yer mother's so upset.'

Sheila stopped crying long enough to blurt out, 'She's resigned from the Show committee.'

'Well, you nearly did too,' Louise sniffed.

'But that was because of the classes. I don't know why *you* nearly resigned. What was it Pat was meaning? And

Linda? She said about the "rectory" and "encouragement". What did she mean?'

Louise pressed her lips tightly together. Her father saw the child in her and remembered the fierce arguments they'd had when she was young. Give him their Brendan any day. He barked at her, 'I'm still waiting for an explanation and I don't care if it takes all night. What have you been doing?'

'I've been doing nothing. It's other people who've been "doing", not me.'

Sheila remembered. 'Is it something to do with Caroline? She was very white-faced. Was it her? Have you been arguing with her?'

'We don't like each other, but it's not her.'

Sheila wiped her nose again and then asked, 'Sylvia then?'

'It's not Sylvia.'

Sir Ronald groaned inwardly. 'That only leaves the rector.'

Louise, with eyes downcast said, 'Don't blame me, I've done nothing.'

Sir Ronald persisted with his quest for the truth. 'Then if *you've* done nothing, what's all the fuss about?'

Louise took a deep breath to control her tears. The truth. She couldn't tell them the truth no matter what. She couldn't admit to rejection once again, not again. 'They all . . . well, Pat Duckett seems to think I've been making overtures to the rector. I haven't, of course not, for heaven's sake, but that's what they think.'

His eyes widened. 'You don't mean the rector's been . . . Lovely chap though he is, and I wouldn't have a wrong word said against him, he does have a certain reputation which probably you don't know about. I can understand he's very attractive to women. Oh yes.'

'I refuse to say anything which might damage his reputation. Now can I go to bed? I'll have my tea in bed, Mother, and I'll have one of those plain biscuits as well . . . please.' Her parents watched her walk up the stairs and when they heard her bedroom door close they looked at each other.

'Ron, I ought to believe her, I am her mother after all, but I don't.'

'You don't?'

'No. I think she's been making all the running and he's been backing off as fast as he can, but she won't let go. There's something strange happened at the bank which she won't tell me about.'

'But she got made redundant, she said so.'

'I know she did, but there's more to it than that.'

'She doesn't usually lie. What do you think happened, then?'

'I don't honestly know anything, it's just a feeling I have.'

'Woman's intuition, eh?' He put an arm around her shoulders and gave her an understanding hug.

Sheila wiped her eyes, dropped the tissue in the metal waste-basket she'd decorated with flowered fabric and trimmed with gold fringe, and whispered, 'Oh Ron, whatever are we going to do? What she really needs is to meet a nice man.' Sheila's eyes glowed. 'That's it! I bet that was it! There was a man involved at the bank.'

'The sooner she gets a job and moves away the better.'

'Amen to that!'

Chapter 13

'Craddock Fitch here, I need to speak to Miss Bissett.'

Sheila's hand trembled as she held the phone. After the upset last night she'd hardly slept a wink and wasn't really braced sufficiently at this early hour of the morning to conduct a conversation with someone so prestigious as Mr Fitch.

'Er, oh yes, er, it's Lady Bissett speaking, yes, I'll get her for you, can you hold the line?'

She raced up to Louise's bedroom, and knocked agitatedly on the door. 'Louise, Louise, it's Mr Fitch on the phone, hurry up! Don't keep him waiting.'

Louise appeared in a second, still in her nightdress, sleep heavily obvious around her eyes, her hair uncombed. Sheila watched her run downstairs to the phone. No, she thought, the rector wasn't at fault. It was all Louise's overcharged imagination, that's what it was. Well, Ron had said she had to deal with it; he'd said after all it was women's talk. Her heart quaked at the thought, and there came a mysterious throbbing in her ears. Oh dear, had she got high blood pressure? If she hadn't now she would have by the time this was all over. She could hear, couldn't avoid it really, Louise saying, 'Yes, of course, Mr Fitch. Certainly. Twelve noon. Of course. Certainly. Oh, how lovely. Thank you. Looking forward to it. Bye bye.'

The receiver went down and Louise came charging up the stairs. 'That was Mr Fitch, he wants to see me at twelve about the Show. He's driving down from London this morning. Twelve o'clock, he said, and then stay for lunch. I'm having a bath and washing my hair. Mind out of the way.'

'But you've resigned!'

'Oh God – so I have! The file! I'll need the file! Damn and blast it!'

What she'd hoped would be a relaxing soak in perfumed water planning how she would impress Mr Fitch, changed into a frantic charge through several rehearsals of how she would extract the file from Pat, without admitting she wanted to be back as Secretary to the committee. Why did he have to ring at such an inopportune moment? A few more days and she could have resolved it, got the file back, been reinstated and carried on as before. Without being on the committee and without the rectory visits she had nothing left and would definitely have to find a job. There was no further excuse. She could make a start on sorting out Gilbert's music, but that would really bring little reward. Though she had promised she would do it. Yes, she'd do it and then that would be that. Louise put a stop to her meanderings. This wasn't working out how to get the file back from Pat without too much loss of face.

A decision to leap out of the bath and get round to the school before Pat left meant Louise was out in Jacks Lane by twenty minutes past nine. She found Pat in the school kitchen hanging up some tea towels to dry on a little rack above the sink. Louise could hear the babble of children's voices, but didn't smile like others did when they heard it; she was too preoccupied searching for the right words.

Pat turned to see who had called her name.

'Oh, it's you! Well, what now?'

'Could I possibly have my file back? I think I must have left some private correspondence in there and I need it, this morning, right now. Please.'

'Not got it, I'm afraid.' She finished hanging up the cloths, then began drying her hands on the kitchen roller-towel.

Startled, Louise asked sharply, 'Not got it? Where is it then?'

'Dr Harris took it. I certainly wasn't going to take over, not on your Nellie! So if you want it you'll have to go to the rectory for it.'

'I see.' Louise swallowed hard. 'I'll have to go there then.'

'You will. Though how you've the cheek to knock on their door after the rector's turned you out, I don't really know. Glad I'm not in your shoes.'

'Mmmmm. Right, well, I'll get round there.'

'See yer then.'

Louise didn't notice the glee on Pat's face, nor did she see Pat dance a little jig right there on the red tiled floor.

She walked slowly out of the school and across the playground, then stood for a few moments in the gateway watching the builders working on the houses in Hipkin Gardens. They were glazing the windows already. How many months had she been at home? Too many. What on earth was she going to do? It was such a feather in her cap for Mr Fitch to want her to go for lunch and discuss the arrangements for the Show, that she couldn't, honestly couldn't, miss out. She'd promised him anyhow, and at least he wouldn't know what the gossips in the village were saying about her. They just didn't understand how she felt. She could make darling Peter so happy, so very happy. There were no two ways about it; she'd have to face up to going to the rectory. It might not be a bad thing, after all; she might even get a chance to have a word with Peter on his own. She'd go home first, have a coffee and a think and then walk across and request the file.

At the rectory the file was on Peter's desk, where he'd left it the night before, after he and Caroline had gone through it when she'd got back from the committee meeting.

'Give credit where it's due, she's an amazing organiser, isn't she, Peter? I can't see how I could possibly be as detailed as this. All these notes, cross references, all this detail. All these coloured stickers, red for this, yellow for that. Brilliant! If she went under a bus tomorrow we'd be able to carry on as if nothing had happened.'

'Caroline! What a thing to say!'

'Well, we would – it's true. But whichever way you look at it, I've got to get her back as secretary again. I simply haven't the time to take all this on, nor am I the kind of person who could keep such immaculate records.' She waved her hand over the file, closed it up and said, 'What a pity her private life is in such a mess. All she needs is a good—'

'Caroline!'

'*Man* I was going to say – a man who loves her for what she really is. After all, there must be more to her than all this.' She waved her hand over the file again. 'Who could we find for her?'

'Michael Palmer springs to mind.'

'Yes, that's a good idea – we could give them those opera tickets you were sent. We're not opera people, but Michael is and she would be, if it meant going out with a man. Yes, we'll give them the opera tickets and follow it up with a post-Show dinner party. That would make a good start for them, don't you think?'

'Caroline! I don't want her anywhere near the rectory, thank you, unChristian though that might sound.'

When the doorbell rang Peter was impatient at the interruption. Caroline had taken the twins into Culworth to buy new shoes and meet a friend for lunch, and Sylvia was using up some holiday which was due to her. He was in the rectory all on his own and taking the opportunity to finalise an article he'd been asked to write for the local paper. As he crossed the hall, he put a welcoming smile on his face and opened the door.

'Ahh! It's you, Louise. Good morning. What can I do for you?'

'Good morning. May I come in?'

Peter had a rule that anyone and everyone was welcome at the rectory whatever the time of day or night. Reluctantly he held open the door and asked her in. However, instead of inviting her into his study as he would normally have done, he stood waiting in the hall to hear what she had to say.

'Actually it's the file, the file for the Show. In a moment of . . . extreme stress I gave it to Pat last night. I don't know if Caroline . . .'

'Yes, she did.'

'Is she in? Could I have a word?'

Peter said she was out, sorry.

'Oh, I see. Do you happen to know where she put it? I need it to get some things out, personal papers I left in by mistake.'

Peter gave her one of his deep searching looks. Louise lowered her eyes and stared at the carpet. Why must he look at her like that right now? She couldn't tell lies when he looked at her like that. 'Well, the truth is, the truth is, I want it back . . . because I want to be . . . oh God! The truth is . . .' Suddenly out of nowhere, abruptly and thoughtlessly she blurted out, 'It's you. Oh, Peter! I can't bear not seeing you, can't bear it.' She took her handkerchief from her pocket and wiped away the tears welling in her eyes.

'Now see here, Louise, you know it's not possible. Simply not possible. We agreed on that.'

'No, you agreed to it with Caroline and Sylvia, you *told* me.'

'Quite right I did. What I said still stands though.'

'Why can't I see you? Whyever not? Just you and me, we work together so well. I wouldn't ask to look after the children. Think how well-organised your parish work would be with me helping you. Oh Peter!'

'I . . . I . . . There's no way this conversation can proceed. I'll get the file and you can take it away. Caroline really rather wished you'd be secretary again. She didn't feel up to the job herself, not when she saw how complicated everything was.'

'No, you see, that's it. That's all everyone ever sees me as – a highly efficient administrator. But I'm not like that underneath. Underneath I'm . . .'

'I'm sorry.' Peter backed away. 'Please, whatever it is, leave it unsaid. There's nothing to be done about it.'

'But there is. You could solve it all for me, for us. You and me. I'm brimming with ideas for helping the parish, to increase the congregation, to reorganise the giving, even ideas for different services. I've given it such a lot of thought. It would be brilliant. I'd see to it that it was, believe me.' Eyes brimming with tears, she looked longingly at him, her soul stripped bare for him.

Peter glanced away. 'I'll get the file.' He made to go to the study, intending she should stay in the hall, but she followed him in and shut the door.

'Why not? I don't understand why not? We work together so well, you and I. We've grown so close, and I've . . . I've . . . Oh, Peter, Peter, please!'

Peter stepped back to avoid her clutching him. God, what a mess! 'I desperately don't want to hurt you. I have the greatest respect for you, you see, but frankly I have no intention ever . . . again . . . of doing anything that would hurt Caroline. Me seeing you and working with you, would endanger my relationship with her. The first day I met her I knew how it was to be. I love her very deeply. We are married for *life*. There is *nothing* that I would do to jeopardise that. I made my promise before God and that promise I shall keep till the day I die.'

He watched the tears begin to pour down Louise's cheeks. When Caroline cried it broke his heart. Seeing Louise cry caused a sick feeling in the pit of his stomach: not pity, nor pain, nor distress, but revulsion. He strove to keep his feelings from his face, but it was his way to be truthful and to expect, and receive, the truth from others, so he was unsuccessful in hiding how he felt. She wiped her eyes and looked up at him again, intending to plead just one more time. He'd misunderstood, he didn't realise she was offering herself to him, but she saw the look on his face and recognised the truth; her tears revolted him.

He handed her the file. She snatched it from him, flung wide the study door, and ran away. Out through the open front door and across the Green to home. If her mother spoke one word to her when she got in she'd kill her. But she did. And they had the row to end all rows. And her father was home too, and said his piece. And Louise wept, desolate, unloved and thirty years old. At a quarter past eleven she remembered she still had Mr Fitch to see. When he saw how efficient she was, he'd appreciate her even if no one else did. She'd drag the last remnants of her self-respect together and get up there and show him what she was made of.

Chapter 14

Pat, still chuckling about Louise's dilemma, didn't bother to cycle between the school and the Store. She left her bike in the school-shed and walked round. Barry was coming tonight for a meal. Dean and Michelle had persuaded her to invite him. It was a thank you for Dean's cupboards, a talk about arrangements for the holiday, and a chance to get to know each other better. Grandad had agreed to go on holiday with them so long as he had a room of his own, and Dean was so delighted to be going away he'd not complained about sharing with Barry.

What was she to cook? Jimbo might have some ideas. She pushed open the door and picked up a wire basket. Jimbo was behind the meat counter sharpening a large carving knife.

'Morning, Jimbo. Can yer knock off for a minute and let me pick yer brains.'

'Just the person I want to see. I'll pick yours first. What on earth happened at the meeting last night? I've just seen Louise racing across the Green, crying buckets, clutching to her ample bosom that file she always takes to the meetings. Is there something I ought to know?'

'Well . . .' Pat told Jimbo the details of the upset. 'So this morning I told her to go to the rectory if she wanted it.'

'I say, what can have happened?'

'Crying, you said? Serves 'er right.'

'Yes, and running like hell.'

'Blimey! He must have told her straight. Only right he should. Anyway, I'm making a special meal tonight. For five. Can you give me any ideas? Not too expensive, but just a bit special.'

'Special meal?' Jimbo eyed her speculatively, his eyebrows raised, his head to one side.

'Now look, Jimbo, I know you like to know everything that goes on, but this time it's secret.'

'Won't stay secret for long, not in Turnham Malpas.'

'Maybe not.'

They discussed the meal at length and when Jimbo had packed her shopping for her and she was paying him, he said, 'He's all right, is Barry, a nice chap. Does the noble parent like him?' He grinned at her and she couldn't be angry.

'Old Mrs Thornton that 'ad this place before you was a gossip, but you're ten times worse.'

'Such fun though and quite harmless. Sorry! I didn't mean to pry.'

Pat settled her forearms on the ledge in front of the till and didn't notice the doorbell jingle. 'Yes, I'm asking him as a thank you for putting up some cupboards in Dean's bedroom. I might as well tell you the rest. He's going on holiday with us to Devon . . .' Jimbo coughed significantly and winked. Pat turned round to find Barry's mother breathing fire down her neck.

'Is that my Barry you're talking about?'

'It is.'

'You're no better than you should be, Pat Duckett. Going on holiday with him when you're not married. Disgusting! Wait till he gets home.'

'And what do you propose to do about it? He's a grown man, he can do as he likes.'

'Not when he's under my roof he can't.'

'Well, he is going on holiday with us, and that's final. First holiday my kids have ever had, and nothing's going to spoil it for 'em. Not you, not anybody.'

'I don't know who you think you are, speaking to me like that.'

'Same as you, ordinary. To put your suspicious mind at rest, your Barry's sharing a room with our Dean, not me. Satisfied?' Pat picked up her shopping and with a brief nod to Jimbo walked out.

It was after ten by the time she'd finally got Dean packed off to bed. Grandad had helped to wash up and then taken a cup of tea up to bed to watch the football in his room.

'Do you want to watch the football, Barry?'

'No, thanks, not tonight. Come and sit next to me here.' He patted the cushion beside him and put his arm along the back of the sofa. He smiled up at her and her heart flipped.

Barry patted the cushion again. 'Thanks for a lovely meal, it was smashing. You're a good cook.'

'Makes a difference when yer can afford the ingredients. Before Dad came, it was egg and chips, beefburger and chips, or jacket potatoes for ever and a day.'

'Been hard for you then.'

'Yer can say that again.'

'I'd like to make life easier for you.'

Pat turned towards him and said, 'You are doing that already by taking us all away. I need to sort out the money for that. Can't let you pay for everything, petrol and that. I'll bring plenty of food with us.'

'There's a supermarket on the site. As far as the money's concerned, petrol's my responsibility and the caravan's free so there's only the food and the entertainment to pay for. Yer dad said he wants to chip in with that so I reckon it won't be that expensive.'

'You been talking to Dad about it then? When?'

'One day, when we met.'

'He likes you.'

Barry asked, 'D'you like me? That's the big question.'

'Yes, I do. You're house-trained, clean, smart and healthy, and you've got all your own teeth.' She grinned at him.

Deflated he said, 'Make me sound like a dog, you do.'

Pat laughed. 'What did you expect me to say? That you put me in mind of Clark Gable, or Rex Harrison or someone?'

'I'd rather you said Harrison Ford or Kevin Costner.'

'I couldn't match up to them! No, they'd be no good.'

'Give us a kiss. Come on.'

'I'm not much good at kissing.'

'I'll teach you, I'm an expert.'

'It is true then – you an' all those girls?'

'No, no. All talk. Kissing's instinct really. All instinct.'

'Is it?'

'Go with the flow as they say.' He hitched himself closer to her and taking her in his arms he vigorously set about kissing her cheeks, then her eyelids, and then several small kisses around her lips. It was Pat who opened her mouth and encouraged him to kiss her 'for real' as she called it. It was Pat who groaned her pleasure at his kisses, it was Pat who moved closer still and it was Pat who didn't object when he opened the buttons at the neck of her dress and began touching her neck and her throat with rapid exciting kisses.

'Oh Barry . . .'

'God, Pat, we'd better stop.' He sat upright and didn't look at her, anywhere but at her. His hands were twisting together as though battling with themselves. She re-buttoned her dress, and sat rigidly upright away from him, not touching him, puzzled by his reaction and disappointed that he didn't find her exciting.

Barry muttered quietly, 'Sorry about that. Really sorry.'

'Why?'

'I'd better go.'

'Go – why? Is it because . . . I didn't do it right?'

'No, no, you were great. This time it's . . .' He took a deep breath. 'Always before it's been sex first and last. This time I'm getting it the right way round. This time it's important to me. You're important to me, that is. Don't know why, but you are. I've always gone for the tarts before, all high heels and boobs. But this time it's differ-ent. More real. I want to get it right.'

'I see. I think that's how I'd like it too.'

Barry stood up. Looking down at her, he said, 'You mean you might take a liking to me?'

Pat nodded. 'But there's the kids. I come with baggage as yer might say. And there's Dad.'

'I know. But I like your kids. Really nice they are. Not at all cheeky and wanting things all the time. You've done a good job there.'

'I've tried. They're not always good.'

'Wouldn't want 'em to be. I'll say good night. Take no notice of Mum, by the way.'

'If you say so.' She stood up and went to see him to the door. 'Good night and thanks, Barry.'

He waved good night and then turned back. 'I just want to say this. Men yer know, at work, talk about the women they've been with the night before. Their girlfriends and their wives too – go into all the detail, for a laugh and to boast, yer know how it is. I did it too. I want you to know I don't talk about you. OK?'

'Right, thanks.'

Pat felt a million dollars. Yes, a million dollars. Beneath all his flirty talk he was a decent bloke. She locked the back door and began to make herself a drink to take to bed.

The kitchen door opened and Michelle was there. 'Mum, I'm thirsty, can I have a drink?'

'You not been to sleep yet then?'

'For a bit, but then I woke up feeling funny.'

'Sit there and we'll 'ave a cup of tea.'

'Mum?'

'Yes.'

'I do like Barry.'

'Good.'

'Do you?'

'Yes, I think so.'

'You know L-O-V-E? Well . . .'

'Yes, go on.'

Michelle stirred her tea. 'Does Barry L-O-V-E you?'

'Not yet, but perhaps he might.'

'I thought there was a big bang and you knew you were in love.'

'Sometimes there is, but when you get older sometimes it happens slowly.'

'I hope you love him. I'd like him for a dad. Could I be a bridesmaid? I've never been one.'

Pat laughed. 'We'll see. He hasn't asked me yet.'

'No, but he will. I can tell the signs.'

'Michelle!'

'I've talked to Grandad. He says the same. He says Barry's smitten, 'cos he's different with you. I think he likes me too, don't you? I should like him to like me. Could I call him Dad?'

'Only if we married.'

'Well, hurry up then. When he proposes will you tell me all about it? What went on and that. I need to know for when I grow up.'

'Cheeky face!' Pat kissed her and the two of them went off to bed.

When she got into her own bed, she stroked the pillow next to hers. She'd kept the bed her and Doug had bought when they first got married. Pat tried to imagine what it would be like to have Barry going to sleep there every night. Feel funny. Been alone for eight years she had. If, and it was a big if, they married she'd have a new bed – one of those big ones, the really big ones, then there'd be plenty of room. She wouldn't want any more kids though. They'd have to have an understanding about that. Not when she was knocking on forty and the other two so old. No more kids. He'd have to understand. Pat took a last look around her bedroom before finally closing her eyes and going to sleep. She admired the flower pictures Dean had bought her to put on the wall over the radiator. She leaned out of bed and dug her fingers into the tufts of the carpet she'd chosen in that big carpet warehouse outside Culworth; she patted the bedspread, pretend patchwork quilt like them American quilts, and finally she switched off her bedside lamp – now that was a luxury. Before, she'd always had to get out of bed to turn off the light.

Yes, things were definitely looking up. One whole week beside the sea, like a real family, and to top it off she was determined she'd win the shortbread prize, because this year was her year.

Chapter 15

The bar in The Royal Oak was packed. Saturday evening, hot summer weather, and the world and his wife were there. The tables outside in Royal Oak Road were filled, and the overspill had taken their drinks out on to the Green and were sitting on the grass, enjoying themselves. Willie and Sylvia were at their favourite table in the saloon, with Jimmy and Vera.

'Pat not coming then?' Vera asked.

Jimmy shook his head and said, 'No, Vera, she's got other fish to fry. That Barry's taking up a lot of 'er time.'

'Good luck to her, I say. He's a nice chap, all that flirting he does though, it's scandalous. Cor, he's had some girls in his time. Got caught in the hayloft at Home Farm few years back. Talk about a carry on, that was. There was mention of a shotgun, but he managed to escape.'

Sylvia put down her gin and tonic to say, 'Well, he seems to have steadied down now. The whole lot's going on holiday together after the Show.'

'No! Grandad as well?'

'Yes.'

'Well, that's a turn-up for the book, that is. Wouldn't

ever have thought Barry would be taking two kids and a grandad with 'im. What a laugh. He must be serious! Any news from the church we ought to know, Willie?'

'Not from the church, 'cept the rector's away. Gone to Devon today for two weeks. Time they both had a holiday. That's all really. But there is news from the school. Did you know Mr Palmer's given his notice in?'

'Mr Palmer given his notice in?' Jimmy couldn't believe it. 'After all these years? Whatever for?'

'Got a new job miles away. Head of a big primary school. Hundreds o' kids.'

'Bit different from ours then.'

Sylvia said she couldn't think what on earth had made him move.

Vera agreed. 'Neither can I. He's been here nearly twenty years, must have been. Yes, twenty at least. He's going on for forty-five or thereabouts. Wonder what's made him do it? I've always thought of him as a permanent fixture, like the school boiler or something.'

'It'll be a big wrench for 'im anyways.'

'Pat always thought him and Suzy Meadows would make it up. Very pally they were when she ran the playgroup at the school.'

'That poor girl must have had enough of men one way and another.' Sylvia felt Willie's knee nudge her under the table as she spoke. She tried to change the subject. 'Still, new fields to conquer and all that. You planned your holidays yet, Vera?'

Vera's mind was still dwelling on Mr Palmer. 'You know, it would have been great for Mr Palmer and her to get together. A readymade family with them three girls, and lovely girls they are too. He's too old to start a family of his own, it would have been just right.'

Jimmy suggested he'd never have the guts to ask her in the first place. 'When his wife killed herself he switched off. Good with the children but dead as a dodo otherwise. Don't yer think?'

'Well, he never does have much to say about anything except school. That's the only time he comes alive. Sad, very sad.' Vera gazed gloomily into her empty glass.

''Nother drink, Vera?'

'Oh, thanks, Jimmy. What it is to have a wealthy neighbour.' She giggled at him. 'Same again, please. We'll drink to Mr Palmer, wish him good luck in his new job. It takes some believing.'

When Jimmy got back with the drinks they toasted Mr Palmer and his big decision to move away from Turnham Malpas, and then had an in-depth discussion on the likely winners of the prizes at the Village Show.

Jimmy summed up the situation in a nutshell. 'Well, yer can all say what yer like but I reckon when all's said and done the Templeton Cup for most points in the produce classes will be won by Willie.' He paused to take a long drink from his glass and then volunteered a piece of information that none of them knew about. 'There's going to be another cup this year.'

'Who says?'

'Louise-know-it-all-Bissett. She's persuaded old Fitch to present a cup for the most points in the flower classes. 'Spect it'll be as big as the FA Cup knowing 'im. The Fitch Flowers Cup it's to be called. The conditions'll be on that amendment sheet they're 'aving to put in 'cos of the classes that got left out by the printer – so Louise says, but we all know it was Sheila Bissett left 'em out on purpose. I'd 'ave 'ad something to say if there'd been no egg classes. My 'ens are laying like nobody's business now they're getting fed better. That new 'ouse of theirs suits 'em a treat.' Jimmy downed the last of his beer and said he'd got to go. 'I'm off to Culworth; there's always plenty of business for a taxi on Saturday nights. I've got a living to earn. Be seeing yer.'

'You shouldn't be drinking when yer driving.'

'I've only 'ad two halves. I'll suck a couple of mints on the way. Nobody'll know.'

Vera shook her head. 'He'll never improve, he won't. Right turn-up for the book about Mr Palmer though, isn't it? Just wish he could find a right nice little wife, not too flighty, but quiet like 'im. Wonder if they've got a replacement? Poor fella, right upheaval it'll be.'

Michael Palmer lay soaking in the bath in the schoolhouse, unaware that he was the subject of speculation in the bar. He'd left the bathroom door open so he could hear the sound of his CD player in the sitting room. There was no pleasure more enjoyable than lying in the bath, alone in the house, listening to good music.

He must remember to feed his roses before he went to bed. This year, his last year, he was determined he'd win something. He'd tried beans and marrows and won nothing, but this year he was trying roses. A Highly Commended would please him greatly – a final fanfare before he left. He sat up to turn the hot tap on for a while. As the comforting hot water passed his feet and began creeping up his legs, he thought about his new school. Three hundred children compared to thirty-eight. What a difference. What a decision. The most decisive step he'd taken in years. He turned off the tap and lay down again.

He still had to tell Suzy. He should have told her before he accepted the job, but somehow he knew he couldn't face a possible rebuff. The school was only fifteen miles from where she lived. Near enough, but far enough away, so if she didn't want to see him any more then they wouldn't be bumping into each other and it wouldn't be embarrassing. On the other hand . . . he did love her. She brought joy with her and gave it to him, joy like he'd never known. The final chords of the symphony bombarded his ears, and as the notes died away he became aware of the telephone ringing. Michael got out of the bath, wrapped a towel round his waist and went to answer it.

'Hello, School House, Michael Palmer speaking.'

'It's me – Suzy.'

His heart leaped. 'Hello, how are you?'

'I'm fine, thanks. I've been thinking.'

'Yes?'

'I haven't seen you for a long time.'

'Four weeks and five days.'

'Is it? That's a long time. I wondered if there might be a possibility you could come over. Next weekend perhaps?'

'I'm sorry, I can't. I've sold my car today.'

'Oh, that's good news. You didn't think you would.'

'No, well, I did and my new one won't be delivered until a week on Tuesday, so I've no transport at the moment.'

'Oh, I see. I am disappointed.'

'So am I. But it can't be helped. It would have been lovely to see you.'

'Michael . . .'

'Yes?'

'I could come to you, I suppose. No, of course I can't, because I wouldn't want to meet . . .'

'Oh, but Caroline and Peter won't be here. They'll be on holiday. You could come. We don't have to advertise the fact. Keep a low profile et cetera. It wouldn't matter, would it?' He'd begun to sound eager.

'Really?'

He controlled his eagerness. 'I don't want you to get the wrong idea. I mean . . . what I wanted to say was, I'm not putting pressure on you . . .'

'Oh no, I know you wouldn't.' He thought he heard Suzy sigh.

Michael rushed on with what he had to say. 'There's the spare bedroom, you see. You could have that.'

'Yes, I suppose I could. Shall I come then?'

'Yes, please, I'd like that. That would be lovely.'

'I'll come Friday night after school and leave first thing Sunday. Can't expect Mother to have the girls all weekend.'

'I'm really looking forward to seeing you.'

'Right, Friday night it is. What will the village say?'

'Plenty. But I don't care. After all, I'm—'

'What?'

'Nothing. Nothing at all. I'll see you Friday night then. I'll give you a ring during the week to confirm. Good night, Suzy.'

'Good night, you dear man.'

Michael, now shivering from head to foot, put down the phone, and dashed back into the bath. He put the hot tap on and warmed up the water again. He felt as though he'd taken a big step. The second big step in the last few weeks. This coming weekend could be the one when he proposed. On the other hand, was he doing the right thing? Yes, he was. Nothing ventured, nothing gained. She did want to come. She was willing to risk a lot to see him, so she must be interested. Yes, definitely, this coming weekend could be one of those turning points.

He was still joyful in school on Monday morning. He couldn't keep the happiness from his face. Pat noticed it. As she slipped her feet into her old school shoes she said to him, 'My word, Mr Palmer – you won the lottery? Million pounds, was it?'

'No, of course not, Mrs Duckett.'

'Well, I don't know what's caused it, Mr Palmer, but you're like a cat who's been at the cream.'

Michael wagged his finger at her and said, 'I'm not the only one. Since you moved to the Garden House, you've been on top of the world, and I don't think it's only the move that's done it.'

'Well, no, you could be right there.'

'I'm glad for you, Pat.'

Pat looked up from the cupboard under the sink where she was searching for a duster. 'My word, something's up. This summer I shall have worked 'ere in this school seven years and that's the first time you've called me Pat. It's always been Mrs Duckett this and Mrs Duckett that. What's up then?'

'Nothing, nothing at all. It must be the weather.'

'Weather my foot! I reckon I'm not the only one who's courting. It's not that Louise Bissett, is it?'

'Good God, no!' The words slipped out without thinking and he looked so appalled by his rapid, thoughtless answer to Pat's question that she burst out laughing.

'Gawd 'elp us, I 'ope not! Desperate she is for a man, so yer'd better watch out.'

'Mrs Duckett! That's most unfair. Not at all kind.'

'Well, just mind you're not *too* kind to her yerself. She's after anything in trousers, she is. The poor rector's having a right time with her. Mind you, I'm not surprised – he *is* lovely. Wonder he's not had trouble with women chasing him before this. Course, he did have, didn't he?' She glanced at him as she picked up the polish from the draining

165

board, and saw he'd clamped down and gone back to how he used to be. Withdrawn and unapproachable. Gawd! That was it. The photo in the drawer. He was moving to be near her. Of course. She'd right put her foot in it this time.

'The windows in the playgroup room – when you have a moment, they need cleaning, Mrs Duckett.' He turned on his heel and left the kitchen. Mr Palmer deserved some happiness. You'd got to grab it while you could. In fact, no one in their right mind should turn down the chance of happiness. Life could be Gawd-awful lonely at times, even if yer 'ad kids, which he didn't.

He made Suzy a cup of tea as soon as she arrived. He'd boiled the kettle three times while he waited for her coming. His expectation was she'd be there by about eight, but it was nine before he saw her car. He watched as she slid it carefully into the narrow parking space by his house wall. In 1855 they didn't build school premises to accommodate cars. He'd taken a deep breath and gone to open the door. Bag in hand, she stood there smiling. She was wearing a dress the colour of wild cornflowers, and with it a matching blue headband holding back her hair from her face. His photograph didn't do justice to the blue of her eyes, nor to her silver-blonde hair, nor the delicate roundness of her cheeks. She seemed smaller than when he'd seen her over five weeks ago, more vulnerable, more hesitant. There was a tremor in her voice when she said, 'I've come as I promised.'

'Come in, come in.' Michael was conscious of being hale and hearty to cover how he really felt. Was he never going to be able to speak the unspeakable? To ask the impossible? Why should this delightful creature want him? He was ten years her senior and not remotely good-looking. Even her husband for all his faults had had a certain air. But he, Michael Palmer, had nothing to offer. His heart sank and he wished this weekend had never begun.

They talked the whole of the evening, Michael putting off the dreaded moment when he had to show her her bedroom and use the bathroom and . . . How would he get over the awkwardness of it all?

He proposed over breakfast. Broke the news first about moving from the village, said how excited he was by the challenge of the bigger school, the urban environment, and mentioned that it was about fifteen miles from where she lived. He'd have to buy a house, though he'd rent first and give himself time to look around and . . .

'Michael! What amazing news! I never thought you'd leave here.'

'I should have left when Stella . . . when Stella died. But I didn't, couldn't face my daily life here, never mind moving away on top of it all. At least everything was familiar here.'

'Something important must have made you decide to move away from here, something quite mind-blowing.'

He put down his spoon, and stared at the remains of his Shredded Wheat. 'Yes, something did. I unexpectedly fell in love.'

Suzy picked up her cup, and before she drank from it, she looked at him over the rim. 'Who's the lucky woman?'

Michael didn't answer immediately. His eyes strayed to the kitchen window and then back to his Shredded Wheat. He picked up his spoon again, filled it with cereal, lifted the spoon halfway to his mouth, put it down again and said so softly she had to strain to hear, 'You.'

'So did I. Fall in love. Unexpectedly.'

*

He took her to his favourite high point. They sat close together bracing themselves against the strong breeze blowing briskly over the fields below.

'I love this place. It's mine. I come here when I'm unhappy.'

'But you're not unhappy today of all days, surely?'

'No, not today. Today I could be on the brink of happiness. Yes, the brink of a lifelong happiness.' He turned his head to look at her, the second time that day he'd looked frankly and openly at her. He asked her bluntly a question he'd formulated a thousand ways in his mind but had never found the courage to ask.

'Peter Harris. Where do we stand about him?'

Suzy snatched her hand from his, and looked away.

He persisted. 'We must have it clear, quite clear, and then it won't be mentioned again.'

'My word, Michael, you're coming right out from behind the parapet today, aren't you?'

'There are times when one must. I can't hide any longer.'

'Neither can I. Seeing as we're being honest . . .' Suzy pushed her hair away from her face and tied the long length of it with a ribbon she took from her shirt pocket. 'I needed comfort and love the day they found Patrick dead. Peter was there, and for the moment he needed me. No, *wanted* me. To his dying day he will regret what happened. I shan't, though. It was a momentary attraction, which by the grace of God, gave Peter and Caroline the children they wanted. Nothing more, nothing less. You need have no worries about regrets or anything, Michael. My only regret is that it's taken me so long to come round to knowing how much you mean to me.'

Michael recaptured her hand, put his arm around her shoulders and hugged her close. The sun went behind a cloud. Suzy shivered and rubbed her arms. She smiled at him. 'It's getting cold. Time to go back to your house. I'll cook tonight, right?'

'Right. Race you to the bottom.'

Suzy laughed. 'Honestly, who am I marrying – a man or a boy?'

'A man, believe me – a man.'

Peter slowed right down when they came to the sharp right-hand bend by the sign to Turnham Malpas. Caroline glanced at the children strapped in their safety seats. 'It's all right, they're both still asleep. What a nightmare journey! I'm so sorry, darling, that we've had to come home. Who'd believe it – chickenpox! I really think the other guests believed they had the plague.'

'We couldn't have stayed. They're much too ill and much better off in their own beds, safe at home. We'll have another holiday later in the year, I promise. Only two more miles and we'll be back.' Peter patted Caroline's leg. She took his hand and squeezed it. 'Thanks for being so understanding,' she said. 'I really did wonder if I was being too "parenty" and worrying too much.'

'Indeed not. Coming home was by far the best decision.'

'Oh Peter, isn't it lovely having children? We'd got very self-centred, you know, before they came. Debating about whether to go to South Africa or the Rockies or whatever. And here we've had one week making sandcastles on a Devon beach and I've loved every minute of it.'

'Same here – every minute. But we mustn't get too smug with ourselves, or we might become dull.'

'You'd be more guilty of that than me. You can be very smug sometimes, Peter, to the point of being positively self-righteous.'

'Oh right, I'll have to watch myself then. I'll park in Pipe and Nook because of the bolts on the front door. The twins are bound to wake up. Can't help that. We'll take out only the essentials. I'm not up to unpacking properly at this time of night. In any case, we'll disturb the neighbours.'

The twins spent a very restless night, asking for drinks and crying for their mother. Caroline hardly slept at all. Twice Peter got up to them to give her a chance to rest, but they cried for their mother and refused to allow him to help them.

Caroline got up for good at six o'clock.

'Look, my darling girl. You stay up till I get back from prayers. I won't go for a run today, I can't find the energy. You settle them back into bed again and you go to bed too and I'll stay on duty while you sleep.'

'Wonderful. Right, come along you two, Mummy get you drinkies and some porridge. You always love porridge when you're not well, don't you? Lovely swirly syrup too. How about that?' Thumb in mouth Beth nodded, but Alex merely ignored what she said and demanded a cuddle.

Caroline had expected Peter back again by seven ready for his breakfast, but he hadn't come. At a quarter past seven the doorbell rang. 'Oh, he's forgotten his key. Coming, darling.' But it wasn't Peter it was Sylvia, worried because she'd seen the car parked in the lane and wondered what the matter was. Caroline explained.

'Oh no! Where are they? Alex, Beth, come to your Sylvie. Oh you poor sweethearts, oh my goodness me! Just look at your spots. Don't scratch, Beth. Don't they look dreadful? No wonder you had to come home.'

'I've been up and down to them most of the night, so when Peter gets back from prayers he's taking over. I shall put them back to bed and then I'll go too.'

'I'm so sorry about your holiday. What was the weather like?'

'Well, it was lovely all the week. Sun shining every day, but then by Thursday the children began to droop, and that spoilt it for us, of course. Anything of any note happen while we've been away?'

'No, nothing at all. Just the same sleepy village. You know what it's like, one week runs into the next. You look tired, I must say. How about I dash home for breakfast and then come back to give you a hand?'

'Certainly not, it's your holiday and I insist we shall manage.'

'If you're sure?'

'I am.' She held open the rectory door and invited Sylvia to leave. As Caroline was about to shut the door, Alex popped under her arm and out into the road. He set off after Sylvia, his pyjama legs flapping furiously as he ran. Caroline stepped out to catch him. 'Young man, you've had me up half the . . . night . . . and . . .' As she caught hold of him she glanced up the lane. Coming out of the lych-gate was someone she had thought she would never see again. Surely not? It couldn't be Suzy, could it? That silver-blonde hair of hers shining in the morning sun – there was no mistaking it. Oh, God! Caroline watched her pause for a moment, saw her turn back to face the church and give a slow gentle wave. There was obviously someone there returning her wave. Caroline snatched Alex back into the rectory, slammed the door shut and stood with her back pressed against it, breathing heavily. The shock of seeing Suzy again so unexpectedly made her heart pump frantic- ally.

What was Suzy doing here? Hoping to see the twins? She wasn't. She wasn't seeing them. Over her dead body would

171

she see them. They were hers, not Suzy's. She'd come to take Peter away from her and to get the twins – that was it. She'd come for Peter and therefore for the twins, they were theirs after all. Otherwise why was she here? What else was there for her to return to in the village, if not for the twins and Peter? God in heaven, *what was she to do*? Caroline felt crushed by the weight of her distress. In her agitation she clutched Alex against her chest and when he protested and struggled to get down she felt desolate, because his hatred of being squeezed felt like a rejection of her. Had he recognised his mother? Was he running to her and not to Sylvia? Had some sixth sense told him who she was? She mocked her own foolishness. Of course not, he didn't know her from Adam. She was being a stupid idiot. But Peter and Suzy had obviously met in the church. What had they said to each other?

He hadn't prayed at the main altar that morning but in the little side-chapel, converted to commemorate the men of the village killed in the First World War. Their surnames echoed those of the villagers of today.

Albert Biggs, William Biggs, Arnold Glover, Cecil Glover, Harold Glover, Sidney Glover, Fred Senior, Major Sir Bernard Templeton, 2nd Lieut. Ralph Templeton.

Dear Lord, what a loss. Four Glover boys. Four sons. How did their parents survive after that terrible blow? His own problems began to fade away, and he slipped into deep concentration and then to prayer.

He didn't hear Suzy's footsteps, and she didn't know he was there, hidden as he was by the oak screen carved in memory of so much horror. It was the sound of her accidentally sending a hymn-book spinning to the floor which disturbed Peter's absorption. He stood up and found himself looking at her through the screen. His heart missed a beat. Convinced he must be dreaming, he watched her walking about the church. What on earth was she doing here? Her lovely round cheeks were thinner than he remembered, but they still had that innocent glow to them; her splendid blue eyes were just as beautiful, and her hair, that lovely silvery-blonde hair, gleamed in the shaft of sunlight coming through the window above the altar. She hadn't changed much except she looked at peace now and not haunted.

He'd feel a fool if she came into the chapel and caught him hiding, so he stepped out from behind the screen and stood by the pulpit. She caught sight of him and he heard the swift intake of her breath. They looked intensely at each other, spanning the years with their memories. It was Suzy who spoke first.

'I'm so sorry, Peter. So sorry. I was told you were away from home. I was surprised to find the door open. I should have known. I've come to say goodbye to Turnham Malpas. You see, Michael's cooking our breakfast. If I'd known, I wouldn't have . . .'

'That's all right, we've had to come home because of illness.' He took a deep breath and making a huge effort to remember his duties as priest said, 'How are you, Suzy? You're looking very well.'

'I'm fine, Peter, thank you. How are you?' She reached out her hand but he ignored it. She put her hands behind her back. 'You're looking well. Everything is fine with me, is it with you?'

'Yes, thank you.' Peter paused for a moment and then said, 'Caroline and I are forever in your debt.'

There was a tremor in her voice as she said, 'No, you're not, not ever. The gift was freely given. I only gave you what was yours. I don't know why two old friends should be so solemn. I'll cheer you up. Michael Palmer and I are getting married in the summer. He's a lovely man, I feel so secure with him. I can depend on him – rely on him, you know.'

'Yes, I can understand that. Married? That's good. Wonderful news. I am glad.'

'This is goodbye then. I shan't be coming here again. I'm driving home this morning straight after breakfast. Don't tell Caroline you've seen me. I don't want her to be upset.'

Peter hesitated for a moment and then said abruptly, 'The children have chickenpox – that's why we've come home. They're covered in spots, and not at all well. She's been up most of the night with them.'

'I see, I'm sorry. Children can be a trial.'

'But worth it, worth it, you know. They are delightful.' He regretted those words the moment they were out of his mouth. What a fool he was to have said that.

Suzy's whole demeanour altered when Peter said how delightful they were. She became agitated. She twisted her hands together, then she put them to her mouth and almost gnawed on her knuckles. Then with her arms by her sides and her hands clenched tightly in her cardigan pockets she said, 'Delightful? Are they really? Are they . . . do they look like . . . like . . . me . . . or you?'

Peter felt himself to be reaching dangerous ground. 'They're both . . . that is, Alex . . . is like me but Beth is simply Beth.'

Suzy half-turned away from him and said quietly, 'Alex and Beth. They sound lovely. What I wouldn't give just for a goodbye peep. Just to say goodbye for ever.' Suzy faced him again. 'I wouldn't trouble you again, honestly I wouldn't and it wouldn't have occurred to me if you hadn't had to come home and been here when I . . . Please, Peter, please let me see them. It would kind of lay a ghost to rest if you would let me. Surely Caroline would . . . She knows I can't take them when they're yours, she knows they're safe. Please, just a peep.'

'No, no, no.' Peter backed away. 'Don't ask me, please don't ask me. Caroline is so deeply attached to them, almost more than if they were her own, if that's possible. The damage it would cause would be immeasurable. You really can't ask it of her. Your seeing them would distress her terribly.'

'But she has them for the rest of her life. I've lost them for ever.'

'You and I have caused her more than a lifetime of agony. It would be cruel, downright cruel of us to ask that of her. I'm sorry but no. Definitely no.'

Suzy came close to Peter and laid her hand on his arm. She looked intently up at him. He recalled the last time she'd laid her hand on his arm, when he'd been totally captivated by her gentle beauty. His innards turned to pulp. She tugged at his sleeve. 'Please.'

Peter brusquely pushed her away from him. 'I'm sorry, Suzy, but the answer is no. I can't let you down gently, I've got to be firm. No, absolutely no, both for her sake and yours. You've never seen them and that's the best way. If you do see them you'll never be free from heartache. This way at least you haven't got a picture of them in your heart for the rest of your life. It's best, believe me.'

He made the sign of the cross on her forehead, took her hand and slowly led her from the church. Her feet stumbled a little as the two of them walked down the aisle, and he sensed her struggle to control the sobs coming from deep within her. By the time they reached the church door, she had mastered her grief.

She turned to him and said sadly, 'Tomorrow, perhaps, I shall know you're right, but today I feel you've been very hard. I would have loved to have seen them, even if only a glimpse. Give them each a kiss from me, will you? Promise?' Peter nodded. 'I'll leave you then to finish your prayers.' When they reached the porch Suzy held out her hand. 'Goodbye, Peter. Be happy.' Peter shook hands, and then impulsively bent his head and kissed her, just one gentle kiss on her forehead, and for a moment he held her close.

'God bless you, Suzy. From the bottom of my heart I sincerely hope that your life with Michael will be tremendously rewarding, full of happiness and a great joy for you both.'

'I'm sure it will. Stay there and wave to me when I reach the gate, just this one last time. Just for me?'

He watched her walking slowly down the path to the gate. Michael was a lucky man. As she stepped out into the lane she turned and raised her hand to him. He raised his in blessing and then went back inside.

Caroline's prayer book was on the shelf in the rectory pew.

He read the words he'd written on the morning of their wedding day and knew how true they were. She was his and he was hers, '*from this day unto eternity*'. No one could part them. Suzy's ghost was at last laid to rest. He sat for a while and then realised that someone had entered the church. It was Willie, come to get ready for early service.

'Oh, good morning, Rector. Sorry you've had to come home. Right surprised we were when we opened the curtains and saw your car there. Sylvia popped in to see if

she could give a hand but Dr Harris said you'd manage.'
Willie peered closely at Peter's face. 'You not feeling too
good, sir? You look peaky to me.'

'Put it down to a bad night with the children, Willie. I'll
be off then. Don't want to upset things with my stand-in.
I'll ring him later today – perhaps I could do Evensong.'

'No such thing. You keep out of the way, sir. It is your
holiday after all. Looks to me as if you could do with some
sleep. I'll see to everything, don't you fret.'

At home the twins were in their beds, eyes beginning to
close. He found a place on Alex's face which was free from
spots and kissed him. He took hold of Beth's hand and
raised it to his lips. Caroline was already in bed. Now he'd
have to find the right words.

Chapter 16

Peter took off his shoes and laid himself down quietly beside her and tried to think how best to tell her what had happened. Once before he'd not told the truth; this time he had to tell her everything, no matter how much it hurt them both. But at least now he could say that he'd seen Suzy and he knew she didn't matter one jot to him because it was she, Caroline, whom he loved beyond all and . . .

'I'm taking the twins up home tomorrow.'

Peter half-sat up, resting his body weight on his elbow. He leaned over her and said, 'Up home? What for?'

'Because I need time to myself.'

'Why?' She didn't answer him. 'They're too ill to travel all that way.'

'They'll survive.'

'You're going to see your mother and father?'

'They should be leaving hospital tomorrow. They need me. You can tell everyone that's why I've gone.'

'But, darling, what help will you be to them with two small children to care for? They are such hard work, the pair of them. Leave them here. I'm off all this week – I can care for them.' Caroline didn't reply. He touched her arm and realised she was incredibly tense. What on earth was the matter with her? 'Look at me.'

'No, I shan't.'

'*Please* look at me.'

Caroline turned over to look at him and the pain in her eyes choked him. In a voice which was scarcely audible she said, 'I saw *her*. She was waving to *you*, wasn't she?'

'Dear God, Caroline, I'd no idea you'd seen her. That must have been the most tremendous shock. Why didn't you tell me straight away? I didn't speak because I thought you were asleep. I'm so deeply sorry that you've been suffering such pain. Please, my darling, believe me when I say I've been lying here trying to decide how to tell you, but I didn't know how. I was searching for the right words.'

'Oh, were you? I think you were hoping I wouldn't know, but Alex ran out into the road after Sylvia, and I went out to catch him and saw her wave.'

'It was goodbye. Before God, I didn't know she was here. Neither did she. Know we were here, I mean.'

'Yes, but you weren't going to tell me, were you?'

'I was. Believe me, I was.'

'It's always her who makes you not be truthful to me. The fact still remains that I'm going home tomorrow. You can tell the parish whatever you like, but that's what I'm doing. I'm terribly afraid and all mixed-up. I can't keep going any longer, so I'm going away. I'm leaving you. I'm leaving Turnham Malpas. I'm leaving the parish. Everything. I'm leaving it all.'

'As God is my witness we only said goodbye.'

'So you say. But I'm going. Going home.'

'Can I tell you what we said?'

Caroline's body jerked with anguish. '*No, you can't.* I don't want to hear. Not *one* word.'

The two of them were silent for a while and then Caroline, her voice strangely tight and jerky, said: 'Did she ask to see them? Because she isn't.'

'She did, but she isn't. I told her quite positively.'

'I would have killed her first.'

'My darling girl, I think maybe you're overwrought through sheer lack of sleep and too much worry, don't you?'

'Overwrought! What do you think I am? Some brainless idiot with nothing better to do than find wrongs to magnify and dwell upon? Peter! You know me better than that. You're reducing a deeply-felt anguish to a petty triviality. You must think me unbalanced. For God's sake!'

Alex, who'd been quietly crying for some time, began screaming.

Peter swung his legs over the edge of the bed. 'You stay there, darling, I'll go.'

'He won't let you see to him. *I'll* go.'

She got out of bed and climbed in with Alex and hugged him close. From sheer exhaustion she fell asleep and so did he. Secure in her arms.

'For one last time, I'm begging you not to go.'

'I am.'

'You're much too tired.'

'I'm not.'

'It's far too far for you to drive with the children by yourself. I'll take you. Please let me take you, and I'll leave you there with the car and come back on the train. If you don't want me there, that is.'

'I don't. Please, Peter, let me go. Just let me *go*.' Caroline grew angry and was within a hair's breadth of losing control. Her white face and clenched fists warned him how close she was to breaking down.

'Very well. But for my sake, ring me when you get there, so I know you're safe.' He reached out intending to kiss her goodbye, but as though his touch would be the last straw, she sprang away from him and jumped in the car.

He stood watching her turn the ignition key, fasten her safety belt; his arms and his heart aching with love for her. The children, still covered in spots and looking flushed and uncomfortable, waved their small hands to him and Beth blew him a kiss. He couldn't bear to see them go and quickly walked back into the rectory before the car moved off. He shut the study door, and stayed in there alone until Sylvia brought him his coffee.

'Here you are. I'll put it on the table for you, shall I? It's nice and hot.' She got no reply. 'There isn't much for me to do today. It looks as if Dr Harris did most of the washing and ironing yesterday. I've dusted round and got some shopping in, so I'll go if there's nothing else. Rector?'

'Thank you. Thank you for all you do. There was no need to come in this morning. You're more than kind.'

'I'll pop by tomorrow as well. Don't worry if you go out, I've got my key.' Sylvia looked at him and sighed. He was sitting so scrunched-up in the easy chair that he looked as though he'd shrunk. He'd shaved, she wouldn't have expected anything other, but his skin had a grey tinge. He looked more like forty-eight than thirty-eight.

'Don't take on so. They'll be back.'

Staring into space, Peter said, 'Her parents still live in the house they had when the girls were all at home. There's plenty of room for them, you see. They've a huge garden, and a dog. The children will be very happy there. So will she. She loves the wildness of Northumberland, especially the sea coast.'

'She'll be back. Trust me. Give her a few days.'

Peter looked at her for the first time. 'May God help me if she isn't.'

'Ron! Ron! Are you there?'

'In the bedroom.' Sheila ran up the stairs as fast as she could, her shopping still in her hand. She closed the bedroom door after her. 'Ron, you won't believe this but Caroline's left Peter.'

'Sheila, for goodness sake! You're spreading rumours again.'

'I'm not, it's true! They all know, they've just been talking about it outside the Store. Apparently Sylvia and Willie know the whole story but, of course, they won't tell. I bet even the Gestapo couldn't get it out of *them*.' Sheila sat down on the bed; in a stage whisper she asked, 'What about Louise?'

Ron looked at her through the mirror as he tied his tie. 'God only knows. More trouble, I expect. When is she blasted well going to get a job? If only she'd move away.'

'I'd better tell her not to go and see him.'

'Don't. She'll do the opposite. Say nothing.'

'All right then. I'm so sorry about it all.' She took her handkerchief from her pocket and wiped away a tear.

'Come on, old girl, they'll sort it out. Storm in a teacup.'

There came a tap on the bedroom door and Louise came in. 'I'm just off to sort out the choir music. I promised I would and I've done nothing about it. It might take all day. I'll come back for a sandwich, but don't make anything for me just in case.'

'Dad and I are going out, so we shan't be here. There's plenty in the fridge.'

'You sound odd. What's the matter?'

'Nothing's the matter. Off you go.'

Louise stopped at the Store to buy some chocolate to see her through the morning. By the till, elbows resting on the ledge in front of it, was a customer gossiping with Jimbo.

'I'm telling you, Mr Charter-Plackett, I saw it with my own eyes. Just out with the dog and I saw her leaving in that big car of theirs. Loaded up as if she's going for a lifetime. Pushchair, the lot. You don't need me to tell yer why, do yer?'

'Don't I?'

'Mean to say you 'aven't 'eard? Yer slipping, you are. Where've yer been this weekend?'

'We've all been away to a wedding. Got back late last night. What's happened then?'

'Well . . .' The customer regaled Jimbo with the whole story, embellished by her own conclusions, but nevertheless the essence of it rang true. 'Sly beggar, is that Mr Palmer. Still, quiet waters always run deep, don't they? So we're all concluding there's been a rupture at the rectory because of 'er coming for the weekend.'

'Rupture?'

'Well, it's certainly not rapture at the rectory, is it, let's put it that way. How much do I owe?'

'Oh right. Better pull myself together. Let's see.' He tried hard not to show how stunned he was by the news of Caroline's departure. He'd been wondering what they'd all been talking about outside on the seat, now he knew. No, he kept telling himself, it was all hugely gigantic supposition on the part of the village. They were prone to that if gossip was a bit thin on the ground. All she'd done was go home because her parents were coming out of hospital. Still, taking two small children with her, with chickenpox . . .?

Louise quietly chose a bar of fruit and nut, paying Jimbo the exact money so she wouldn't be delayed at the till and find herself betrayed by her boiling emotions. Safely out of the Store, she went swiftly over to the church. Caroline had gone! For whatever reason, she'd gone! Best of all, it wasn't her fault but Suzy's that she'd gone. That put her, Louise, in the best possible light; because she wasn't to blame, she could rightly sympathise. Right now his nerves would be raw. Absolutely raw. He would need a salve for his wounds. He would need understanding and — dare she say it? — comfort. She, who loved him, would have to serve that need.

In the choir vestry Louise took her big Oxford notepad out of her briefcase, two pens, sticky tape and scissors, some coloured stickers, a highlighting pen and her fruit and nut. Where to begin? When your heart is thumping with joy it's difficult to assemble your thoughts. *She'd gone! She'd left him!* Best way to tackle it was to make piles, give each pile a title and then sort each pile individually, check all the pages were there, mend torn ones, throw away sheets beyond repair, but make a note in case Gilbert wanted to buy replacements. *She'd gone! She'd left him!* When she'd got it all written down on paper then she could put it into the computer, and he'd have a complete schedule of the music. *She'd gone! She'd left him!*

Gradually her heart slowed to a normal beat and she became absorbed in the music. At eleven o'clock Louise went to sit in the church to eat her chocolate, because every chair and every bit of floorspace in the vestry was covered with music. She was hot and sticky with clambering over the piles of music, so she chose a pew where she could rest her shoulder against the cool stone of a pillar. There was only one square of her chocolate left when the heavy church

184

door opened and, caught by an unexpected gust of wind, slammed shut with an earth-shattering clang. Louise peered round the pillar to see who had come in.

Oh God, it was him! She shrank back behind the pillar; she couldn't face him. She looked such a mess. You didn't have meaningful, crucial meetings with the man in your life, when your skin was hot and sticky, and your hair tousled and wringing with sweat, and your teeth gooey with chocolate. She ran her tongue round her teeth to clear them but what she really needed was a drink of water to get them clean. She hid behind the pillar and waited to see where he would go. Peter walked slowly towards the altar. He was wearing jeans and a blue shirt; his red-blond hair was in disarray. He looked like a small boy who'd been severely reprimanded, and was at a loss to know how to recover his self-esteem. Indeed, he did look smaller than usual. How could he? That was ridiculous. But he did. He'd shrunk. He looked defeated. He stood before the altar, hands by his side, head bent, motionless.

She couldn't get up and creep away; the slightest movement would be heard in the deep silence of the church. Louise, rigid with tension, her trembling hands clasping the chocolate wrapper tightly, daring it to rustle, longed for him to go. But he didn't. He knelt to pray on the altar steps, his head thrown back, his arms outstretched for a while and then his hands clasped to his chest, his head bowed. Louise asked herself how could Caroline do this to him? How could she hurt him like this, reduce him to this? When someone loved you like he must love her, you didn't leave them, no matter what they'd done. Caroline was destroying him. It seemed an eternity that she waited. She watched him cross himself and then he stood up and went to leave the church.

Louise was horrified by the expression on his face. She almost cried out with the pain of seeing him so consumed by his anguish. Never in a million years would she have the capacity to suffer as he was suffering at this moment.

She held on to her tears until he'd closed the door behind him, then they began to roll down her cheeks. Hot scalding tears – tears for his agony, tears for the love she finally realised he would never be able to return, tears for the unfairness of life in not endowing her with the ability to love as deeply as he. Bitter tears for her own foolishness in thinking she could ever win him for herself with her organisation and her lists and her highlighting pen. What a total idiot she'd been; she'd had absolutely no conception of how deep and enduring passionate love like his could be. There were tears for lots of things . . .

So noisy were her sobs that she didn't hear the church door open for a second time. It was Muriel, come to search for her umbrella. She'd lost it times without number, but it had a charmed life and always seemed to turn up again in the must unexpected places. Hopefully it might be in church; it had a habit of appearing there and Willie was so good with lost property – she knew it would be in the vestry if he'd found it. She heard the weeping as soon as she closed the door, but couldn't see anyone there. As she crossed in front of the pulpit, she spotted Louise, crouched by a pillar, hidden from view, her head bent almost to her knees.

'Louise, my dear.' Muriel went to sit beside her. She placed her hand on her arm and gently shook her. But sympathy made Louise cry even louder. Muriel dug in her pocket for a fresh tissue.

'Here you are, my dear, use this.' She sat stroking Louise's hand, waiting for the tears to stop.

Louise howled like a stricken animal. 'I can't bear it! I can't bear it!'

'Gently now, gently now. If you want to talk I'm willing to listen. When you're ready, that is.'

Louise's red eyes peered at her over the tissue. 'How can I? I can't tell anyone.' Fresh storms began and Muriel sat quietly waiting. Ralph would be wondering where she was, but dear Ralph would have to wait: Louise needed her more than he.

'I'm the soul of discretion, I truly am. I'm top of the class where keeping secrets is concerned. I shan't tell.'

'You won't, will you?'

'No, of course not, my dear. But perhaps your mother would be the best person . . .'

'Oh no, not her. She wouldn't understand.'

'I think maybe mothers are more understanding than daughters realise.'

'Mine isn't.' Louise made up her mind. 'It's Peter, you see. It's Peter.'

'Ahhh, right, I thought perhaps it might be. He needs all the love and prayers he can get right now.'

'So do I. So do I.'

'Surely not as much as he.'

The whole story came out, burbling and tumbling over itself, like a stream in full spate, here deep and bottomless, there shallow and swift, swirling along, hurrying here, idling there, and Muriel listened to it all in silence. Finally the stream of words fell still and Louise sat drained, awaiting the comfort of Muriel's words.

Muriel stroked her hand while she searched for words of wisdom. Before she married her dear Ralph she wouldn't have been able to understand even one jot of how Louise must be feeling, but marriage and love had given her an insight into feelings she never dreamed existed before she met Ralph.

'My dear Louise. Peter and Caroline are two very privileged people. They've found the one person in the world who means everything to them. They could no more be separated than . . . than . . . well, I can't think of it now, but they're welded together. It brings tremendous joy but also tremendous heartbreak sometimes. You've got to realise that you having Peter is impossible, so it's no good going down that route either in your thoughts or in what you do.'

Louise cried, 'I know that now.'

'Of course you do, you're not a fool, my dear. Now you've got to take yourself in hand, make a new life for yourself. Get a job, search out things to keep busy with, and build on the pain to make yourself a better person. Don't, whatever you do, become *bitter*. Not bitter. That's the worst thing to have happen. Bitterness twists everything. Now's the time to step forward bravely and take hold of life. Don't look back at the past, but ahead to the future because the future is yours. Don't waste your life grieving over someone you know you cannot have.'

'Oh, but I *am* grieving – for me it's as though Peter has died. I've lost him, you see. Though if I think rationally I never really had him in the first place, did I?'

'No, I think perhaps you didn't. He and Caroline belong, you know. One day you'll find someone like that and then you'll be privileged too. You've to put all this behind you and get on with life. Perhaps what's happened will make you more understanding, more sympathetic. *Build* on this experience, use it as a foundation of something new, don't let it destroy you. I'm quite sure you've plenty of courage. You'll do it if you try hard enough. There, I've talked for far too long.' Muriel stood up, giving Louise's shoulder a last comforting pat. 'Now I've got to find my umbrella. I expect Willie's put it in the vestry – I'll just go and look.'

It was half-past two before Louise had finished cataloguing all the music and storing it away again in the cupboard. She was beginning to feel hungry. She'd had a drink of water from the tap in the vestry wash-basin; it tasted bitter and flat, but she didn't mind – it was all part of her punishment. There was still lots more to do; neat packages of some kind were needed to keep all the copies of one sort together, but the essentials were done. When she got home she'd get on the computer and make her lists for Gilbert.

The air was cooler now, and she enjoyed the walk across the Green. Some tourists were taking photographs by the stocks. They looked expectantly at her, so she went across and let them explain the workings of their camera to her and she spent a few minutes taking snaps for them and chatting about the village. Some children from the school were out sketching by the old oak tree and she smiled and waved.

She pushed open the cottage door, glad to be home. It wasn't such a bad place really. 'Hello-o-o! I'm home!' Ron and Sheila looked at each other in amazement, rapidly straightening their faces when she came in. 'I'm back. Just making myself a sandwich and then I'm typing up this stuff I've done for Gilbert. Had a good morning?'

Sheila was surprised, as she'd fully expected to be asked to make lunch for Louise. 'Yes, thanks,' she said. 'Have you?'

'Yes, thanks. Excellent. Would you like a cup of tea?'

Ron said he would and so did Sheila; it was hard to disguise the fact they were in shock. Sheila listened for sounds of Louise in the kitchen and when she heard the kettle being filled, she whispered, 'Does she know, do you think?'

'I can't tell.'

'There's something fishy going on.'

'Let's keep quiet and make hay while the sun shines.'

'You don't think she's been to see him and they've . . . you know. Got an understanding?'

'Sheila, for heaven's sake! With the best will in the world you couldn't think for one minute he'd be interested in her.'

The disdainful tone in Ron's voice cut Sheila to the quick; after all, she was their daughter. 'Sometimes you're very unkind. She's not a beauty, I know, but she's attractive in her own way. It's just her *attitude*.'

The telephone rang. It was Mr Fitch for Louise.

Chapter 17

Louise made the coffee at the next committee meeting, having arranged to do so with Caroline before she went to Devon. How on earth she was going to tell them what had happened that very day up at the Big House, she didn't know. These last four days had been hectic for her. The phone call Mr Fitch had made on what she now called her 'Revelation Monday' had changed her life. Of course, it was only supposed to be a temporary job but between themselves they knew it would be permanent because Fenella, his receptionist, sadly had terminal cancer. Louise was therefore in an admirable position for being the first to hear about the new development. The conclusion she'd arrived at was that they might as well cancel the entire Show.

Jimbo, Michael and Linda arrived together.

'Isn't it exciting, Mr Palmer, you moving away. And such a big school too.'

'I don't know about exciting, Linda. Certainly it's challenging.'

'Where will you live?'

'I'm going to rent somewhere to begin with, till I've had a

chance to look round and find somewhere I like. I've never been a homeowner before.'

'Alan and I are moving in to Hipkin Gardens next week. It'll be so lovely, having somewhere with a bit of space. Alan's got all sorts of ideas for the garden. The cottage is a bit big for just the two of us but,' she giggled, 'hopefully we shan't be there on our own for long!'

'Seems I'm not the only one with a challenge then.'

Jimbo thanked Louise for his coffee. 'Two months and this Show will be over. Let's drink to its success. Old Fitch will have something to say if it isn't. If he could order the weather he would. No stone unturned is his motto.'

Louise didn't join in the general enthusiasm. She'd wait until they were all there to break the news. Barry came next, disappointed that Jimbo had taken his seat on the committee again; still, he was seeing Pat afterwards, and he'd brought her a present from London too. He tapped his pocket to make sure it was still there. Then came Bryn and Jeremy together, and her mother arrived last. Louise hadn't told her; if she had, Sheila would have been round to the store in a jiffy spreading alarm. She'd have been right too; it *was* alarming.

Louise tapped her spoon on her cup. 'Right, ladies and gentlemen. Can we be seated, please?' When they were settled she drew in a deep breath and said, 'I'm afraid I have some disquieting news.'

Barry interrupted, 'Don't tell me, bet I know: the sewers won't be finished in time. Been doing a job up in Mr Fitch's London flat. Only got back this afternoon – didn't look like much progress to me. They'd all stopped working.'

'Actually, yes, you're right – they *had* stopped working. This afternoon,' she cleared her throat, 'they found what looks like Roman remains.'

Sheila said, 'You didn't tell me! Do you mean bodies?'

'No, I don't. I mean remains of a building. Well, there might be bodies, but I don't think so.'

Jimbo was aghast. 'I can't believe it! This Show is destined not to happen. First sewers and now this. I thought they'd taken all possible precautions to make sure they *didn't* disturb anything.' He shook his head in disbelief.

Bryn twirled his moustache and said, 'Is there anything else fate could throw at us? It's just not possible.'

Sheila, affronted that all her well-constructed plans might come to nought, said matter-of-factly: 'Why the blazes can't they just pretend they haven't found anything? Lay the sewer-pipes and fill it all in. No one will be any the wiser. We can have the Show and the building or whatever it is can stay there. Who wants blessed Roman remains anyway? Just a few old stones. If they've been there for centuries let's leave 'em in peace. It won't make any difference to them, will it? This Show's a lot more important.'

Linda said, 'Oh, you can't do that. I know someone in Culworth whose house is close to Chantry Gate and they were digging to make a pond in their garden and found funny pottery an' that, and before they knew it the place was full of archaeologists and nearly the whole garden got dug up. Weeks, it took.'

Jimbo slapped his forehead with the flat of his hand. 'Thank you, Linda, for that contribution.' He asked Louise whereabouts the remains were.

'Under the front lawn beyond where he had the gravel laid for the car parking, just where we'd planned to have all the stalls. It's been a lawn since the year dot, so it's never been disturbed, literally for centuries. The trouble is, they don't know how large an area it might cover. It could be a terribly important find, or very minor and not worth bothering about. It's not on any of the maps, you see; so they didn't know it was there. The sewer people refuse to ingore it – more than their job's worth, they say. Right brouhaha there was the last time this happened and they tried to cover it up and say nothing. Some busybody leaked the news and there were questions in the House, they said. With working there this week, I had the job of ringing Mr Fitch to let him know. I don't mind telling you there was an awfully long silence. I swear the phone grew hot.' Louise grew uncomfortable at the memory. 'His language! He can't decide whether to be thrilled to bits or completely devastated.'

Barry said in a disgusted tone of voice, 'They'll be digging for months.' He ran his fingers through his hair and stared at the floor. 'All that wood and all that work I've done with the stalls. It can't be true.'

'Well, it is.'

'What about Gilbert?' Michael asked.

Puzzled, Louise echoed: 'What about Gilbert?'

'Well, he's an archaeologist.'

'Is he? I didn't know.'

'Well, he is. He'll probably be called in. He's only home at weekends at the moment. He's doing a dig out Salisbury way. He finishes this week, he said, and then the engineers are covering it over and getting on with the road. It's been delayed eight weeks to give them a chance to rescue what they can. Peter's been standing in for choir practice.'

Linda, latching on to something they were all bursting to talk about but hadn't, said, 'Isn't it a pity about Dr Harris? So sad. He looks like a lost soul. They say he's back at work, as you might say, on Monday but how he'll manage no one knows. Poor thing.'

Jimbo, seeing a gossip session in the offing, said firmly, 'Let's get on with deciding what we shall do about the Show.'

Sheila said, 'If *they* can shovel it under tons of earth, why can't we do the same with this one? No one will know if we don't say anything.' Jimbo and Bryn looked at her sceptically; the thought of Sheila not saying anything was almost laughable.

Jimbo said, 'Look, Louise, you're up there at the hub, you keep your ear to the ground as you might say, and let us know. We'll keep everything on hold until a decision's been made. Everything's organised thanks to you, so we can accelerate our plans at the last minute, surely?'

'Yes, but . . .'

'It's all right saying that . . .'

'How about if . . .'

Jeremy protested, 'But we've ordered the marquees, and the deposit's paid.'

'The printer has to be paid, too.'

'I can't bear to think about all the work we've done . . .'

'Neither can I.'

'It's in the Red Cross schedule as well. Mrs Redfern hates her schedules being mixed up.' This from Linda who had been looking forward to sporting her new uniform in front of all the people she knew.

Louise took the lead. 'Look, there's nothing we can do tonight, that's a fact. I'll keep you well-informed. We've just got to sit tight and hope. The one plus tonight is that the sewer people are working fast, or at least they were. I'm seeing Gilbert on Saturday morning about the choir music I've been cataloguing for him so I'll have a word with him, see what he has to say. We'll tentatively arrange an emergency meeting for next Thursday and I'll let you know.' Diaries came out, the date was written in and they left in a babble of speculation.

Barry said before he left, 'I think I'll stop work on the stalls for the moment. Just wait and see. What do you think, Louise?'

'Might be an idea. I'm sure Mr Fitch would let you have time to make a final burst with them in the last week, don't you?'

'I'm sure he would. What's it like, working in the Big House then?'

'Well, of course I'm still finding my feet. It's not really my kind of work but I didn't mind stepping in, in the circumstances. Poor Fenella, such a lovely person – it's really tragic. I'm just sorry it's her illness which has meant I've got the job.'

Barry nodded in agreement. 'Very attractive girl, Fenella was – *is* I mean. Very attractive. I'm off. See yer.'

Barry climbed into his van, kicked a couple of pieces of chipboard out from under his feet, started it up and drove hell for leather up to the Garden House. He slewed to a stop, narrowly missing Dean's bike which he'd left laid on the concrete by the estate mower. Barry went to stand it up for him. Poor old Dean. Exams, that's what it was – exams. He didn't know what he was doing.

He knocked on the back door and opened it wide, shouting, 'It's me, I'm back!'

Pat came into the kitchen. 'Oh, it's you. Hello, long time no see.' She grinned at him, unsure about how enthusiastic she should be. Maybe he'd changed his mind since he'd been up in London and seen all those smart women.

Then he opened his arms wide and she went into them and they hugged each other. 'By Jove, Pat, it's good to be back. I've brought you a present.'

'You shouldn't have. What is it?'

'Give me a kiss first.'

'You and yer kisses. Sex-mad you are!'

'Naughty but nice though, isn't it?'

'Go on then. But for real.'

'Well, well, getting choosy are we now? This makes a change. What's happened to the Pat who thought kissing meant a peck like in them nineteen-thirties' films?'

'You won't get one at all if you don't hurry up. Four days I've been without a kiss.'

'I've a mind to make you wait.'

'You won't, 'cos you can't wait to give me that present that's digging into my ribs.'

He laughed and slapped her bottom for her and she wriggled away. 'Not that, Barry, not that.'

'Not what?'

'Using yer 'and to me. I'm not having that.'

'I was only having fun. I didn't hurt you, did I?'

'No, it didn't hurt, but I'm not 'aving it.'

Barry looked hard at her and comprehension dawned. 'You mean your Doug used to hit you?'

Pat's eyes shut tight and she nodded her head.

'The sod! As God is my judge I have never and will never hit a woman, and more especially you whom I respect. You need have no fear of that from me. Honest to God'.

'I'm sorry, I know you won't. I'm sorry I spoke.' Pat swallowed hard and to divert his mind from his anger she tapped his pocket and asked, 'Well, what is it then?'

'I was going down Oxford Street and there was this chap with a suitcase open on the pavement and he was selling watches, five pounds with a free pen thrown in. He was having a shutting-down sale, so I got one. I think you'll like it.'

He took the box from his pocket and watched her face as she opened it. He knew she'd tried to cover her disappointment when he'd told her the tale about the suitcase and he couldn't wait for her to realise he was pulling her leg.

'Barry! Oh Barry, you daft 'aporth. This came from a proper jewellers. It's beautiful, really beautiful. My watch broke months ago and it wasn't worth paying for it to be mended. How did you know I needed one?'

'You looked at my watch a while back and I realised you hadn't got one of your own, and I thought, one day I'll buy her one she'll be proud of. Here, let me put it on for you.' He fastened it securely on her wrist and stood back to admire it. 'There, what do you think to that? Perfect.'

'It is, it's lovely. Just lovely.' She put the watch to her ear and listened to it. 'It's got a lovely tick. You shouldn't have.' Then to lighten things she began thumping him playfully. 'Telling me it was from a man with a suitcase, you cheeky devil you.' He twisted and turned, shouting his protests till she had him cornered by the kitchen door. Then he grabbed her and kissed her like she'd wanted in the first place.

'Cor, Pat, you smell great. It's real come-and-get-me perfume.'

'It's our Michelle, she bought it for me. Determined, she is.'

'What about?'

'You and me.'

'Keen then, is she?'

'Oh yes, she is. I don't know about me though. Not yet.'

Barry kissed her and said, 'Not another word. Wait till

you've had that week away with me and we'll see how we feel then.'

'Cup o' tea?' Barry nodded. 'How did the meeting go?' She was admiring her watch while she said it. 'You're very generous, Barry. I've never bought you a thing.'

'No matter. I'm glad you like it.' He watched her fill the kettle. She was getting the milk out of the fridge when they heard footsteps. The door opened and it was Dean in his pyjamas.

'Hi, how's the exams going?'

'Hello, Barry. Not bad, thanks. Can't sleep for worrying though. Is there a cup of tea going?'

'Yes, love. Won't be a minute. Look what Barry's given me.' Pat held out her arm. The watch gleamed in the fluorescent light.

Dean whistled. 'Wow, Barry, that's great.'

'Bought it from a fella with a suitcase in Oxford Street.' His eyes twinkled at Dean.

'You never did. That cost a bomb. It's lovely, Mum.' He talked about his exams for a while and then decided to take his tea to bed. Dean grinned and said, 'Wouldn't want to cramp your style, you two.' As he was closing the door he added, 'It's like our Michelle says, and as the man of the house I agree with her for once. You two were made for each other.'

Pat went red and shouted, 'Get off to bed, yer cheeky little devil!' He hastily shut the door and they could hear him laughing as he went up the stairs.

'I suppose I should be grateful your children want me here. Some chaps would meet nothing but resentment.'

'Says a lot for you, I suppose.'

'If we . . . er . . . you know . . . I wouldn't want any more children. Yours will do for me.'

'If we . . . er . . . yer know . . .' she laughed, 'I wouldn't want any more either.'

'That's settled then.'

'So what did 'appen at the meeting?'

Chapter 18

Rumours were rife in the village about the Roman ruins. In the Store on the Friday morning, Jimbo had the story *ad nauseum*. Most were of the opinion that the Show would have to be cancelled, others that Mr Fitch would cash in on the discovery and they'd be having coach parties coming to view the ruins and a reception centre built with a display and tea rooms, and public lavatories all over the place and . . .

'Hold on a minute!' Jimbo protested. 'They were only discovered yesterday. Could be they're so insignificant that they rescue some bits, put them on a shelf in a storeroom at Culworth Museum, fill in the hole and we hear no more about it, and all it'll be is a dot on a map at County Hall. In any case, a few more tourists would be a good idea.'

'Oh yes, and we all knows why. Why don't you build some public lavatories just outside 'ere and then tempt 'em in 'ere and make even more money. The only one to do well out of it would be Mr Charter-Plackett.'

'I say, that's a bit under the belt.' Jimbo was beginning to get angry. 'What have I done to deserve that?'

'Well, nothing really, but it just seems that at every turn, that chap up there and you is making money.'

'I see. Well, there you are then. Two of the biggest employers in the district and still we're at fault. It takes some understanding. Now, what can I get for you? Anything else? No? Right then, we'll add up.'

When the irate customer had gone, the next customer in the queue said, 'Take no notice, Mr Charter-Plackett. She's only mad because her daughter wanted that receptionist's job up at the Big House, but Louise Bissett got there first. It's not you really.'

'Thank goodness for that, I don't like being *persona non grata*.'

'Well, whatever that is, you're not it. You're lovely and we all love shopping in here. Brought life back into this village, you have and no mistake. How we'd manage without this shop . . .'

'Store, please.'

'This Store, I don't know. Two pounds of best steak, lean as poss.'

'Having a party?'

'My daughter's prospective in-laws are coming. Got to make a good impression.'

'Well, you will with two pounds of best. As a token of thanks for your compliments, could I give you a box of after-dinner mints?'

'Oh thanks, thanks very much – that'd be lovely. A right finale that'll be.'

'All part of the service.' Jimbo raised his boater and bowed to his customers. They gave him a round of applause and good humour was re-established.

Sylvia came in during the morning. Jimbo waited until she was his only customer and then he said, 'Sylvia, can I have a word?' He invited her into his storeroom and sat her on his stool, put his boater on top of a case of strawberry jam, folded his arms and said, 'Well?'

'She's not back yet. This is the fifth day. I'm worried sick.'

'How is he?'

'In a terrible state. He's supposed to be back in harness on Monday, but at the rate he's going he'll end up in hospital.'

'Bad as that, is it?'

'It is. I don't know what to do. I keep thinking I should ring her, but Willie says no.'

'No, I don't think that would be right.' He stood gazing out of the window deep in thought.

'He won't eat except bits and pieces when I insist. I'm not supposed to be working this week, but someone's got to do something. I can't just leave him, can I? I can understand her being hurt, but she knows, deep down she knows, there's nothing in it.'

'I wonder if I went to have a word?'

'I don't think he'll see anyone. He won't even answer the phone. Not that she's rung, not while I've been there anyway. I asked him this morning if she'd rung last night and he just shook his head. He won't ring her, you see; they seem to have this arrangement whereby they don't trespass on each other's ground. She's made this decision so it's her he has to wait for. Seems daft to me. They tell each other they're both free to make their own decisions, but they're not really; they're like two halves of the same thing. You'd have a shock if you saw him.'

'Hell's bells. I'm beginning to feel quite angry with Caroline, letting him get like this.'

'Well, I don't feel that, but I do feel helpless. He's such a dear man, such strong faith, devoted to the church, but without Dr Harris there he's like a ship without a rudder. I think it's guilt you know, for what happened. You know what I mean. And it's the children, too. He's missing them and so am I.' Sylvia took a handkerchief from her pocket and wiped her eyes. 'Anyway, I'll finish his shopping and get back.'

'If things get desperate, let me know. I might be able to say something which will give him a boost. Such a delicate matter though, isn't it?'

'It is.'

Jimbo looked at her severely. 'I sincerely hope Louise Bissett hasn't been round.'

'Oh no, she hasn't, much to my surprise, but then she has stepped in up at the Big House. So sad about that receptionist, isn't it?'

'Dreadful. Beautiful, beautiful girl. I sometimes have great difficulty in understanding this world. However, by the sound of it I've got customers. Don't forget – if you get in a fix, let me know and I'll come across. Any time, can't stand by and see him sink.'

Sylvia stood up. 'Thanks for listening to my troubles. You're most kind. I'll get back to him.'

Around midnight on Sunday night, Peter, unable to sleep, went out into the garden. Caroline's cats followed him out, tails up, twisting and turning around his legs, pestering for attention. He bent down to stroke them.

'It's no good, you won't find her out here. You miss her too, don't you?' By the light coming through the kitchen window he could just see well enough to wander about the garden touching her plants, admiring the pots of bright pink geraniums she'd bought this year, loving the deep blue delphiniums she'd planted their first summer. 'No country garden is complete without them, in any case I love them,' she'd said. He went to inspect the low wall which she'd filled with nasturtiums, laughing to himself when he remembered her daily battle against an unexpected plague of caterpillars. God, how he longed for her to be home. *Caroline, please come home.*

Out of nowhere a decision burst into his thoughts. He no longer cared for all these ideas about not trespassing – hell, it was his marriage, his life, his children that were at stake! The parish would manage. He'd burn his boats and go. If he went he laid himself open to rejection but if he didn't . . . if he didn't he might lose everything. Maybe that was what she needed to see, that she was more than life itself to him. Yes, that was it. Intelligence and logic and agreements didn't come into it any more. No, dammit! He would go up there, see for himself. He wouldn't even tell her he was coming. He'd simply go. It couldn't make matters worse; they couldn't *be* any worse.

The practicalities of his decision raced round his mind. He'd have to let people know he wouldn't be here, couldn't just depart when he was officially back. Say he had a family emergency, which in truth he had. Heavens above, what was losing your wife, the only one he would ever have on this earth, and your children, other than an emergency? Contact the vicar in Culworth, let Willie know, rearrange the two evening meetings he had for this coming week, and the Friday morning school prayers. He could be away by lunchtime at the latest. He'd have to go by train. Then, God willing, he could drive them all back.

Peter went straight back into the house, showered, and set the alarm for six-fifteen. He slept soundly for the first time since she'd left.

★

Sylvia, who'd come in at eight as she usually did when she was working, was delighted at his decision.

'You start making your phone calls, I'll pack you a bag and I'll take you into Culworth if you like. My car's just been serviced so it's not likely to break down.'

Peter couldn't resist teasing her. 'That'll make a change.'

'Rector! I love that car.'

'I know, I'm sorry.'

'I'm not, not if it's made you laugh.' She flapped her hands at him, grinning. 'Go on, get things organised.'

Despite his energetic endeavours he had the greatest difficulty in contacting the people he needed to speak to before he left. He seemed thwarted at every turn. By eleven-thirty he'd made his last phone call.

Sylvia insisted he had something to eat before he left. 'You've had next to no breakfast and a bite to eat now will stand you in good stead. A big chap like you needs good solid food.' He began to protest, he wanted to be off. 'I insist, never mind those wretched sandwiches British Rail serve, all clammy and sweating in those plastic packets. Sit down, it's all ready. And you've to let me know when you're coming back and I'll have everything ready for you all.'

His face changed and she saw him withdraw back into his anguish again. She could have bitten her tongue out. He pushed his plate away and stood up. 'You eat this, I can't.' The phone rang. 'I'll answer that, it might be—' He hurried to the study.

Someone in the parish had died. Finally, at half-past twelve, Sylvia left to get her car while he went to the bathroom to check his shaving kit and put it in his bag. The cats were watching him, as though they knew they were going to be deserted. They mewed and padded about after him, getting under his feet as he moved between bathroom and bedroom. Suddenly they left. He went to the top of the stairs carrying his bag and saw them race to the front door. It opened and there stood Beth and Alex, and behind them Caroline.

'Dada! Spots going. Beth better now.' She pulled up her T-shirt so he could see her chest. 'Look!'

'Dada, Dada, look Granda buy Alex boat, look Dada.'

Caroline and Peter looked gravely at each other, he from the top of the stairs, she from the hall. In the soft light they couldn't quite read one another's thoughts but their eyes devoured each other, measuring, weighing up, estimating the ravages of the last week. She was alarmed by his appearance; he was drenched with relief by hers.

To cover his shock he spoke to the children first.

'Hello, darlings, have you had a good holiday? Daddy is pleased to have you back.' When he reached the floor of the hall he put down his bag and hugged the two of them, kissing them and admiring Beth's receding spots and Alex's boat. They rushed off to look for Sylvia, leaving him and Caroline to greet each other.

'Are you going somewhere?'

'Actually I decided in the night I would go up to Northumberland, but I got delayed. Someone chose to die, and things . . . and . . .'

'I'm glad they did. We'd have looked pretty silly, you up there and me down here.'

'Yes, we would. Very silly. You've come back then.'

'Of course. I made up my mind in the night. I thought, There he is, that darling man of mine, and he's wanting me and I'm wanting him and I'm going to him. I could see you, for some daft reason, in the garden by the nasturtiums laughing about the caterpillars. Stupid, aren't I? And I wondered how my garden was and . . . and whether you were well and that . . . that sort of thing.'

'Whatever time did you leave?'

'I got up at five and packed like a maniac and the children wake early anyway, so we set off. We're dying for something to—' The door opened and in came Sylvia, her face alight with relief.

'You're back!' Sylvia, who'd always maintained a certain reserve in her relationship with Caroline, opened her arms wide and went to hug her. 'I'm so glad, so very glad you're back.'

Caroline embraced her and said, 'So am I.'

'Would you like a cup of tea, something to eat?'

'Oh yes, please, you're my saviour. Thank you.'

Sylvia went to the kitchen to greet the children. Caroline stood close to Peter. For the moment she couldn't kiss him or hug him; their estrangement had been so severe, they'd have to come to that later that night when they were alone, but she touched his face with her fingers. 'What have I done to you? My beloved darling.'

'Nothing your being here won't heal.'

Her eyes intently searched his face, looking warily for his reactions. She said, 'Mother told me off – called me a fool. She was right. Said I didn't deserve a man like you. Said it was only idiots who ran away from love. Said you are her bestest son–in–law to date, and if I ever do this again she'll turn me straight round and send me back.'

'I've always approved of your mother's common sense. How is she?'

'Frustrated by inactivity but bossing us all around as ever. They've brought help in so they're going to be all right. Dad isn't too perky; Mother won't let him rest, she will make him do things that he's not really up to yet. But they'll have to sort themselves out.' Caroline grinned at him. 'When Mother heard me packing in the night she shouted from her bedroom, "And not before time".'

Peter laughed. 'Only she could have survived such a serious accident so brilliantly.'

'Yes.' She smiled and made as though to kiss him, but changed her mind. Her voice shook as she said, 'I'll go and give Sylvia a hand.' He followed her into the kitchen, where the children were already seated at the table drinking from their Bunnikin cups, waiting for Sylvia to finish making their lunch. The sun had come out again and was shining into the kitchen, welcoming them all back. Sylvia looked at the two of them as they went in. She turned back to the worktop to finish putting the sandwiches on a plate and said, 'Can I invite the children to tea this afternoon? I've bought some things at the Red Cross sale they might like to play with. Make a change for them, wouldn't it?' She looked at Caroline. 'I could take them straight after they've finished lunch.'

'Thank you, Sylvia, that would be a lovely idea.'

'Bring them back about six after their tea?'

'Thank you, yes, thank you.' Peter recognised the unspoken message between them. Without it being mentioned, the two of them had arranged time for him and Caroline to be alone.

The children were eager to see what Sylvia had bought for them and they rushed off hand-in-hand with her, without so much as a backward glance.

'Be good, the two of you, be good.' Caroline closed the door and stood with her back to it. She was glad to have time alone with Peter, but it would have been a relief to have been able to postpone their reconciliation until her tiredness had lifted. She could hear Peter clearing the lunch away. She'd make a fresh pot of tea, just to have something to do to stop herself from clutching hold of him and never letting go. They must sort things out before that happened. 'I'm making myself more tea, would you like some?'

'Yes, please. They've found Roman ruins up at the Big House, by the way. The Show is in jeopardy yet again, I'm afraid.'

'Oh no! I don't believe it. What has . . . Louise . . . to say?'

'My darling girl, I have no idea, I haven't seen her. She's replacing someone up at the Big House so she's very busy. This Roman ruin caper has certainly upset the apple cart. There's an emergency meeting this Thursday, Sylvia says. You'll find out then, I expect.'

'Yes, I expect I will. Mr Fitch must be going mad.'

'I imagine so. I haven't seen anyone to ask.'

'I see. Here's your tea.'

'Let's go into the sitting room, the chairs are more comfortable.'

'Right.' Caroline led the way, Peter carried the tray in and placed it on the coffee table. They sat together on the sofa. When it had brewed he poured them each a cup.

Together they both said, 'Darling . . .'

'Sorry. You first.'

'No, you first.'

Peter put his cup down and began, 'I'm going to tell you what we said that morning. Every word. And you've to listen and then I'll listen to you. OK?'

'Yes.'

He told her word for word as best he could remember, even the kiss and the cross he made on her forehead and her sadness at not being able to see the twins, and how she'd sobbed and that she was marrying Michael and how he'd given her his blessing as she left, and how she meant nothing to him now.

Caroline told him about her fear. Fear that, seeing Suzy, he would want her and they'd take the children and go away and how it would crucify her if they did. After all, seeing her again he might realise it was Suzy he wanted more than her, but she couldn't live without him and his children. And did he think that now might be the best time to tell them because they'd *know* without *understanding*; the understanding would come in time but wouldn't, hopefully, hurt so much if they already *knew*. 'I feel as if we have to put things straight and then they'll stay straight for the rest of our lives. I went away partly because I was so distraught and partly because I wanted to get the children away from you both so you couldn't take them from me. I may not have given birth to them, but they are mine, believe me they are mine. This problem with Louise, too. I felt so threatened and like a fool I ran away instead of standing and fighting for what was ours.'

'You had nothing to fear. Nothing at all. There is never any question of that. Please believe me. You're right about telling the children. We'll tell them together when the right moment comes, I don't know how we'll put it to them, but we will somehow. Then we shall be straight, as you say, for the rest of our lives. God bless you for coming back.'

She rested her head against his shoulder and closed her eyes. He began to touch her, remembering her anew. He stroked her hand, kissed her hair which smelt of sea and sand, he ran a finger down her bare brown arm, he kissed her fingers. Trying not to disturb her head he turned himself gently towards her, and put an arm across the front of her, around her waist. He savoured the living life of her, the beat of her pulse, the smell of her flesh, perfumed and

211

sweet. His hand touched her breast and he rubbed his fingers back and forth, enjoying the warm firmness of it. She took that hand in hers and with eyes still closed she kissed the palm, and then put it back.

He raised her up and put an arm around her shoulders so she rested half on his shoulder, half on his chest. He held her like that while she slept.

Chapter 19

'Well, Mr Fitch, I had a word with Gilbert Johns, he's our tame archaeologist around here, and he said nothing must be done till a team can get here to investigate.'

'You told him?'

'Well, of course I did. We need this solving.'

'I never gave you permission to do that! There is one thing you must understand, no, not understand, *accept!* I decide what happens around here, not you. Right?' Louise nodded, gritting her teeth at his male arrogance. 'I came back here last night with the intention of persuading,' he indicated inverted commas with his fingers, 'the men to lay the pipes and cover it all up and mum's the word.' Mr Fitch rubbed his forefinger and thumb together as though he was feeling twenty-pound notes. 'You know?'

Louise did know, but she couldn't let him do it.

'Yes, but . . .'

'Yes, but nothing. I'm going out there now and just watch me get my own way.'

She watched him march out of the office door and across the hall. Masterful he might be, but she'd a nasty feeling that it would be Gilbert out there. He'd said as much on

Saturday morning when she'd showed him his well-organised music cupboard.

'My dear Louise, I shall be grateful to you to my dying day. What a miracle! If I'd done it, it wouldn't have been half so well organised as this. I just meant to make piles and leave it at that. But these wonderful plastic folders and the list. Amazing. I didn't know we had half this stuff. How can I ever thank you. It's a wonderful gift you've given me, it really is.'

Louise had blushed. 'It was nothing, really – not once I'd worked out how best to do it. Have you seen the handwritten anthems? I don't know enough to identify them, but you will. Look, here they are.' She'd checked the catalogue she'd made and then found the right shelf and pulled them out for him to inspect.

Gilbert had sat down to study them and she'd stood by awaiting his comments. He was so scruffy. No, not scruffy, kind of untidy in a scholarly way. Despite the chilly morning all he wore was a pair of old cotton trousers and a bright burnt-sienna shirt open almost to his navel, which meant she had glimpses of a seriously hairy chest. The sleeves were rolled up, showing dark brown sinewy arms. All that digging, she thought. On his bare feet were a pair of sandals, scarcely more than a couple of leather straps fastened to a thick hard-wearing sole. She noticed his toenails were scrupulously clean and neatly cut. Her nostrils kept catching a trace of his earthy scent as she stood waiting for his verdict; it stirred her inside in a strange kind of way. His face was striking. He wasn't handsome like . . . Peter, but the hollows of his cheeks, and the prominent cheek-bones and the piercing brown eyes were intriguing.

She noticed his hands were trembling. He looked up at her. 'What a find, listen.' Gilbert hummed a few bars. 'No, that's not right, no. Look, bear with me, we'll go and try them on the organ.'

She followed him into the church, unable to appreciate how someone could grow so excited over a few handwritten crotchets and quavers. He swung his legs over the organ seat and switched on. Gilbert then looked at her with glowing eyes. 'You never know, you could have found something of real value. Unknown, never performed. What a triumph!'

Louise began to catch his excitement. 'Really?'

'Oh yes. Now here we go.' Gilbert could only play the organ as he would a piano, but the melody was enchanting. 'Here are the words. You sing your part, I'll sing mine.'

The two of them had tried it. They'd had several stops and starts before they got it right and in parts Gilbert had difficulty reading the notes because they were so faded, but together they worked it out.

'It's wonderful! By the style, it's late eighteenth- or early nineteenth-century, I should think. Wait till I tell people about this. No composer's name though, what a pity.' Gilbert turned off the organ. 'With a bit of work on it I could use this in church. Clever girl, clever girl. What a find.'

She was warmed by his enthusiasm. 'That's not the only bit of news.'

'No? What other treasures are you about to unearth?'

'That's a highly appropriate way of saying it, actually.'

'Yes?' He put his head on one side, reminding her of a heron she'd seen once, watching for fish by the beck on the spare land.

'There's been what we think are Roman ruins found under the lawn up at the Big House.'

215

She almost jumped back with shock at his response. He appeared to have been electrified. *'At the Big House?'*

'Yes. They were digging to put in these new sewers, and they found interesting bits and the men won't go any further. They've had trouble before, you see.'

Gilbert paced about the aisle with excitement. 'I want to see. Not been to the office for my messages. Got back too late. Don't know anything about it. This could be a major find. Oh yes. I don't suppose we could . . . No, of course not.'

'Could what?'

'Go and take a peep. Just a little peep, don't you know.' He'd begged with the innocence of a child wanting to peep at a birthday present before the day.

'I work up there now, for a while anyway, so perhaps . . . I know exactly where it is.'

He eyed her speculatively. 'Let's, shall we?'

'There's only a skeleton staff with it being the weekend, so no one of any importance will see us.'

'Let's go.'

Louise had noticed Gilbert blanch when he saw the diggers. 'Oh my God! They've got to be stopped.'

'Don't worry, they have stopped. It's a question of whether Mr Fitch will permit anyone to investigate. He wants everything finished because of the Show. It's to be his grand gesture in his Lord of the Manor campaign.'

Gilbert waved his hand in disdain. 'That! That's nothing, nothing at all. Trivial at best.'

'What is, his ambition or the Show?'

'Both.'

'Both?' Louise was horrified by his attitude, and for a moment rendered speechless. She stuttered and gasped and eventually came out with, 'But I've put an awful lot of work into the Show, and everyone's looking forward to it. We've got Morris Dancers . . .'

He waved his hand dismissively. 'I know about them.'

'Hot-air balloon, children's fancy dress, tug of war, you name it. So many people are involved, so much work. We *can't* cancel it.'

'If this proves important, nothing can be done till we've fully excavated it. Come on, jump down, let's see what we can find.' Louise had looked down into the trench. She could see bits of mosaic here and there and what appeared to be something earthenware poking out of the side.

Fascinated, despite her dislike of dirt and mess, she'd allowed him to grip her hand and help her in.

Her mother had been at home when she got back.

'Louise! What on earth have you done? Where *have* you been, you're filthy! Good heavens. Take your shoes off – don't put them on the carpet. I'll get a newspaper. Mind your skirt on the wall. Better just take your dress off and give it to me. Oh dear.' Louise didn't get a chance to explain until she'd showered and put on fresh clothes.

'Come on, then,' Sheila Bissett demanded. 'What's all this about?'

'If you laugh I shall never forgive you.'

'I won't.'

'I've been up at the Big House with Gilbert Johns looking at the Roman stuff in the trench.'

'You've been digging?'

'Well, not digging exactly, but he found one of those trowel things in his pocket and we had a bit of a poke around.'

'Bit! You look as if you've been laying the sewers singlehanded.'

'Not quite, Mother.'

'Not far off. So what does he say?'

'They mustn't lay any more pipes till he's had a chance to investigate properly. Gilbert being Gilbert says the Show is a minor consideration. I could have slaughtered him for that.'

'Did he indeed! Minor consideration! What about all my ladies and their flower arrangements? One of them's been all the way to Wales to get a piece of slate exactly the right shape for her display. I can hardly tell *her* it's all off.'

'We'll have to see. Mr Fitch will sort it out.'

From her position behind the reception desk she could see Mr Fitch striding back. Perhaps she was getting fanciful but she thought she could see smoke coming out of his ears.

'Do you know this bloody Gilbert?'

Feeling like a traitor she said, 'Vaguely. Seen him in church on Sundays.'

'Thinks he's got power – well, he's seen nothing yet. Get my MP on the phone pronto.'

'The one in London or the one here?'

Mr Fitch snorted. 'Both!' He stalked into his office and shut the door.

All week Mr Fitch struggled to make some common sense out of the situation. To Louise's dismay, it was Gilbert who came with a team of people to start the dig. Every morning Mr Fitch stood at the window nearest the reception desk watching and waiting.

'I'll get the measure of this chap before the week is out. Bloody man. Never argues, never shouts. I could deal with him if he did. Just gets on as if I haven't spoken. Never been ignored like this in all my life. He's a menace or a maniac, I don't know which. Married, is he?'

'No.'

'Thought not. Divorced?'

'No, never married at all.'

'Oh I see, he's one of those.'

'He most certainly isn't.'

'How do you know?'

'Well,' Louise thought quickly but couldn't come up with anything more decisive than, 'he isn't, that's all.' Then she blushed. Mr Fitch eyed her curiously.

'Where's he live?'

'Just outside Little Derehams, I think.'

'Rented?'

'No idea. I've said I don't know him that well. I'm sorry.'

'Choirmaster?'

'Yes.'

'I'll get him somehow. I know – do the boys need new surplices?'

'Sir Ralph bought them some a while back.'

Mr Fitch impatiently turned away from the window. 'He would! Is there anything else they need? Anything I could buy to put pressure on him to do as I say? Organ need repairing, updating – you know the sort of thing. I'll buy this or that if you'll . . .'

'Not that I know of. I could always ask.'

Mr Fitch looked speculatively at her and made a decision. 'You do that.' He approached her and, staring her straight in the eye, barked out: 'But remember whose side you are on. *Mine!*'

Louise quailed a little at his threat. It wasn't often she was intimidated by a man, but Mr Fitch could do just that. She made up her mind that in her coffee break she'd go and have a word with Gilbert.

'Here! Take a look at this.' Louise looked down into the

trench where he was working. He'd cleared an area about three feet square, and exposed an almost intact piece of mosaic flooring. 'Brilliant, eh?'

'Definitely!' The colours weren't distinct because the soil was only partially cleared away, but she could see heavenly rusty red and a kind of grey-white colour in the pattern.

'Gilbert.'

He looked vaguely up at her and said, 'Yes?'

'Mr Fitch wants to know if there's anything you need for the choir. Like new robes or music or anything, or the organ updating.'

He stopped his gentle scraping of the mosaic, wiped his hands on his trousers and gazed at her. 'I hope he doesn't imagine he's dealing with a fool.'

'Oh no, nothing like that, but that's the message. He asked me to enquire.'

'There's nothing, thanks all the same.' He called an instruction to one of his team working just beyond him in the trench, then said to her, 'There's no way he can stop this work going ahead, you know.'

'Yes, but when will it be finished? We need to know. *I* need to know, not just Mr Fitch. All our plans are on hold, you see.'

'Have your Show next year instead then.'

'Gilbert, that's no answer!'

'It is. I've said postpone till next year. This,' he pointed to the exposed floor, 'could be of national importance.'

'If it's just this little bit, we could fence it off and make a detour with the pipes and then the men could finish the sewers and you could have your bit of fun too.'

'*Bit of fun?* And there was I, thinking I'd found someone with a soul.' Gilbert shook his head and sadly turned his back on her and began working again.

'Oh, you have, but you're not being fair. I was only trying to work something out to everyone's benefit.'

'I have no idea at this moment of the extent of this site. It could be just this bit or it could cover acres.'

'Acres? Mr Fitch won't have that.'

'Oh, won't he? You just wait and see.'

In The Royal Oak the Roman ruins were discussed with fervour. Vera decided that Mr Fitch would want to cover everything up.

'He'll do like they do when there's a preservation order on old trees. It was in the paper a while back. Builder wanted to cut some old oaks down, Council said not on your Nellie, so he felled 'em about five o'clock one Bank Holiday Monday morning. Daft Council said they couldn't understand him doing it at a time when no one was about to stop him. I sometimes wonder about these councillors.'

Jimmy asked what on earth trees had to do with Roman ruins.

'Same thing but different. He'll get some other company to come, at the weekend of course, and get it all filled in and then look us straight in the face and say, "What Roman ruins? Where are they?" There'll be no answer to that because they won't be there no more and the Romans haven't left an address book have they, to let us all know?'

'Gilbert Johns is digging up there,' Willie said.

'Well, he's about as much use as a yard of pump-water. My cousin Dottie cleans for 'im. She's not allowed to move a thing. There's old rubbish all over the place. As soon as one lot goes another lot takes its place. Drives her mad, it does. And books, they're everywhere. If she says should she sort some out to go to a jumble sale he nearly lies down and dies. "Dottie," he says in that sad voice of his, "these are my children, my life's blood. How can I thrust them out into an uncaring world?" Still, he pays well and never complains if she has one of her turns and can only flick 'er duster.'

Jimmy shook his head. 'Seems funny to me. How can yer make a living poking about with bits of old stone and that? Beats me. It's not like a man's job, is it?'

'Takes all sorts, Jimmy.' Willie shook his head. 'Talking of which, what's Louise doing about the Show?'

'Latest is they're still waiting to see what's happening about the ruins. They say old Fitch is nearly blowing a gasket. Blazing, he is. Told her off for telling Gilbert. Asked her who exactly it is she's working for.'

'Yer start to lose interest in growing stuff, when yer don't even know if there's going to be any Show.'

Jimmy shook his head sympathetically. 'Don't worry, Mr Fitch'll sort something out. Ridiculous state of affairs, you can't please yerself on yer own land now. Things is coming to a pretty pitch. When my grandad was a boy you were master of yer own destiny and what you owned you owned. Not nowadays, nowadays, it's . . .'

Vera shuffled about impatiently. 'You two going to put the world to rights, because if you are, I'm off. It's not the same since Pat stopped coming in.'

Jimmy felt annoyed by Vera's uncharitable attitude. 'You should be glad she's found someone.'

'Oh, I am, but . . .'

'Well?'

'I am, I said!'

'There's more to it than that. I can tell.'

'No, there isn't.'

'There is. Go on, tell us, we've a right to know, Willie and me. We've looked after 'er interests all these years.'

Vera hesitated only for a moment. It wasn't often she knew the gossip before these two did, and it really was a juicy piece of news. 'Well, they do say there's someone in Little Derehams after him for money.'

'You mean he owes 'em some?'

'No, I mean . . .' With her hand Vera draw a large arc around the area of her stomach and nodded knowingly.

'You don't mean . . .'

'I do. That's what she says. You'd think she was 'aving quads she's that big, so they say, and it's early days yet apparently. I don't know whether to tell Pat or not.'

Jimmy leaned across the table and pointed his finger at Vera. 'You keep well out of it, understand? Don't interfere. It could all be a tale. She could be naming him 'cos of his reputation; maybe she daren't name who it really is.'

'OK! So what if it's true?'

'Say nothing, please. Right? Just this once mind your own business.'

Willie, curiosity getting the better of him, asked, 'Who is it anyways?'

Vera looked warily at Jimmy and then whispered, 'Simone Paradise.'

Willie, amazed, shouted in a stage whisper: 'Simone Par—'

Jimmy nudged him. 'Shut up, keep yer voice down.'

'I don't believe it, I really don't. Her and him have nothing in common.'

'Well, they have now, or so she says!' Vera chuckled and then tapped Jimmy's arm, adding, 'Pat'll know soon enough, but *I* shan't tell 'er. I'm off. Don's bringing fish and chips home tonight, we're warming 'em in the microwave when he gets back. Wish we had a fish and chip van here. Be grand, that would. Toodle-oo. We don't

223

get far but we do see life, don't we?' And she left the bar laughing.

Sure enough, Vera didn't get the chance to tell Pat. She found out for herself the next morning.

Chapter 20

Pat went into the Store to have a quick check with Jimbo about when she would be required for his next list of functions. It was a busy morning and Jimbo and his assistant were having a hard time keeping up with the flow of customers. While she waited to speak to him, Pat wandered along the shelves trying to think of a little treat for Dean, seeing as he'd finished his exams. Chocolates? He liked them special ones in the gold boxes, but they were too expensive; he'd have the box finished inside five minutes. No, they wouldn't do. What on earth could she buy for him? She'd reached the stationery shelves, and was thinking of a nice new pen when she bumped into Barry's mother. They'd had an uneasy truce since Pat had informed her that she and Barry weren't sharing a room on their holidays.

'Morning, Pat.'

'Morning, Mrs Jones. How's things?'

'Fine, thanks. I'm thinking of entering the shortbread competition – any chance I might win?' She smiled a kind of crooked smile, half-teasing, half-serious.

'With me on a winning streak, perhaps not.' They both

laughed. Then they fell to discussing the weather, the Roman ruins, the . . .

'Hello, Grandma!' A neighbour nudged Barry's mother and chuckled.

'Who are you calling Grandma?'

'Not me, that's for certain!' Pat joked.

'You,' she nodded in Barry's mother's direction. 'It's you I'm meaning. Thought you'd have been the first to know.'

Mrs Jones drew herself up to her full height and asked for an explanation.

'Oh dear, things is more serious than I thought. Not like you not to be in the know. It's your Barry got her in the club, she says.'

Mrs Jones turned and looked piercingly at Pat, who replied by raising her eyebrows and shrugging her shoulders. Mrs Jones asked her sharply. 'Do you know who she means?'

'Don't ask me, haven't a clue.'

The neighbour nudged Mrs Jones again. 'Yer know, Simone Paradise. It's 'er – she says your Barry's to blame.'

Pat went white as a sheet. Mrs Jones hit her neighbour a smart stinging slap across the face, followed by a swipe with her handbag, which sent the other woman's basket spinning out of her hand and the contents all over the floor. A bottle of tonic water smashed and spewed its contents over Mrs Jones's tights.

As she leaped back out of the way, Mrs Jones shouted, 'Don't you dare make disgusting accusations like that! Simone Paradise is a tart and my Barry would never go with a tart. My Barry's a good boy. Whatever she says isn't true. D'yer hear me? *Not true!*'

'Ask him then. She swears it's him. No good coming all indignant with me, the evidence is there for all to see. It'll be number five. Course I'm not saying they're *all* his, but . . .'

Mrs Jones almost boiled with anger. 'None of 'em's my Barry's. Believe me.'

'Little white hen that never laid away, is he? Come off it, Mrs Jones, we all know what your Barry's like, and your Kenny,' she paused for dramatic effect, '*and* your Terry.' The whole store was listening and the air was filled with sniggers at this last statement.

Pat, who'd been standing white and shaking during this argument, turned on her heel at this and left. Jimbo called after her but she ignored him. He then went to sort out the row.

'Now, ladies, shall we finish our shopping and then leave. I don't like to have this kind of confrontation in here; it upsets the other customers.'

Someone waiting at the meat counter shouted, 'Yer wrong there, this is why we come in 'ere. Good bit of nice clean fun it is, better than the telly any day.' There was a gale of laughter at this remark and Jimbo could feel things were definitely getting out of hand.

The neighbour said indignantly, 'And who's going to pay for this broken bottle? Not me, that's for certain. Put it on Mrs Jones's bill, will yer, Mr Charter-Plackett?' She gave a triumphant smile in the direction of Mrs Jones, who writhed with indignation.

'This is on me. No one pays for it. Just step out of the way and mind your shoes on the glass. Thank you, ladies.'

The assistant came to clear up the mess, and Jimbo returned to the till. Mrs Jones went home with her shopping only partly done; half her heart was feeling sorry for Pat, the other half for herself. She'd kill that neighbour of hers! No, she wouldn't – she'd kill the neighbour's pea plants instead. That would hurt her a lot more, watching her peas dying inch by inch, oh yes . . . a slow torturous death. Coming on lovely they were, be just right for the Show, 'cept she'd do for 'em once and for all. Saying that about her Barry. Weedkiller she'd put on 'em, all over 'em – the leaves, the stalks, every inch. She'd plenty in the shed, and she'd use it double strength. That'd sort her out.

Pat collected her bike from the school cycle shed and stormed home. Halfway up the drive she began to cry. That woman had punched a hole clean through her future. How could she have been such a fool as to think for one moment that he could have the slightest serious interest in her and her children? He'd been fooling her all this time. She'd been a complete and utter idiot. All the signs, everything she'd ever known about him she'd simply pushed to the back of her mind, ignored them, scorned them.

She'd believed all his talk about it being different with her, which come to think of it, it was. It really was. He'd never tried anything on. Always been restrained, even sometimes when she'd been tempted he'd said no. So what was he playing at? What's more, what was Simone Paradise playing at? It was that French grandmother of hers who was to blame. The Paradises had always been a queer lot, but the French blood had made them even odder.

She was beautiful though, was Simone. That long dark hair, almost to her waist when she'd not taken the time to roll it up into that great plaited bun at the back. The slow swinging walk, with her layers of beads jingling at every step, the roll of her hips, the gaggle of little children at her long swaying skirts. Always dreamy, relaxed, come day go day. The children she dressed at Oxfam; Pat's had been too, but Dean and Michelle didn't manage to look like Simone's kids, all peasant and gypsy-like. They said she and the children lived on pasta and beans. There were bins of them in the kitchen and great swathes of herbs hanging up to dry. Funny woman she was and not half.

In front of the mirror when she got home, Pat studied herself. OK, she was short, slimmer now since she'd dieted, though Barry said he liked something to get hold of so he didn't want her to get too thin, brown hair cut short – in a thousand years hers would never grow as long as Simone's – skin mediocre, nice straight nose, her mouth could be a bit more generous. Simone's was rich and soft and moist and ruby red without the aid of lipstick, but he wouldn't want that great gaggle of kids, would he? Oh no, Simone Paradise wouldn't be a marriage proposition. He didn't like pasta anyway – he'd told her as much. And that cottage was crammed to the thatch with kids, all of them in two bedrooms. Oh no! Pat Duckett was a better proposition from the point of view of comfort. Nice four-bedroomed house, all mod cons, two children soon off her hands, money in the bank. Oh yes, she could see right through it all now. He was coming for tea tonight . . . well, she'd show him!

She wore the long skirt she'd bought years ago and never had the brass cheek to wear, topped with a long baggy brown blouse from Oxfam – no, it was from Cancer Research. She put on four necklaces, the biggest, heaviest ones she could find, then carefully applied eye-liner and eye-shadow, leaving her skin smooth and shining. She put on every ring she could find, including some of Michelle's, and then she boiled a great pan of pasta and emptied a large jar of tomato stuff onto the mince and added almost a whole tube of tomato purée. That'd show 'im.

When he came he politely made no comment at her appearance. She flung her arms round him and kissed him in front of the children and her dad. He returned her kiss, somewhat surprised because she was usually very circumspect about touching him in front of the family.

When they sat down to eat Michelle noticed her rings. 'Mum! You've got my rings on!'

'Only borrowed 'em, that's all. Like pasta do yer, Barry?'

'Er . . . yes thanks. I'm not keen on it usually, but this is good. Very tasty.'

'Well, yer'll be used to it, I daresay. They tell me she cooks a lot of it.'

'Who does?' He began to grow wary.

Grandad looked at the two of them. 'What's up?'

'Nothing,' Pat said as she shovelled pasta into her mouth, pretty certain it was going to work itself into a clump which she wouldn't be able to swallow.

Barry stoically struggled with his food. He had a nasty feeling that Pat knew about the rumours. She hadn't given him a chance to explain. He couldn't in front of the kids, didn't want them to lose faith in him.

'Finished, Dad?'

'Yes, thanks. Very nice that was – bit heavy on the tomato, but very nice.'

'Well, now.' Pat cleared away the plates leaving Barry's because he hadn't finished. 'Lemon meringue pie?' She looked round the table and Grandad, Dean and Michelle nodded their heads. 'And what about you, Barry? Perhaps some goat's cheese and oat biscuits with fresh fruit would be more to your liking – more natural-like?'

'Mum!' Michelle protested. She sensed things were wrong but couldn't understand what.

Now Barry definitely knew she'd heard the rumours. But this new Pat had jammed up his ability to talk. He wasn't on her wavelength at all. She came to stand beside him. His plate of pasta and mince was still not finished. He looked up at her. 'Now, Pat, what's up?'

'What's up? This is what's up!' She picked up his plate and emptied the contents on his head. Barry sat there, with tagliatelle and tomato sauce and meat sliding down his face.

'Now get out.'

'Mum! Mum! Don't! Poor Barry! I'll clean you up, Barry. She didn't mean it, did yer, Mum?'

Pat ignored Michelle's pleas. 'Out, and don't come back for the next thousand years.' She leaped towards the back door and opened it wide. 'Go on out. You lying, cheating sod. I can't believe I was such a fool as to believe yer.'

Barry stood up. He'd made no attempt to get the pasta and tomato sauce off himself, so it slid uncomfortably around his collar and down his shirt-front.

He slipped on a splodge of tomato sauce and almost fell, but Dean put a hand out to catch him. 'Barry, don't go.'

'Don't you dare stop 'im.'

Michelle began to cry. 'Barry! Mum! Grandad, stop her, please!'

'It's nothing to do with me.'

'It is! I want him for a dad.'

When Barry had left, Pat slammed the door after him, sat down and burst into tears.

Dean was angry. 'Well, what made you do that?'

Through her tears Pat said, 'You wouldn't understand.' She dragged all the rings off her fingers and the beads from her neck. She scrubbed her eyes, smearing the eye make-up, then hauled Michelle's flipflops from her feet and stood up and said, 'You lot can clear this up. I'm off to bed.'

'Mum, what have you turned him out for? What's Barry done?'

'Been spreading it around . . .'

Her father shouted, 'Pat!'

Contrite, Pat sat down again. 'I'm sorry. I thought I was the only one, but I've found out I'm not – he's got someone else. I know you like Barry and want him for a dad but there's things happened . . . and I'm not having it.'

Michelle wailed her disappointment. 'I'll never get a dad now. I want a dad. I want a dad. I want . . .'

'Come and sit on your Grandad's knee. Perhaps I'll do for now.'

Michelle snuffled a little longer into her handkerchief and then decided to sit on his knee.

Dean argued she'd been too hard. 'It was a nasty trick you played, Mum.'

'What kind of a trick do you call what he's been doing?'

'But what's he done? Or is it that you've listened to all those gossips in the Store that you talk about?'

Pat instantly realised the common sense of what Dean had said. But she brushed it aside because she was so angry. 'Never you mind.'

Michelle gave a horrified shriek. 'Our holidays! It's all spoilt now because of you! I hate you, Mum! I hate you! I want Barry back!'

Up earlier than usual the following morning because she hadn't slept properly, Pat was thoroughly at odds with herself. Michelle had fallen out with her over the holiday, and because of it she hated herself. She'd thrown away the best chance of a holiday they'd ever had. She'd been stupid playing that daft trick on him, with the pasta and that and her clothes and the rings and things. In retrospect she wished she'd behaved with more dignity. Pat opened the back door to let in some fresh air. It was going to be hot today. Make a change.

On the doormat in the porch was an envelope addressed to her. The handwriting seemed familiar. The letter read:

Dear Pat,

I was planning to tell you about the rumours going round but I realised last night you'd already heard.

I want you to understand, they are only rumours. That baby is not mine. I'm not saying I haven't, you know, but I haven't lately and the baby is nothing to do with me. I'm going to see her today, and ask her to stop telling these daft lies. I'm really sorry about all this. I don't want you hurt.

You know I'm fixed on you, and since we've been going out I haven't been with anyone else. Please believe me. Am I forgiven? Let me know how you feel.

Love and kisses. Barry. XXXXXXXXXXXXXXXXXX-XXX

She tore the letter into tiny pieces and threw them in the bin. The whole village would be laughing at her, and brightness had gone from her life – all because she'd been jealous and stupid and listened to gossip. And she'd never given him a chance to explain. Serve you right, Pat Duckett, she thought, just serves you right. She'd thrown away the best chance she'd had in years. Pat Duckett was a fool.

Chapter 21

The whole village had noticed the difference in Louise since she went to work up at the Big House. She was slimmer, she was livelier, she was kinder and more sympathetic, and above all she didn't look down on everyone as she used to when she first came back to Turnham Malpas. The change in her had been sudden and nothing short of miraculous. Malcolm the milkman even swore he'd seen her out running early one morning, but they'd all dismissed that as fantasy.

In the rectory they put it down to the accessibility of the pool and the fitness rooms at the Big House. In the Store they attributed it to her having a lover; it must have been quite five minutes before anyone was capable of speech, they'd laughed till tears were running down their cheeks. Sheila put it down to the voluntary work Louise had recently taken up with the homeless in Culworth. Though Sheila had to confess she didn't know where the homeless *were* in Culworth, because it didn't seem quite that kind of place. But coming home in the early hours after taking the soup and bread rolls round was certainly exhausting. Louise always slept late on those mornings. Once she'd helped out on a weekday night and Sheila had had a terrible time getting her up in time for the office. With Mr Fitch still on the rampage about the Show and its possible cancellation, that would be the last thing he'd need, his receptionist turning up late for work.

But at least, thought Sheila, she wasn't bothering with the rectory any more, and Caroline had found a nice retired secretary who was willing to come in, as and when for a few hours, and help out with the parish typing. So that little problem was solved, and working up at the Big House seemed to have turned out rather well. Louise was earning good money and enjoying the job, and she'd been out the previous Saturday and bought some lovely flattering clothes too. Best of all, she was much happier and easier to get on with. Sheila wasn't quite sure why she'd mellowed, but whatever the reason she was glad. Altogether life was much improved.

That was how Louise felt too. Life had taken a definite upturn. She lay in bed one morning in the middle of June smoothing her hands over her hips and right down her thighs thinking about Gilbert doing just that. He always ran his hands over her body, fingering her hip-bone, moulding his palm over the bone in her shoulder, smoothing his fingers over her elbows, running his hand down her spine. When he'd counted her vertebrae then she knew the real foreplay was about to begin and the anticipation of what was to come excited her more than she had ever imagined. You could read about it in books, see it on film and television, but actually experiencing it was something out of this world. The more often they made love the more her pleasure increased.

Gilbert had this strange earthy scent to him which she found incredibly stimulating. The first time she'd noticed it was when they'd been in the church trying out the handwritten music she'd discovered, but it was in the close proximity of his house when she'd called with a letter from Mr Fitch, that it had really hit her. He'd invited her in and his body aroma had made her crave his touch.

He'd recognised the look on her face and he'd unhesitatingly planted a soft response-seeking kiss on her lips. Her body had reeled with the shock of the intimacy she so powerfully desired, and he'd caught her elbow as she staggered. From that moment there was no going back. She was undressed and in his bed almost before she knew it. It was all so tremendously beautiful, her need for love so great, his approach so teasing and amusing that she was carried on the crest of a wave into a world of exquisite experiences the like of which she had never known before. When they'd finished, she'd lain beside this total stranger with her eyes closed, still shuddering with pleasure, thrilled by her daring, a slave to his sex drive.

She'd quickly learned the ways of love and desperately hoped, though never asked, that she satisfied him as he satisfied her. But there never was a post mortem for Gilbert, no analysis. It had happened and that was it. She knew that her appetite for him would always be insatiable.

Sitting in church the first Sunday morning after they'd become lovers, she'd watched Gilbert come in with the choirboys, his white surplice immaculate, his eyes downcast, his hair falling over his forehead as it always did. Who would have imagined, she thought, that he could be this wonderful lover of hers; that he could make taking off her dress into an act of worship? There was no hint of his sinewy strength nor his passion. Louise had looked round the congregation and said to herself, 'No one here knows the real Gilbert Johns, only me.' She then looked at Peter as he stood on the altar steps, waiting to speak. She was startled by the fact that she could look at him and feel only a small sadness, nothing devastating, just quiet regret. But when she gazed on Gilbert, her insides heaved and she longed for him to meet her eyes. But Gilbert didn't glance in her direction; he behaved as he always did when he was choirmaster – quiet, unassuming, absorbed in his music . . . a watchful eye on his boys, and his long, sensitive fingers conducting with such style.

Suddenly Louise recognised the music they were singing. It was the piece she'd found in the music cupboard on Revelation Monday and which had thrilled Gilbert so wonderfully. As the incredibly beautiful sounds reached the rafters of the church on their way to Heaven, Louise flushed with excitement. She was seized by the idea that Gilbert must have chosen to sing that particular piece, on this particular Sunday, as an offering to her. What more glorious tribute could he give her! Louise wept quietly for joy.

One Monday morning, Mr Fitch had said, 'This Gilbert Johns . . .'

Louise jumped at the mention of his name.

'Miss Bissett?'

'Yes, Mr Fitch.'

'I said Gilbert Johns is on the point of calling it a day.'

'Calling it a day?'

'Yes.'

'Oh! Is he?'

'About the Roman ruins.'

'Oh, the Roman ruins. Ah, right! Oh, is he? I didn't know.'

Mr Fitch smiled wryly. 'Seeing as you don't know him very well, I don't expect you do.'

'No, that's right. So, right. The Show. We can carry on then?'

'He says it's definitely a very minor find. He's rescued everything and the items are being catalogued or whatever they do with these things and they'll be sent to Culworth Museum. Heaven alone knows what kind of a mess he'd have made of our lawns if it had been a major find – he's dug trenches all over the place as it is. However, it's all turned out for the best. Thank goodness. The sewer people have promised to work night and day to finish laying the pipes and then the work in the house and surrounds can carry on and it won't affect the Show at all. So we've got the go-ahead: there's nothing to stop us now.'

'I'm so glad. I'll get a piece in the *Culworth Gazette* – let everybody know it's definitely on.'

'Yes, good idea. I want this Show to be the best ever. It's more than fifty years since the last proper Show at the Big House, and that wasn't anything like the size of this one. It's just got to be the best. I know I can rely on you, Louise.'

'You can, Mr Fitch, certainly. I'm so pleased. We've all done so much work and everyone's so involved with growing things and everything . . . what a relief. Thank goodness. It's all organised right down to the last detail. We just have to press the "Go" button.'

'Good. That's how I like things to be – in smooth running order. Have we invited the rector to sit on the platform? I think it would only be courtesy to do so.'

Louise found that her heart didn't even blip at the sound of Peter's name and the prospect of close contact on the platform. 'We haven't, but we can if you wish.'

'See to it, please. A courteous invitation – we must

observe the niceties of village life.' Unusually for him, he smiled at her. 'You and I will get on very well together. Shall we agree between ourselves that this is a permanent job? Would you be willing to accept it?'

Thinking of Gilbert she said, 'Oh yes, of course I would.'

'You can get a letter done to that effect then, there must be a sample contract somewhere in the files. I'm afraid Fenella hasn't long to go now. Very sad.'

'It is.'

'However, life goes on. How are you finding village life, Louise? Not very exciting, eh?'

'I don't know about that. There's always something happening. For instance,' she lowered her voice, 'someone's had weedkiller poured on the peas they were growing for the competitions.'

'No! Really?'

'Oh yes. There's been a terrible upset about it. It happened in the middle of the night and they got caught. The police were called.'

'The police?'

'Yes, because there was a fight. Barry's mother, you know Barry the carpenter,' Mr Fitch nodded, 'and her neighbour Carrie Evans were fighting. Apparently they were both in their nightdresses in the alleyway between their houses. Barry came out, and one of his brothers, and the neighbour's husband and there was a real dust-up. Mrs Jones flatly denies she poured weedkiller on the plants but they were wilting unto death, *and* she was caught with the watering can in her hand.' Louise was laughing so much she had to wipe her eyes.

Mr Fitch was appalled. 'I didn't know these things were taken so seriously.'

'Oh yes. These competitions bring out the worst in people. Heaven alone knows what the neighbour will do to Mrs Jones's flowers in retaliation. She goes in for the cut-flowers class, you see. Been winning prizes at the Culworth Flower Show for years with her cut flowers.'

There came the sound of a gentle step in the doorway, and Gilbert entered carrying an outsize cardboard box. This morning he was wearing a vivid red shirt, open almost to his navel as usual, with the sleeves rolled up above his elbows. On his head was a stiff-brimmed Australian bush hat without the corks. To Louise he looked so vital, so vibrant, that Mr Fitch's dynamism faded into insignificance.

'Good morning. Good morning.' He nodded briefly to Louise. 'Brought some things for you to look at, Mr Fitch.' He put the box down on Louise's reception desk.

'Just a few, there are more, but these are some of the best pieces. This here is a very nearly complete wine jar.'

'Complete?' Mr Fitch queried the odd collection of bits Gilbert held in a small box.

'I know it looks nothing now but it will be when we've finished with it. The mosaic we found is in a crate, too heavy to carry in. Very pleased about that. Now here in this box waiting to be cleaned up are these . . .' he tenderly lifted some knobbly almost unrecognisable items and laid two of them on Louise's hand and two on Mr Fitch's. 'Those in your hand, Mr Fitch, are hairpins, and those you have, Louise, are rings – women's rings. Gold, I suspect. I think there'll be a carving on that larger one; we'll see when it gets cleaned up. Aren't they beautiful? Not seen the light of day for something like possibly sixteen or seventeen hundred years.'

'We're very privileged then.'

'You are indeed, Mr Fitch. And so am I, to have a job like this. Here's a brooch, this here is part of a spoon, and this, and this spoon is virtually complete. All quality stuff which, with the mosaic flooring we've found, makes me know it's the corner of a small villa, and not a peasant's house. Pity it's not complete, but there we are. Once the Romans had gone home the villas were looted for their stone and anything the owners had left behind, and over the years they were ploughed up and that kind of thing. So this appears to be all we're left with. There's lots of other bits and pieces I haven't brought in. County Hall have established the exact position on the map and so now the diggers have got the 'all clear'. I've had a word with the site manager and they're getting ready to restart tomorrow.'

He smiled at Mr Fitch. 'The Museum is going to make a special exhibition of all this, once we get it sorted. They'll be buying new display material to exhibit it. I don't suppose . . . ?' He looked at Mr Fitch with that curious 'heron' look Louise had noticed before; she almost expected him to be standing on one foot.

'You mean would I contribute to it?'

'Well, I was thinking of it being called the Turnham Malpas Fitch Collection.'

Mr Fitch couldn't conceal his delight. His face lit up and he beamed at Gilbert. 'Really? I hadn't thought of that. What a splendid idea! Really put Turnham Malpas on the map, eh?' He chuckled. 'I say. Never thought my name would finish up in a museum! The Fitch Collection. Marvellous. No expense to be spared. Remember, send me the bill. Well, well.'

Mr Fitch turned away and walked towards his study as nonchalantly as he could. He didn't need to think twice about it; he'd pay – oh yes, he'd pay! No matter what it cost.

He was delighted beyond belief. It would give him more pleasure than all the big deals he'd brought off over the years. What was it about this village that had so captivated him, and got him so excited about a few broken remains found on land he owned. Ah! that was it. *Land he owned.* He now had three cottages of his own in the village — Pat Duckett's and the two weekender cottages. Soon, soon, he'd have the lot. Well, almost.

Gilbert waited until the door was safely shut. Louise was standing leaning against her desk. He looked at her from his deepset eyes, pushed his hair back from his forehead and came to stand beside her — close, so close. Louise's heart began thumping thunderously; he really shouldn't, not here at work. No one knew, and she didn't want them to know, and how long she could go on deceiving her mother about the homeless of Culworth she couldn't tell, but they mustn't find out about him, not yet at least. It was all too precious, too fragile to be shared. For a moment she leaned away from him but then she couldn't resist his touch. He kissed her without any preliminaries, a heart-stopping, blood-pounding kiss. She slipped her hands inside his open shirt and relished the slight sweat on his skin: something which, with anyone else, would have repulsed her, but with Gilbert it added to his attraction.

The door from one of the lecture rooms burst open and out came some of the students, laughing and joking on their way to lunch. Louise couldn't believe that they didn't know what earth-shattering things were happening to her. She was on such a high she was convinced there must be visible beams of passion radiating out from her. But the students were quite oblivious.

'Gilbert, you must go.'

'See you later then? Hmmmmm?'

'About eight?'

'Bye for now.' And he sauntered out with his cardboard box, apparently unaware of the turmoil of emotions he'd left bubbling in Louise.

Chapter 22

The news that the Show would definitely be going ahead was round the village like wildfire. Willie Biggs, who'd been giving Caroline a hand to dig out a rosebush which had succumbed to some dread disease, said, 'Now the Show's back on, why don't you enter the cut-flower class? You've got some lovely blooms here.'

Caroline laughed. 'I'm not up to that standard, Willie. Heavens above! They would laugh themselves silly at my flowers.'

'No, they wouldn't. It's time that Mrs Jones had some real competition. You've got them lovely delphiniums – they'd be good for a start. Another week and they'll be at their peak. Think about it.'

'Well, I'm really flattered and it would be fun. Shall I?'

Willie chuckled. 'Go on, give it a whirl.'

'I will then. Yes, I will. I shall be so nervous. I've never done anything like it before.'

'I've got a spare schedule, I'll pop it through the door.' He lifted the bush into his wheelbarrow. 'There we are then. I'm 'aving a bonfire tomorrow with churchyard rubbish.

I'll put this on it, got to burn it else whatever it's got will spread.'

'Thank you, Willie. You're most kind.'

'Not at all. Glad to 'elp.' He looked at her as though deciding whether or not to say something else. Then he made up his mind. 'My Sylvia loves working for you. Them children's like her own grandchildren. Forever telling me stories about the tricks they get up to, she is. I just hopes yer here for a long time.'

'Oh, I hope so too. I've been asked to do some morning surgeries at a practice in Culworth while someone's on maternity leave. It'll be after Christmas when the children go to playgroup. Under no circumstances can I ask Peter to take and collect the children, he's too busy and it's just not on – but do you think Sylvia would mind? I haven't spoken to her yet.'

'Believe me, whatever you do will be all right by her. She just loves working here.'

Caroline thanked him and then said, 'I wouldn't have survived without her.'

Willie knew she meant things other than housework. He bent to take hold of the wheelbarrow handles, to hide the fact there were tears in his eyes. 'All the village love you both, the rector's made such a difference to us all. Even those who don't go to church of a Sunday, think the world of yer. There's something about 'im that brings out the best in people. It's that look he 'as. Yer can't tell fibs to 'im. Remember what I said about the flowers.' Willie set off to walk round by Pipe and Nook Lane.

'Don't do that, Willie. Let's wipe the wheel and then you can take it through the house. It's a ridiculously long way round otherwise.'

'I'd carry it round, 'cept I don't want to dump all the soil.

It's best to get rid of everything all round the roots, just in case.'

After he'd gone, Caroline put her idea of covering the surgeries to Sylvia.

'It would be three mornings and the twins would be going to playgroup three mornings to start with, so I'd have to leave before they went and wouldn't be back till roughly half-past one. What do you think?'

'That's fine. I'd have nearly three hours to get done in, wouldn't I? 'Cept in the holidays, that would be more difficult.'

'Yes, I realise that. Think about it?'

'Of course. You like the idea then?'

'Once a doctor always a doctor, it's in the blood!' Caroline went back into the garden to study over Willie's idea. She might, just might, do what he said. After all, it wasn't the Royal Horticultural Society, was it? Only a village Show. Even so, she wouldn't want to enter something which would make her look a fool. Yes, why not, she'd enter. What fun. She decided to go to the Store and announce her intentions; best find out the opposition.

Alex and Beth clamoured to go with her, so they wandered across the Green, hand-in-hand and into the Store.

Harriet was in there, behind the till and Linda was coping with a long queue at the post-office counter.

'Cut flowers? You're being ambitious, aren't you?'

'Harriet! Don't put a damper on my enthusiasm!'

'Sorry, but the competition's stiff in the cut-flower department. Believe me.' She leaned across the till and whispered, 'Mrs Jones always wins.' She nodded her head in the direction of the queue and Caroline saw that her main rival was next to be served.

'Oh right. Got to give her some competition then.' The two of them laughed and then Caroline's attention was taken by the twins who were busy filling one of Jimbo's wire baskets with all manner of sweets.

Beth's voice could be heard saying, 'Beth like choccy.'

'Maybe, but we can't possibly buy all these, we'll have to put some back. Now, which shall we choose?' But Caroline's placatory approach didn't please Beth, who promptly stamped her feet, and when Caroline attempted to put back some of the sweets, she flung herself down on the floor screaming, 'No! No! No!'

Alex kicked at her thrashing legs to stop her screaming, which made her yell louder still. Sadie came out from the mail-order office to see what the commotion was, and everyone in the post-office queue craned their necks to see this magnificent display of temper. Caroline, unable to quieten Beth, picked her up and gripping her firmly under her arm marched out, with Alex holding her spare hand. Beth's arms and legs were pumping vigorously as Caroline squeezed out through the door. The people in the queue could hear her screams fading away in the distance.

'Well, really, and them the rector's children!'

'Never heard such a row.'

'What an exhibition!'

'You'd think she'd manage 'em better than that. Spoiled to death, they are.'

Barry's mother turned contemptuously on her scandalised compatriots. 'Never 'ad none of your children throw a paddy, then? Always been quiet and well-behaved, 'ave they? I like to see a bit of spirit. She handled it right, she did. She's doing a good job there.'

'Well, she does love them children, I'll give yer that.'

'Of course she loves 'em. Who couldn't, they're that lovely. And I reckon she did right by the rector. Must 'ave been hard but there we are. She's a true Christian, she is; that's what being a Christian is. I admire her.'

'Yer mightn't be so keen if she wins the cut flowers. I've just heard her saying she's entering. That right, Mrs Charter-Plackett?'

Harriet agreed it was.

'I see. Well, all's fair in love and war. May the best man win. My pension, Linda, please and this parcel to post, while yer at it.'

As she weighed the parcel Linda said, 'How's Barry nowadays?'

'All right. Why?'

'I heard he'd blotted his copy book with Pat and they weren't seeing each other.'

'There's a sight too much gossip in this village. They've all got nothing better to do.'

The person behind her in the queue said, 'Hark who's talking!'

'And you can keep yer trap shut. I've heard about the trick you're getting up to with yer pot-plant entry.'

'And what do you mean by that?'

'You were seen sneaking round that new Garden Centre out on the by-pass last Sunday, eyeing their best begonias. We all know yer going to enter the pot-plant class.'

'So, what if I am?'

'You're going to buy one from the Garden Centre and enter it as yer own – pretend you've grown it. I wasn't born yesterday, even if the judges were.'

'Well, I never! What an accusation! That's libel!'

'I shall be watching out, believe me. I'll have my eye on them pot-plant classes.'

'What about you putting weedkiller on them prize peas then, eh? What about that?'

'I never.'

'You did.'

'I never.'

'Oh no! I bet!'

'Thanks, Linda. I'm off. Leave you to sort 'em all out.'

Barry's mother sauntered out with as much dignity as she could muster. They were all a sickening lot and she was fed up with 'em. She'd go home, have a nice cup of tea and sit where she could see her flowers and contemplate which ones she'd enter. That was it, yes. Do her nerves a power of good. As she passed the new houses Sir Ralph had built, and had inspected the front gardens that the tenants were now licking into shape, Pat came out from Jacks Lane on her way to the Store. Mrs Jones waved. 'Hello, Pat.'

'Hello.'

'Have you time for a word?'

Pat got off her bike and stood waiting.

'Our Barry's right upset, yer know.'

'I daresay.'

'He's off his food.'

'Oh dear.'

'He can't sleep.'

'Oh dear.'

'I don't know what to say to him next.'

'Neither do I.'

'He says it isn't his.'

'Does he.'

'Yes. 'Ow about it Pat?'

'How about what?'

'Letting bygones be bygones.'

'No. I've enough on without asking for trouble.'

'He's different about you, yer know.'

'So they say.'

'I'd have liked some grandchildren.'

'Well, there's always your other two. They might turn up trumps sometime.'

'I've been too good to 'em. Made life too comfortable. Barry's me favourite, yer know.'

'Is he?'

'Yes. Always has been. He can twist me round his little finger.'

'Well, there's one thing for certain. He isn't twisting *me* round his little finger.'

In a pleading tone Mrs Jones said, 'All men who are men have a little fling now and then.'

'There's flings and flings. I'll be off then.'

'They say your Dean's very clever, that the school says he'll be doing ten GCSEs, and two of 'em a year early.'

'Yes, that's right.'

'Nice that, having a clever boy. None of mine were interested. Couldn't wait to leave and get a job.'

'Your Barry's done all right.'

'Oh yes, but the other two are a waste of time.'

'I'm off then. I've a lot to do.'

'Think about him will yer, Pat? He hardly ever goes out now. Stuck in mooning about. Miserable, he is.'

'Can't help that.'

Pat felt a certain degree of satisfaction that Barry was taking her rejection of him so hard. Serves him right. But at the same time, deep in her heart, she regretted the lost opportunity. She could have easily been persuaded to marry him, very easily, but there was no way she was marrying someone who could beetle off and be getting his rations with someone else when he was supposed to be courting her. Then she remembered his beautiful teeth and that kind of antiseptic smell they always had. His thick dark hair and his laughing eyes. His strong legs and his powerful workmanlike hands. Hands that could be so gentle and inviting. She'd better stop this before she began seriously to regret her decision.

Michelle had not forgiven her yet, nor Dean. Pesky state of affairs when your children wanted you to marry someone that you didn't. Still, she'd sorted the holiday. Nice cottage by the sea. Bit off the beaten track, but never mind. They'd have a good time without him. Then she remembered he'd promised to take Dean fishing, and she recollected the comfort of his arm around her shoulders and she weakened. Maybe she *had* been too hard . . . Next time she saw him she might, just might, speak to him. After all he *and* his mother had said that Simone was telling lies. Maybe she was.

Chapter 23

It was the Thursday before the Show, and Louise sat checking and rechecking her lists, determined that nothing and she meant *nothing*, could possibly have been over-looked. The telephone at the Big House had been in use nonstop almost all day. Mr Fitch had kept coming out of his office with yet another thought he'd had, and she'd had to check it all over again.

It was taking care of all the silly little things, like who was responsible for putting out the chairs on the platform and around the arena, which made for success. Had the Morris Dancers got the time right? Had Jeremy remembered he was in charge of collecting the money and putting it in the safe at regular intervals? Couldn't leave it till the end of the Show, that was asking for trouble leaving money lying about. Where would they put the bouquets for presenting to Mr Fitch's guests? Had they allocated sufficient parking space? With all the advertising Mr Fitch had insisted on, they'd probably have the entire county there. Small matters in themselves but so important on the day.

She let her mind drift off to eight o'clock that night. Her mother had already said she was an idiot to be going round with the soup and rolls so close to the Show. 'You'll need all the sleep you can get, you'll be so busy on the day.' But Louise had pooh-poohed the idea. She needed Gilbert just as much as Gilbert apparently needed her. She sucked the end of her pen and gazed out over the garden. Through her open window she could see her father watering the roses, and hear her mother supervising and criticising; an angry gesture here, hands-on-hips despair there. She wondered what made her father stay with her. What feeling they had left for each other . . . or didn't it matter when you got older? Was it all habit? Or when love mellowed, maybe you each couldn't live your life without the other. Or was it because there was nowhere else to go? Maybe that was it. You stayed simply because there was no choice.

And she and Gilbert? What had they got between them? Passion? Lust? Love? She decided yes to the first two questions, but no to the third. It wasn't love like Jimbo and Harriet had. Their love was tough – a firm anchorage, a belt and braces love affair. It wasn't love like Caroline and Peter's; that was all-adoring, all-giving, all-enduring. Not one of them could leave each other and walk away for ever, they'd no choice but to stay. She still had choice. Choice to stay, choice to go and be glad. Muriel Templeton had said . . . what was it she'd said? 'Find out who you truly are.' Perhaps that was what she had to do, despite her hunger for Gilbert. And it was a hunger and no mistake. She craved him. Poor Muriel – her face when she'd confessed to her about Gilbert. They'd met outside the church one midweek morning. There'd been only herself and Muriel around and they'd sat side by side on a gravestone and talked.

Muriel had been appalled at first, then she'd wiped her

face clean of shock and become sympathetic. 'I have to tell you I can see the need. Before I married, I couldn't have done. I would have thought you sinful, but somehow marriage and . . . and . . . love have adjusted my thinking. But it really isn't right for it to be just . . . well, just wanting a man. It ought really to be for love. That's the best.'

'I know it is.'

'Gilbert's a lovely man. He deserves more than just wanting.'

'Yes, he does. You see, the trouble is I don't know what I am any more. This business with . . . Peter completely threw me. I thought I knew where I was going, but now I'm aware that I didn't. One half of me is eager to organise things, pleased to be praised for my success at it, but somehow there's another person emerging and I don't know really what she is.'

Muriel stood up to go. 'Then you need to sort her out, this new person you talk of, my dear. Think about finding who you truly are.'

Muriel was right. Perhaps she'd take her advice. She seemed so unworldly did Muriel, but somehow she'd hit the nail on the head. Louise felt quite exhilarated with the thought of finding out who she really was. The Show would be her one last brilliant administrative success, her swansong. She'd be relieved when it was over. Lists and highlighting pens and coloured stickers didn't hold quite the fascination for her as before; Gilbert had changed all that. Now when she looked at the sky it was bluer than she'd ever realised, the flowers bloomed brighter, the crystal-clear water of the beck sparkled more enticingly, the houses round the Green looked more beautiful than she could have believed possible. She was even tempted to buy a pair of the dreaded green wellingtons and walk over the fields . . .

Louise rested her elbows on the windowsill and breathed in the country air. She recalled the thick smell of the air in the city when she'd worked at the bank. You didn't open windows there, the fumes would have constituted a serious health hazard, but here in Turnham Malpas, opening a window was sheer joy.

A ladybird crawled busily along the sill. Before Gilbert she would have angrily flicked it off and to hell with it, but now, with her finger she eased it towards a stem of the climbing rose framing her window, and watched it meandering up till it went out of sight. This philosophising wouldn't do. She'd check her lists one last time and then she'd get ready to go to Gilbert. Already in her nostrils she could smell his strange earthy scent; her insides churned with longing.

Sheila had begun to get cold feet. Decorating a church for a flower festival or organising a flower-arranging competition, she'd done that before, but this was scary. She'd begun to lose sleep over it. What she dreaded most was everything going wrong and having to face Mr Fitch and explain. She knew he was intimidating, in fact he must be because there were times when even Louise had been wary of him; she needed no more proof than that. The biggest worry was, did she have enough space for everyone who had entered? She'd just got home with the last of the entries when she heard Louise using the shower ready for going on the round with the soup and rolls. She found her reading glasses and sat down to try to make sense of it all. Why had she refused help from Caroline? She'd offered to help sort it all out, but Sheila had been too proud, and what's more too embarrassed because of Louise's behaviour, to accept.

She spread the entry forms out on the table and began to look through them. There were far more than she had anticipated. Mr Fitch's advertising campaign might well backfire if they got more people than they'd catered for. She had finally got everything into piles and was beginning to count the number of entries in the Victoria sponge section, when Louise came in to say she was off.

'I must say I wouldn't be wearing that if I was going out to help the homeless. It's so flimsy.'

Louise looked down at her dress and realised she'd made a bloomer. 'Well, we have to cheer them up, you know. It's no good wearing old things. It looks insulting, as if they're not worth bothering for.'

Sheila put down her pen. 'Look here, Louise, I'm not stupid. You're not going to see the homeless. If I didn't know any better, I'd think you were going out with a man.' She laughed at her little joke. Louise blushed bright red and glanced away from her mother's scrutiny. 'You're not? You are! I can tell by your face, you are!'

'What if I am? Don't sound so surprised, it's not very flattering.'

'I'm sorry. Who is it – anyone I know?'

Louise debated what to do. Tell her and the entire village would know by Saturday night. Not tell her and she'd be hurt, especially if she found out from someone else. She would be hurt anyway, not to say appalled, if she, Louise, told her exactly what it was she was really doing.

'Look, it's very delicate. You know how these things are, at the beginning. Do you mind very much if I don't tell you? Just till I'm more sure.'

'So you haven't been helping the homeless. You've been going out with someone.'

'You could say that.'

Sheila stood up and went across to Louise. Their physical displays of affection were very limited but tonight Sheila put her arm round Louise and gave her a kiss. 'I'm really pleased for you. Really pleased.'

'Thanks. I'll be off then.'

Sheila went to the door to watch her leave. She waved and smiled as Louise's little car disappeared in the direction of Penny Fawcett . . . Now, who could it be? Who lived in Penny Fawcett . . . ? In fact, Louise was going the long way round to Little Derehams. There was, after all, no point in telling her mother too much. She might be dim, but not *that* dim. And Mother must be pleased at her news; she didn't often earn a kiss and a hug.

Sheila finished sorting the entries and decided that it was going to be a success after all. What's more, her competitions would be the biggest attraction – yes, she'd bring the people in and no mistake. Mr Fitch would definitely be pleased with her. Fancy Louise having a boyfriend! She'd tell Ron when he got back from Newcastle; he'd be pleased too. Who on earth could it be? She'd find out soon enough. Perhaps he might be at the Show.

Barry was putting the finishing touches to the last of the stalls. They'd have them all erected tomorrow. Hope to God it didn't rain. Twenty stalls he'd made. The cost was astronomical but Mr Fitch had said if a job's worth doing . . . so he'd done a good job. Up at six o'clock tomorrow. His mum had cut all the crêpe paper for the stalls, he'd bought all the drawing pins and sticky tape, and he couldn't wait to see how good they looked. Barry took another mint imperial out of the bag in his pocket, propped his shoulder against the doorjamb of the estate workshop and stood looking out across the yard thinking about Saturday.

There wasn't going to be a lot for him to do on the actual day; he'd done his bit already. All he'd have to do was enjoy himself. Huh! Fat chance. He'd been round to see Simone and she'd laughed and said all right then, she'd deny it was his and leave everybody to guess. He knew she had no idea who the father really was. Well, for him those days were over. He wanted Pat. Pat Duckett and stability, and a family and a permanent relationship. No, that was the wrong word to use; it meant all kinds of things to all kinds of people nowadays. He wanted marriage. Marriage to Pat and a son and a daughter and even, he had to admit, a father-in-law.

This Saturday would see a turn-round. He wasn't going on like this any longer. She'd refused to see him, but this Saturday he'd sit in the refreshment tent from two o'clock till they closed up. He'd speak to her, if it was the last thing he did. He'd make her see sense. They were made for each other, and he couldn't think why he hadn't realised it years ago. But maybe the time wasn't ripe and maybe they'd neither of them been ready before now.

He was determined the kids shouldn't miss out on a holiday. He'd get them on his side. Michelle liked him and so did Dean. He'd bumped into Michelle once or twice this last week or so, and she'd been really glad to see him – and Dean had been such a help with the stalls since he'd finished his exams. A nice bright chap he was. A son to be proud of. Having made his decision, Barry locked the workshop door, jumped into his old van, kicked the bits of stuff laid on the floor out of his way, and made for home, more light-hearted than he'd been for some weeks.

Caroline was in the garden making her final decision about which flowers to use for her entry.

'I must be mad entering this blessed Show, Peter. Totally crackers. My flowers won't be a patch on Mrs Jones's and all I'll get will be understanding glances and I shall want to crawl away. Will you go in the marquee for me and see if I've won anything? I shan't dare go. It'll be so embarrassing if I get sympathetic looks.'

'My darling girl, it's only a village thing, not Chelsea.'

'I know, but it feels terribly important, and it is to everyone in the village.'

'Even more so to Mr Fitch!'

'You're right there. He's all of a dither, apparently. He's a funny man, so dynamic, so rich, with so much power over people's lives and yet pathetically eager that this Show should be a success.'

'He's quite a decent chap underneath all that authority. I'm sorry he never sees his sons. That must be dreadful.'

'What do you think to this one? It isn't blemished in any way, is it?'

'Can't see anything wrong with it. You know I'm on the platform, don't you?'

'I do. I think I'll chain the children to me, it's the only way. They're murder in a crowd.'

Peter took hold of her shoulders and turned her around. He kissed her and said, 'Love you.'

'I love you too.'

'I hope this clinic business won't be too much.'

'It's only for a few months. It'll be all right, you'll see. I promise you faithfully if the children show signs of objecting I shall stop immediately.'

'I know you will.'

'You would never ask me to stop, I know that, Peter, but if you really, *really* feel you'd rather I didn't, I won't. But I do want to do it. Pathology got rather tedious, you see, and I'd like to try general practice again. It's such a golden opportunity to try my hand at it, isn't it?'

'Absolutely.'

'I have to stage my exhibit some time between nine and eleven on Saturday morning. Will you make sure you're free then? I shan't be able to do it if the children are with me.'

'Of course.'

'I'm so looking forward to this Show. I wonder if he'll hold it every year?'

'Probably. Especially now with Louise working for him.'

'Of course. So convenient. She's done a brilliant job, you know. Nothing can go wrong, I'm sure.'

'That's her talent, isn't it? Organisation.'

Pat had made one batch of shortbread the night before the Show, then decided to get up really early and make another lot before breakfast and see which she thought was the best.

She'd have to take her entry in by nine o'clock because she'd need to be in the refreshment marquee in good time. Her nerves were playing up something dreadful; she'd hardly slept. It was the first time she'd been truly in charge of an event and the responsibility was weighing heavily on her mind. Jimbo was lending her a mobile so she would be in constant touch with him, so that was a relief. Hopefully she'd only need to make contact if she began running out of supplies. She switched on the oven and got out her scales, and began. Last night's was in a tin so before she started weighing the ingredients she peeped inside it to see how it had fared through the night. Oh, it looked good, very good. Yes, she was pleased with that.

Butter, nothing less, caster sugar, plain flour – four ounces, two ounces, six ounces, pinch of salt. It was just going in the oven when Michelle came down to inspect, for the umpteenth time, the necklace she'd made of sweets. 'Wasn't it lovely of Grandad to find this jewellery box to display my necklace in? He says it had a necklace in he bought Grandma when they got married, so it's very old. It looks real, doesn't it, my necklace? Do you think I'll win?'

'You can only hope, but I reckon it should. It's lovely. Grandad up?'

'Yes, he must be, I can't get in the bathroom. He's sure to win something, isn't he?'

'He'd better, or Mr Fitch will want to know the reason why.'

'He's all right, is Mr Fitch. I like him.'

'Well, I wouldn't touch 'im with a barge-pole.'

'Mum, if Barry's there I'm going to talk to him.'

'If yer want.'

'Will you?'

'Might and then again I might not.'

'I did want him for a dad.'

Pat hugged her on the way to the fridge. 'I know you did. I'm sorry. Start yer breakfast.'

'I know what they say he did, but he didn't.'

Pat was appalled. Children nowadays! 'Michelle!'

'Well, he didn't, honestly he didn't. I asked him.' She swallowed a spoonful of cereal and grinned.

Pat was scandalised. 'You *asked* him?' Michelle shuffled her feet in her slippers and wouldn't look up. 'You'd no business discussing things like that.'

261

'Someone's got to talk to him about it. I mean, wouldn't it be nice if he was coming down to breakfast now? Him and you and me and Grandad and our Dean if he ever gets up. The shortbread's smelling.'

'Oh Gawd!' Pat swiftly opened the oven door. 'I've put the oven too high, it's already too brown on top and it's not even cooked. Blast it. Oh well, I'll have to use the one I made last night. Serves me right for trying to be too clever. I'll be too busy today to see to you, so stick with our Dean or Grandad. Isn't it maddening ruining it like this? What a waste.' She scraped the burnt shortbread into the pedal bin.

'I shall stick with Barry.'

Pat sighed. It really was aggravating that Michelle liked Barry so much. Dean too. And Dad. He came downstairs in his working clothes.

'Hurry up, Pat. I've a lot to do to get my plants ready. Old Fitch thinks he's going to laud it round the marquee showing his guests all the prizes he's won, so I must put my best foot forward today. Barry's done a grand job with the stalls. You'll be surprised when you see 'em.'

'Shan't have any time for going round, I'll be too busy. Still, I'm getting well paid. I'm just going to ring round and check none of my waitresses is crying off. Get yer breakfast.'

Grandad raised his cup to Michelle and she raised hers to his and they clicked cups and winked and he said, 'Here's to us, the champions!'

262

Chapter 24

By half-past one, the crowds were already beginning to arrive. With the opening ceremony at two o'clock it looked promising. Louise had been working since half-past seven. Rushing here and rushing there, checking and organising. At half-past twelve she had gone home to shower and change and grab a bite to eat before returning to sit looking cool and calm on the platform to hear Mr Fitch give his opening speech. She rather felt she'd never feel cool and calm all the rest of the day. No way would she ever take on such a task again. What it would have been like if she wasn't a well-organised person, she didn't know. As it was, the chap listed for putting out the chairs round the arena hadn't turned up and she'd press-ganged Rhett Wright, odd sort of a boy, along with some of his friends to do the job for her. The one good thing was that the sky was a brilliant blue and there wasn't a cloud to be seen. Culworth's Summer Bonanza the previous Saturday had been a complete write-off. It had rained both on the day and the day before, so the site was a quagmire and the crowds almost non-existent.

Louise slipped on her dress and went to look at herself in the mirror. She'd lost almost a stone since she'd come to the village last November. She had a fine-boned jawline now, and when she turned sideways her bottom was no longer her dominant feature. Even her legs had slimmed down and her ankles were slender too. Altogether there'd been a vast improvement. Not only outside, but inside also. Gilbert had awakened a sensitivity in her, which was flowering wildly, and radically changing her outlook. There was no longer any true satisfaction, not deep-down satisfaction, in being an efficient administrator. It had felt good to be appreciated for it, but the real satisfaction came from the way her soul had been opened up by the first worthwhile illuminating relationship she had had with another human being.

She really wasn't going to wear the hat her mother had persuaded her to buy. She thrust the hat-box to the back of the wardrobe, put on her sandals, collected her handbag, picked up her file – couldn't go without that – and shouting to her mother that she was leaving, slammed the front door behind her.

The entire park and Home Farm field were looking magnificent. The stalls Barry had made were perfectly splendid. She'd doubted his idea about uniformity but he'd been right. Mr Fitch had organised a long series of flags of different countries lining the path to the square of stalls. They were blowing briskly atop their tall poles and drawing everyone's attention. The grass in front of the platform had been filled by Greenwood Stubbs with huge pots of vivid flowers, and the bunting which Barry had put up jerked and jumped in the summer breeze. Such a satisfying sight. The car park was already filling up and Louise smiled at the sight of the Scouts with their official red armbands and caps, provided by Mr Fitch to give them prestige, directing the cars.

She could see at the corner of the car park that some of the Morris Dancers from Penny Fawcett had already arrived, and faintly across the grass came the sound of their bell-pads jingling as they tied them to their legs. Thank God they'd arrived. That was one less problem. The marquees were sparkling white against the emerald green of the grass, and the pennants on their topmost points fluttered briskly. Louise could see the waitresses gathered in the open doorway of the refreshment marquee, watching the crowds arriving. Obviously Pat had got things in hand there. She just hoped the table for the VIPs' tea was looking good. Maybe she ought . . . No, Jimbo knew what he was doing, it would be OK.

She parked close to the Big House and went inside to meet Mr Fitch's guests. He'd provided long cool drinks for everyone and Jeremy was busy, with Venetia's help, handing round silver trays with tiny finger buffet delights on them. Louise shook her head; she thought she might just throw up if she ate anything now. Right in the middle of a conversation with a cousin of Mr Fitch, a dreadful cold feeling scrunched her stomach. Oh God, the loudspeaker system. She'd forgotten to . . .

'Excuse me for a moment, would you?' She sped out through the front door and across the lawns towards the platform. Mercifully there was Barry about to say 'one two three' into the microphone. 'Barry! Everything OK, is it?' He gave her the thumbs-up. 'Thank heavens. I'd forgotten all about it. You're an angel.'

'No problem.' He leaped down from the platform. 'It's all going to be fine. Don't worry.'

'I do hope so. I'm feeling so nervous.'

'Don't be. We all know what to do. If you need me I'll be in the refreshment marquee all afternoon.'

'Are you helping there then?'

'No. Not exactly.' He stuck his hands in his pockets, gazed at the sky for a moment and then said, 'It's Pat.' Barry rattled the small change in his trouser pocket. 'She won't speak to me so I'm going to wear her down by sitting there all afternoon.' He laughed ruefully at Louise.

She looked thoughtful and said, 'You do that, Barry. I've come to the conclusion that there comes a time when you've to take life by the scruff and *make* things happen. Good luck!'

When Louise returned to the Big House her mother was chatting to Mr Fitch. Louise's heart sank. She'd have to own up to the fact that she was her mother, but oh, help! Sheila was wearing a claret-coloured lace dress with long sleeves and a low, low neckline, which exposed her crinkled cleavage. On her head was a matching straw hat with a huge brim, decorated with claret-coloured lace and an enormous pink cabbage rose. Ron stood beside her twisting the stem of his glass in his fingers and trying to look as though he wasn't really there. Would Sheila never learn? At least she hadn't bought the matching parasol which she'd told Louise she was tempted to buy.

At that moment Peter came in. He was wearing light-grey trousers with a short-sleeved grey shirt and his clerical collar. Both his height and his looks with his fair skin and his red-blond hair drew everyone's attention. Louise took the bull by the horns and went to welcome him.

'Good afternoon, Peter. Aren't we lucky to have such a lovely day?'

He shook her hand, looked deeply into her eyes with that penetrating stare of his, smiled his kindly loving smile, and said, 'We are lucky indeed. It's a privilege to be alive today, isn't it? So many good friends having a great time. All thanks to you.' Catching Mr Fitch's eye he said, 'Ah, Mr Fitch . . .' The way he'd told her, 'All thanks to you' left Louise feeling completely forgiven for the trouble she'd caused him, and she knew she had his blessing.

Mr Fitch looked at his watch, cleared his throat and announced, 'The platform, ladies and gentlemen – shall we proceed? Will you lead the way, Louise? Lady Bissett?' He crooked his arm and invited Sheila to accompany him to the platform. She hid her nervousness behind a beaming smile, desperate not to put a foot wrong.

Mr Fitch suggested a tour of the competition marquee as soon as the opening ceremony was concluded. Sheila, flustered by the heat of the glaring sun and the tightness of her dress, nodded enthusiastically but with a sinking heart. All she really wanted was to sit down with a cup of tea, with plenty of sugar in it, and to kick off her blessed shoes. She'd been here at the Show since half-past eight, organising this and that, answering questions, smoothing the ruffled feathers of the competitors as they put their entries on display. Much of the aggravation was caused by people taking more space than they'd been allocated, and others complaining their entry was in a corner and could they move it out, please? She'd had no idea how irritating people could be. She'd used a whole roll of sticky tape and a complete box of pins and her stapler had run out and . . . She vowed she'd never do this again. Behind her she could hear Mr Fitch telling his elderly aunt that he'd be running this every year from now on. Oh yes? thought Sheila cynically. He really means we will, Louise and me. We've done all the work.

Mr Fitch's elegant cousin had taken a liking to her and was glued to Sheila's side as they toured the marquee. Sheila pointed out her own arrangement with its seaside theme. She forebore to mention that she'd won First Prize.

'Lady Bissett – this is your arrangement? How wonderful! I love those muted oranges and yellows, and the sand. What a good idea! The shells are fabulous, surely not from an English beach?'

'No, I got those when Sir Ronald and I were touring in the States.'

'What does it say on the card?' The cousin put her reading glasses on and read the judges' card. 'Oh, what a pity! They've said "Excellent try, but . . ." I think it's by far and away the best.'

'"Excellent try but . . . ?"' Sheila shrieked. She recollected herself and said in restrained tones, 'I think you've read it wrongly. I won First Prize.' She fumbled in her bag for her own reading glasses and perched them on her nose. 'Someone's changed the cards round. This says "Mrs Carrie Evans". Just a minute.' She bustled further down the trestle table and found her own card in front of what she would have described as a pathetic attempt at throwing flowers into a vase and missing it. She swiftly changed the cards back again, swearing vengeance on Carrie Evans at the next flower arrangers' meeting, oh yes! She'd have her drummed out, just see if she didn't. Honour restored she smiled at Mr Fitch's cousin and they progressed around the rest of the entries.

Sheila called out, 'You've done well, Mr Fitch. That's the second First-Prize card I've seen with your name on.'

His cousin claimed he'd always had green fingers. This was said in the hearing of Greenwood Stubbs, Head Gardener at Turnham House, who winked at Sheila; she had the gravest difficulty in resisting winking back. How could Mr Fitch stand there and take all the credit? At that moment he went down in Sheila's estimation.

But then he came and took her arm and said, 'A cup of Charter-Plackett's excellent tea, I think, for this charming lady who's worked so hard to make this whole thing,' he waved his arm in a great swoop, encompassing the entire marquee, 'such a blinding success. If it wasn't for your competitions we wouldn't have nearly so many people here, would we, Sheila, my dear?' He squeezed her arm and bending down to reach under the brim of her hat, he planted a kiss on her cheek. 'It's ladies like you, Sheila, who make village life so rich and so rewarding.'

His cousin and his elderly aunt clapped their hands in appreciation and a few of those around also joined in. Sheila blushed and her cabbage rose bobbed as she acknowledged the clapping. 'Really, Mr Fitch, you're too kind. I shall be ready and willing next year, should the need arise.' She laughed graciously and followed Mr Fitch out of the marquee into the blazing sun. At last she'd finally arrived. She'd been re-cognised, in public, as an essential part of village life.

As Jimmy was pushing through the crowds at the entrance to the competition marquee, he bumped into Willie and Sylvia. He raised his tweed cap to Sylvia and then asked, ''As my eggs won, Willie?'

'By Jove they 'ave, and no mistake. Certificate of Merit as well!'

'Never! Well, I don't know. Certificate of Merit. Well, I never. I've got to see this. Certificate of Merit! 'Ave you won anything?'

'I 'ave so. First with me raspberries, me beans, and the vegetable selection. And to top it off I've won the Largest Potato! My Sylvia reckons I must be in line for the Templeton Cup. I'm that delighted I'm like a dog with two tails.'

'Who's won His Nib's cup for the flowers?'

'Looks as if it might be Sadie Beauchamp. She's swept the board with her roses. Beautiful they are. Mine's not in the same street. And she's won a sweet-peas class as well. Reckon it'll be 'er and no questions asked.'

'Wonderful! What a day, what a day. See yer tonight in the bar. We'll have a celebratory drink. You as well, Sylvia.' Jimmy pushed his way through the crowd and disappeared in the direction of the produce displays.

Willie Biggs, flushed with delight at his success in the competitions, pointed out to Sylvia that the hot-air balloon was just returning to earth.

'What do yer think, my Sylvia?'

'It looks lovely. They make the balloon bit so colourful, don't they?'

'My prize money easily covers the cost, and we'll have some over for a slap-up cream tea after.'

'Cost of what?'

'A ride.'

'A ride! Oh Willie, I don't know about that. A ride up there?'

'Go on, let's live dangerously.'

'Commit suicide, you mean.'

'Don't be silly. Yer'll be all right, yer with me. How about it, eh?' He squeezed her hand to encourage her. 'Go on, Sylvia love.'

'Oh Willie, I don't know. I like terra firma. Floating about up there . . .' She pressed an anxious hand to her diaphragm.

'You've been in a plane.'

'I know, but that was different. It had an engine and I'd taken my travel-sickness tablets.' Sylvia looked into his face. He had the eager, longing look of a small boy. He

270

reminded her of Alex when he was trying to persuade her to let him do something she didn't want him to. Bless him. She couldn't deny him his pleasure. 'All right then. I'll give it a whirl. Come on.'

It was the powerful tugging motion as the balloon took off that she didn't like, but once they were up there floating, floating, floating, she couldn't believe how wonderful the world looked, how strong the colours, how blue the sky. Willie held her hand tightly and she loved him for it. His face! She wished she had a camera to capture his delight. He looked like he'd done on their wedding day when he turned to take her hand as she arrived at the altar. Filled to the brim with joy, no room for anything else.

Sylvia peered over the edge at the Show down below. Hundreds of people! And all the cars . . . like myriads of multicoloured ladybirds from where she was. The arena was a clear emerald-green square, and there right in the middle, the tug-of-war teams were busy straining. She knew The Royal Oak team were wearing red T-shirts, and The Jug and Bottle had chosen bright blue; it was the bright blues who were flat on their backs, legs waving. One up to The Royal Oak then. She cheered – *'Hurrah!'* Willie put his arm around her shoulders and laughed. It wasn't possible to be any happier than he was at that moment.

In the refreshment marquee the customers had been coming in even before the opening ceremony. Pat had gained confidence after a pep-talk from Jimbo and was actually beginning to enjoy being in charge. Nothing had been left to chance and she couldn't think why on earth she'd been so worried. The only fly in the ointment was Barry. He'd come in just as the opening ceremony had finished. Now he was sitting at the table nearest to the cash desk with a cup of tea and a cake, neither of which he'd touched for the last ten minutes. All he did was look at her. At first she was indignant, after half an hour she was furious but too busy to deal with him. There was a healthy sound to the consistent *ping!* of the till and she was feeling thrilled with her success.

'Tables to clear, Moira, if you please. Trace, more clean cups please, we're nearly out.'

Barry liked the sound of authority in her voice. This was his Pat finding her niche, and he loved it. Who'd have thought she'd be so good? Next she'd be giving up the school and just doing this for Jimbo. He got rather a kick out of the outfit she wore too. That frilly bow just above her backside added a certain something. He grinned at her, but she ignored him.

A crowd of women came in, and damn and blast, there was Simone with all the kids. Despite her long, loosely flowing dress it was obvious she was pregnant. He kept his head down, not wanting her to come across. He ate a piece of his cake and sipped his tea to make his presence more authentic. When next he looked up, Pat was talking to Simone at her table. The kids were all deep into cream cakes and making a thorough mess which didn't bother Simone one jot. He knew it wouldn't, she was like that. Pat was looking annoyed and then she smiled and then she looked serious. He watched her glance momentarily at him and then she shook her head and walked off. Blast it! What was it Simone had said? He wasn't leaving, he wasn't giving in. No way! He was staying to the bitter end.

His mother came in. She looked round, spotted him at his table near the cash desk and came across.

'We've got to celebrate, my lad. I've won the Victoria sponge! There were ten entries and I've come top.'

'Oh great, Mum, that's great.'

'Get us a cup of tea then, eh?'

'I'm really pleased. What about the cut flowers?'

'Second. Dr Harris won First Prize and though I say it myself, she deserved it. Lovely they are. Have you been in the Show tent?'

'No.'

'Been here all the time, have yer?'

'Yes.'

'Hoping she'll speak to yer?' Barry nodded. 'Leave it to me, I'll have a word with that Pat.' She half-rose to go but Barry pulled her back down again.

'No, don't. Please don't. Anybody says anything it's me. I'll get that tea. Cake as well?'

'Yes, if you like.'

Pat saw them talking but she was too busy to bother. He could sit there all day if he wanted, she wasn't giving in. Sending Simone to plead his case. Huh!

'One in the eye for Sadie Beauchamp for all her special seed from that grower. She only won one sweet-pea class; Mr Charter-Plackett won the other. Just goes to show.'

'What?'

'That it's the technique that counts. You'll never guess who's won the raspberries. Willie! And he's won the beans too. I reckon he might win the cup.'

'Really?'

'Are you listening to me?'

'Yes.'

'No you're not, you can't take yer eyes off Pat. Time you got her out of your system.'

Barry looked at her. 'Honest I can't. It's her or no one.'

'Hmmm. I see Mademoiselle Simone's here. How she's got the barefaced cheek I don't know. Oh look! There's Michelle. Over 'ere, Michelle love.' She shouted and waved her arms, so Michelle, glad to see Barry, came across. 'Sit next to Barry and tell him what yer want, he'll get it for yer.'

Michelle, her face alight with triumph, said: 'Barry, yer'll never guess, I've won the necklace competition. And a Certificate of Merit!'

'Well, that calls for a celebration and not half. Does yer mum know?'

'Yes. I'll have an orange juice and a slice of cream cake please, Barry.'

'Your wish is my command.' He bowed from the waist, winked and went to join the queue. When his turn came it was Pat serving.

'Tea and a slice of cream cake for Mum and an orange juice and a slice of the cream cake, please, for Michelle. Hasn't she done well?'

Pat looked at him and said, 'Yes, she has. I'm really pleased for her. That'll be one pound eighty-five, please.'

'Thanks Pat, keep the change.'

'I don't need your tips, thank you very much. Here, fifteen pence change.'

'Pat, please.'

'It's neither the time nor the place.' And she turned to serve the next person in the queue.

Barry took the tray back to the table and found his mother and Michelle deep in conversation.

'And yer Mum's won the shortcake, I am pleased.'

'She is as well. And Mr Fitch has won some prizes too. Well, it's Mr Fitch on the card but it's my Grandad really, you know. I'm going to be a gardener when I grow up. I'm going to plan gardens with lots of lovely trees, and big gorgeous flowers in brilliant colours that make people think they're in Africa, but really it's good old England.'

'Are you now. You're a bit young at eleven for thinking about your career.'

'I know, but I am. I've got green fingers Grandad says, and he should know. Barry, is Mum talking to you yet?'

'No.'

'I don't know what we're going to do about her. She's that pig-headed . . .'

It was when Louise saw Gilbert disappearing in front of her at a great rate of knots, wearing Morris Dancing clothes and carrying a melodion, that she realised something might have gone awfully wrong. He was scarcely recognisable. She knew him more by his gait than anything. He was wearing an old jacket, to which, for some reason she couldn't quite comprehend, he'd fastened gaily-coloured strips of material, almost obliterating the black cloth of the jacket. On his head was a bowler hat covered with brightly coloured feathers and badges.

'Gilbert?'

He heard her shout and turned round. 'Hello, there.'

'I can't believe it's you! Your face is black! Why have you done that to your face?'

'All part of my costume. Tradition, you see. Where've you been?'

'Sorting out the Portaloos, for my sins. I didn't know you actually danced?'

Behind the Portaloos there was no one about and he greeted her with a long sensuous mouth-massaging kiss which made her feel as though her toenails were curling up. His hat got in the way, and his melodion dug into her ribs.

'Not in broad daylight in full public view, Gilbert! My face will be all black. Is it?' He gently wiped her mouth clean, making a lover's gesture of it.

'Thanks. Back to business.' She fanned her face with her file.

'Made your heart flutter, did I?'

'More than my heart. So-o-o-o, you've never said you were a Morris Dancer.'

'I don't tell my lover everything, got to keep some mystery. I am and have been for years. I love it. Mediaeval and pagan and all that.'

'So you're with the Penny Fawcett side?'

'Certainly not. They're mixed; we're the Culworth Sceptre side and we're traditional. Men only.'

A panic-stricken voice boomed out, 'GILBERT!' and he rushed off before Louise could clear her thoughts. If he was not in the Penny Fawcett side then who . . . Oh good Lord, the ones she'd seen in the distance in the car park were wearing red waistcoats and yes, there'd been two women there too, and they hadn't black faces. When her thumping heart had calmed, she thought, Oh well, it'll make for a better display. The two sides can dance together – even better.

Her watch said it was almost four o'clock. In that case the dancing would be about to start. She hurried out from the back of the Portaloos and headed straight for the arena. She found a space amongst the crowd and watched as the two sides came into the arena from different ends. Whether it was the burning sun, or the dazzle of the colourful clothes the dancers were wearing, or the noise of their bells jingling, or something ominous in the shouts of the crowd . . . Louise had a sudden dreadful premonition that things would not work out as she had hoped.

Gilbert headed straight for the other team. There was a heated discussion, made worse by the fact that they were all carrying sticks in preparation for their first dances. The crowd shouted encouragement as they watched the confrontation. She'd never seen Gilbert so angry.

'Excuse me, please.' She squeezed through the crowd and lifted the rope and stepped into the arena. There was a loud cheer as she walked towards the Morris Dancers.

'Please . . . there's been a dreadful mistake, I don't know how it happened, but—'

'There's no way we are dancing with a mixed side.'

'But couldn't you dance here and the other side over there and do the same dances?'

'*Same dances?* We're Border tradition, love – they're Cotswold. How could we do the same dances? In any case, we're all male, and they're mixed.'

'Well, obviously I can see that, but is it important?'

A woman from the Penny Fawcett side said, 'Look, we don't mind, let's take turns. Give us a chance for a rest in this heat at the very least.'

'Well, now,' said Louise. 'They can't say fairer than that can they?'

She turned to Gilbert's team and waited for an answer. They stood there, sticks at the ready, belligerent and almost begging for trouble, the black on their English faces seeming to emphasise their anger. The men all shook their heads. The tallest one with the recorder in his hand said, 'Sorry, we don't recognise them.'

'Oh, I know them all – I'll introduce them if you like,' Louise offered. 'They're lovely people.'

Gilbert sighed. 'He means we don't recognise them as real Morris Dancers.'

'How can they be anything else? They're all dressed up and ready to go.'

The crowd began to boo. Mr Fitch came marching across the arena. 'What exactly is the holdup?'

Louise explained. Mr Fitch rapidly came to the boil. 'I have never heard such arrogant nonsense in all my life. You're *all* Morris Dancers, so bloody well get on with it and sort something out. The crowd is getting restless.'

'We're getting more than restless. We've been booked for months. It really is only right that we should dance.' This was the Penny Fawcett side.

Gilbert said, 'And so have we, Mr Fitch.'

'LOUISE! How did this come about?'

'I only booked the Penny Fawcett side. I don't know why Gilbert thought I'd booked them . . . him . . . er, them. Look, please, just dance and we'll sort it out later.'

One of Gilbert's dancers stepped forward, stick in hand, and repeated: 'I'm sorry, not with them.'

Before Louise knew where she was, she and Mr Fitch were in the midst of an angry crowd of would-be dancers. All of them, sticks raised, were shouting. The crowd began to cheer. Bells were a-jingling, voices were raised, feet stamped and Mr Fitch, swearing loudly, came within an ace of being struck by a stick.

Suddenly Gilbert raised his voice. 'This won't do. Most uncivilised. My side will retire and leave the field clear for the Penny Fawcett team. There's obviously been a serious misunderstanding. I'll see you later, Louise.' He gathered them all together and marched his side off the field to the cheers and boos of the crowd. Louise and Mr Fitch followed in their wake, after they'd reassured themselves that the Penny Fawcett side would dance. The crowd clapped and cheered and the dancing began.

'My office, if you please.'

Louise, with broken heart, followed in Mr Fitch's footsteps all the way from the arena to the Big House.

When they got inside his office, he burst out laughing;

peal after peal of hysterical laughter. Louise, who'd been expecting a dressing down, was stunned. All her planning, all her notes, everything in ruins and all he could do was laugh. Between his bursts of mirth he gasped, 'Never shall I forget this!! Never!! Oh God!!' He sat down in his chair, holding his side. 'I don't know when I've laughed so much! Oh Louise, I really thought we would have a fight. What on earth are they talking about – won't dance with each other? And I was so looking forward to it. I thought it a really interesting, colourful, heart-of-the-village touch. Brilliant idea of yours. Oh yes. Go and look outside – see if it's all right now. I'll pour us a drink.'

Louise went to look at the arena from the front door. The crowd had settled down and the dancers were dancing, and the music was playing, and it looked all English and mediaeval with the stalls and the crowds, and the flags; oh my word, the setting was absolutely right. Her heart repaired itself and she began to smile. How could they have made love all those times, and never mentioned Morris Dancing? Such a blasted stupid mistake. She'd have to apologise.

'Well, Louise, all right is it now?'

'Oh yes, come and look.' He did and he was pleased, so very pleased. 'How absolutely fitting, Morris Dancing at a village Show. I wonder how many years that's been going on?'

'Hundreds – right from the dawn of time, some say.'

'You can't get more English than that, can you? And tell that Gilbert to get himself better organised. Oh, of course, you don't know him, do you?' He winked and handed her a gin and tonic. 'You deserve that, my dear.' He smiled and they stood together in the doorway listening to the music and watching the ribbons flying, the sticks crashing, the feet prancing, and above their heads the hot-air balloon swaying steadily up into the bright blue sky, its red and yellow and orange stripes echoing the colours of the Morris Dancers on the grass below.

A group of young men who'd spent too much time in Bryn's beer-tent came in looking for trouble. Pat cast an anxious eye in their direction and decided to treat them politely and hope it would calm them down and they wouldn't cause trouble.

'Hello, my darling! Three teas, two lemonades, and what shall we have to eat, boys? Almond slice, cream cakes, butterfly buns, sandwiches? What will it be?'

They argued and then decided on sandwiches and an almond slice for each of them. When Pat told them how much they owed they were flabbergasted. 'Ten pounds? You've added up wrong, love. It's never ten pounds.'

'It is. One pound each for the sandwiches, fifty pence each for the drinks, and fifty pence each for the cake.'

'Cor, that Charter-Plackett fella must be making a packet. You overcharging and putting something in your own pocket?'

Pat began to grow cold. 'No, I'm certainly not. That's the charge, it's here on the blackboard. You can see for yourself.' Two of the men had already begun to carry the trays to a table, and two of the others followed. 'Just a minute. I want paying first,' she said firmly.

'All in good time, my darling. 'Ere you two, lend us some money – I ain't got enough.' He poked his finger amongst a collection of coins in the palm of his hand. ''Ere you are, seven pounds and seventy-two pence, and that's all I've got. Come on, you two, give us some more.'

'Shut yer face, it'll do.' Pat was about to acquiesce and let them have it to save more trouble, but the one left standing at the till shouted, 'Come on, let's be having yer, cough up.'

The smallest of the five men shouted a reply. 'Shut yer face, Fatty, and sit down.'

'Don't you call me Fatty, you little sod.'

'Little sod, is it? Right?' He stood up, pushed back his chair with a crash and lunged towards the man at the till. Pat hastily got her mobile out and dialled for Jimbo. Michelle, who'd been watching the argument from her perch on Barry's knee, said, 'Barry!'

He tipped her off onto the grass and quietly stood up. The fighting began with the big man punching the smaller one in the face. He reeled around for a moment trying to regain his balance, and then fell helter-skelter onto the trestle table laden with the clean cups and saucers. The table collapsed under the shock of his weight and there was a tremendous crash as the cups and the saucers and the man fell to the ground.

The heat had been almost unbearable before the fight, but now Pat felt as though the marquee was on fire. The customers began shouting, and some started to hustle their children and old grannies out before things got any worse. Pat shouted, 'This won't do, please stop it!'

This was when Barry decided to take charge. He strode forward and took hold of the T-shirt of the big man by the till. 'Out, you. Out!' He marched him towards the exit and then came back for the man laid unconscious on the ground. He pointed to the other three men. 'You lot, get him to the first-aid tent, pronto.' None of them made a move.

'Did you hear me? First-aid tent. NOW!'

As the three of them approached Barry threateningly, Pat came out tiptoeing her way between the broken crockery. Determined she wasn't going to let Barry rescue her, she shouted, 'Look here, just get out and we'll say no more about it. Go on – HOP IT!'

One of the men roared with laughter. ''Ark at 'er! Come 'ere, love, and give us a kiss. I like a woman with spirit.' He grabbed her by the arms and tried to kiss her. Pat brought her knee up hard into his groin and he loosened his grip and swore. His hand came back to strike her. Barry saw her cringe and begin to back away, and Michelle screamed, 'Mum!' Barry leaped forward and deflected the blow with his arm. From nowhere, it seemed, Jimbo arrived with the two men who'd been taking the money at the gate. Between them, they each took hold of one of the men and marched them out. The one who was unconscious on the ground began to come round, moaning and wincing as he gingerly touched his mouth, feeling the place where his lip had been split.

Michelle flung her arms round her mother and cried, 'Oh Mum, oh Mum.'

Pat rubbed her back and stroked her hair. 'That's all right, love, I'm OK. Don't worry.' She looked at Barry and mouthed, 'Thanks.'

Jimbo returned. 'Pat, you all right? Sorry about this.' He looked down at the man sitting on the floor. 'You can get up and go. The first-aid tent is just past the stalls. And don't come back, right? Here, Pat, have a nip of this.' He took a silver flask from his back pocket. 'Brandy, do you good, sit down here. Trace, Moira, Denise, look after things, will you? Anne, you be on the till. Chop! Chop! Business as usual. I'll get someone else to clear this lot up. Don't touch it, you'll only cut your hands. Thanks, Barry, glad you were on the spot.'

'That's OK. They'd had too much to drink, that's all.'

'Mmmm. One of life's hazards, I suppose. Look after

Pat. I'll get someone with a shovel and some cardboard boxes.' He stabbed a finger at the broken crockery. 'That's a large slice of the profit gone, dammit.'

Pat tried to apologise. 'I'm sorry, Jimbo, I just didn't handle it right.'

Barry protested. 'She did, she did it absolutely right.'

'I'm sure she did. Worth her weight in gold. Time you recognised that.' He gave a brief nod in Barry's direction and strode out.

Pat blushed, Barry grinned and Michelle looked at them both. 'You two speaking again then?'

Pat said, 'Might be.'

'Yes, we are,' Barry told her. 'Aren't we?'

Pat thought for a moment and said, 'We could be.'

'The holiday's on again then?' Michelle asked excitedly.

Barry raised his eyebrows at Pat. She gave a nod and all three of them hugged each other. When Dean came in with a shovel and a cardboard box, a pair of gardener's gloves on his hands, he grinned at them all and said, 'Better get your fishing rods out, Barry. Looks as if I shall be needing some lessons before we go on holiday.'

They all four laughed, Pat the loudest of all. She screwed the top back on Jimbo's flask, stood up quickly but the brandy had affected her head and she almost keeled over. Barry caught her and planted a kiss on her cheek and said, 'With Jimbo's recommendation I've no alternative but to ask you to marry me.'

Michelle jumped up and down. 'Say yes, say yes.'

'All right then. Yes, I will.'

'I'm going to have a dad!' She danced out of the marquee to tell the world.

Mrs Jones, having removed herself with her tea and cake to a table in the furthest corner as soon as the trouble began, sipped her tea and smiled. She'd get her box of patterns out tonight and look out one for a jumper for Michelle. She'd plenty of time to finish it before the winter set in. Perhaps she'd even do one for Dean. One day in the future she'd be able to say 'my grandson at University', and 'my granddaughter, the one who designs gardens'. Now that was something to be proud of.

An army of boys, enticed by Mr Fitch's promise of great rewards and equipped by him with bin bags and plastic gloves, had begun clearing up the lawns and Home Farm field. The tractor had made dozens of journeys pulling the trailer stacked high with trestles and tables and chairs. The crêpe paper had been torn from the stalls, the pots of flowers returned to the greenhouses, the platform with its banners and flags dismantled, the marquees emptied, ready for taking down and carrying away by the hirers. Mr Fitch and Louise with his guests were toasting their success.

'To Louise! Many many thanks for all your hard work!' There were murmurs of agreement. 'Excellent! Wonderful day! Splendid!'

'Thank you. I can't make a speech because I've nearly lost my voice, sorry.'

'And no wonder. Brilliant feat of organisation. I'm lucky to have you working for me. Keep all your notes, ready for next year!' He raised his glass in recognition of her talent. Louise smiled and excused herself.

She went to her car. Sitting in the front seat was Gilbert. Louise got in and put her key in the ignition. In a husky whisper she said, 'I'm so tired, Gilbert, and my voice has all but gone.' She laid her head back against the seat and closed her eyes.

Gilbert took hold of her hand. 'Sorry about that damn

foolish mistake over the Morris Dancing. I don't really know how I managed to make such a gigantic mistake. After all, you didn't definitely fix it with me, and knowing your propensity for having everything totally organised I should have known to query it. It was all my fault. Didn't really intend to cock it all up.'

'I'm sorry we never spoke about it properly.'

'Too busy doing other things.' He chuckled and she had to open her eyes and smile at him. 'You know, Louise, there's a whole bright shining wonderful person inside you . . .'

She placed her finger on his lips and whispered, 'It's thanks to you she's there at all. You discovered her.'

'That was my privilege. You only needed someone to unlock the door.'

'You've changed me, completely. I'm a new person.'

Gilbert looked steadily at her, his head on one side, his eyes studying her face. 'You're going to let her out onto the sunlit slopes then?'

'I think maybe this whole new person can already feel the sun on her face.'

'Wonderful! I rather thought so. There are moments in life which, when you look back on them, you know, yes *know* that they were completely special and terribly important to the rest of your life.' He kissed her fingers and then laying her hand on his knee and holding it there he said, 'I'm sorry I refused to have you in the choir. It's this all-male thing with choirs, you know how it goes. But I can't bear to hurt people's feelings.'

'It doesn't matter any more.'

'Good. I was going to suggest that tonight we go to my cottage, and you allow me to cook for you. I've something rather special in mind.'

'I didn't know you could cook.'

'My dear Louise, you don't know everything about me, not yet.'

Tentatively Louise said, 'Question is, do I . . .'

'Yes?'

'Oh, never mind.'

'You sit and relax whilst I cook and then we'll spend what's left of the evening reading or something, and go to bed early. To sleep, right? I think that's what you need most of all, isn't it? A good night's sleep.'

'You're absolutely right there. Oh yes. That's what I long for.'

'Do you . . . that is, would you . . .'

'Yes?'

'Could you ever get round to thinking long-term about me? *Very* long-term about me? Like . . . for always long-term about me?'

Louise didn't answer immediately. She stared straight ahead through the windscreen at the Big House and at Mr Fitch standing outside on the gravel saying goodbye to his guests. Then she turned to look at Gilbert. 'I think that might be a distinct possibility. In time, you know, in time. With you . . . yes, I might. Quite definitely.'

'I know Keeper's Cottage isn't exactly top of the shop where design is concerned nor convenience for that matter, but there's a lot of love going spare and that's what life's about, isn't it? Love.'

'You've taught me that, Gilbert. I'll go home and get my things.'

'Don't bother. I'll lend you my Father Christmas night-shirt with the matching nightcap, and you can borrow my toothbrush.'

Louise laughed. 'Better give Mother a ring or she'll worry.'

'You can do that from my house.' Gilbert kissed her full on the lips, leaped out of the car and went to find his own. Louise watched him walking away. Who'd have thought she would find a lover here in this village which she used to so despise. She'd only come back out of desperation – no job, nowhere to live, broken-hearted, home to Mother like a wounded child.

There was something undeniably captivating about Turnham Malpas. In her mind she could see the old oak tree still stout and hearty after what – five, six hundred years? The cottages equally as old, the stocks, the pond. The Store where she'd had that hint of the villagers' collective anger, the church where she'd experienced Revelation Monday, and the rectory where she'd loved and lost. There was something uncannily magnetic about this village; it drew people unto itself and enfolded them for ever. Something strong and comforting and healing – yes, that was the word, healing.

Gilbert tooted his horn as he reached the drive and Louise started up her engine and made to follow him. Yes, she'd stay because there was quite simply nowhere else in the world she wanted to live.

TURNHAM MALPAS SHOW

Turnham House,
Home Farm Field
July 10th
commencing 2 p.m.

MAYPOLE DANCING
HOT-AIR BALLOON RIDES
CHILDREN'S FANCY DRESS
MOTORCYCLE DISPLAY
CHILDREN'S RACES
PUB TUG OF WAR
MORRIS DANCING
STALLS

REFRESHMENT MARQUEE ICE-CREAM STALL BEER-TENT

PRIZEGIVING FOR ALL COMPETITIONS AT

5.30 p.m. ON THE PLATFORM

(see schedule)

FREE CAR PARKING

Entrance 50p Adults
Children and OAPs free

ARENA EVENTS

2.15   Opening Ceremony
2.30   Children's Fancy-Dress
       Parade
3.00   Tug of War between
       Turnham Malpas and
       Penny Fawcett
3.30   School Display
4.00   Morris Dancing
4.30   Demonstration by the Police
       Motorcycle Display Team
5.00   Children's Races
5.30   Prizegiving from the platform

During the afternoon there will be an opportunity to take rides in a hot-air balloon. The
charge will be £5 per adult and £3 for OAPs
and for children under fourteen years. All
proceeds to charity.

REMEMBER!! VISIT THE STALLS AND SUPPORT YOUR FAVOURITE CHARITIES

SCHEDULE FOR
COMPETITION CLASSES

A certificate of merit for best exhibit in
each group of classes.

The Templeton Cup for the most points
in the vegetable classes.

The Fitch Flowers Cup for the most points
in the flower classes.

All judges' decisions are final.

Entries   by 7 p.m. Thursday 8th July
Staging   9.00–11.00 a.m. on day of show
Judging   11.00 a.m.
Show opens   2.00 p.m.
Prizegiving   5.30 p.m.

EXHIBITS MAY NOT BE REMOVED
BEFORE 4.30 p.m.

ALL EXHIBITS TO BE CLEARED
FROM THE COMPETITION
MARQUEE BY 5.30 p.m.

COMPETITION CLASSES

Large Flowered (HT Type) Roses
1. One vase of one bloom.
2. One vase of three blooms.
3. One vase of six blooms.

Cluster Flowers (Floribunda) Roses
4. One vase of three stems.
5. One vase of five stems.
6. One bowl of roses (any type) three stems.

General Floral
7. Three vases of cut flowers, three distinct types.
8. One vase of cut flowers, mixed, up to fifteen stems.
9. One vase sweet peas, same colour, up to six stems.
10. One vase sweet peas, mixed, up to twelve stems.
11. One pot plant, flowering.
12. One pot plant, foliage.
13. Hanging basket.

Fruit
14. Twelve raspberries, one variety.
15. Twelve gooseberries, one variety.
16. Twelve strawberries, one variety.
17. Six bunches blackcurrants, one variety.
18. Bowl of any three varieties of soft fruit.

Floral Art

19. Seaside.
20. The Royal Albert Hall.
21. Notting Hill Carnival.
22. Japanese Garden.

Children's Classes

UNDER 12 YEARS

23. Four scones, arranged on a plate.
24. Four gingerbread men arranged on a plate.
25. A necklace made from sweets.
26. A vase of flowers from a country garden.
27. Miniature garden.

12–16 YEARS

28. Four butterfly buns.
29. Four rock cakes.
30. Pot plant grown by exhibitor.
31. Greeting card.

Vegetables

32. Six kidney beans (French).
33. Six potatoes, matched for size, one variety.
34. Largest potato (judged by weight).
35. Smallest potato (judged by weight).
36. Six pods peas.
37. Selection of vegetables displayed on a dish (Maximum six varieties).

ADDITIONAL CLASSES TO THE ORIGINAL SCHEDULE

Eggs

38. Six matched brown eggs.
39. Largest egg (judged by weight).
40. Brownest egg.
41. Six matched bantam eggs (one variety).

Cakes

42. Victoria sponge with jam filling.
43. Single round of shortbread.
44. Six fruit scones arranged on a decorative plate.
45. Six sausage rolls arranged on a decorative dish.
46. Fruit cake (undecorated) no larger than eight inches across.

SAME COMPETITION RULES APPLY

All Orion/Phoenix titles are available at your local bookshop or from the following address:

> Mail Order Department
> Littlehampton Book Services
> FREEPOST BR535
> Worthing, West Sussex, BN13 3BR
> *telephone* 01903 828503, *facsimile* 01903 828802
> *e-mail* MailOrders@lbsltd.co.uk
> (Please ensure that you include full postal address details)

Payment can be made either by credit/debit card (Visa, Mastercard, Access and Switch accepted) or by sending a £ Sterling cheque or postal order made payable to *Littlehampton Book Services*.
DO NOT SEND CASH OR CURRENCY.

Please add the following to cover postage and packing

UK and BFPO:
£1.50 for the first book, and 50p for each additional book to a maximum of £3.50

Overseas and Eire:
£2.50 for the first book plus £1.00 for the second book and 50p for each additional book ordered

---

BLOCK CAPITALS PLEASE

name of cardholder ....

address of cardholder ....

....

....

postcode ....

delivery address
(if different from cardholder)

....

....

....

postcode ....

☐ I enclose my remittance for £............................

☐ please debit my Mastercard/Visa/Access/Switch (delete as appropriate)

card number ☐☐☐☐☐☐☐☐☐☐☐☐☐☐☐☐

expiry date ☐☐☐☐   Switch issue no. ☐☐

signature ....

prices and availability are subject to change without notice